Praise for 43 Light Street

FOR YOUR EYES ONLY

"Few write suspense like Rebecca York."†

FACE TO FACE

"Harlequin's first lady of suspense…a marvelous storyteller, Ms. York cleverly develops an intricate plotted romance to challenge our imaginations and warm our hearts."*

PRINCE OF TIME

"Get ready for the time of your life.… Breathtaking excitement and exotic romance…in the most thrilling 43 Light Street adventure yet!"*

TILL DEATH US DO PART

"Readers will delight in every page."†

TANGLED VOWS

"A bravura performance by one of the best writers ever of quality romantic suspense."*

MIDNIGHT KISS

"A sizzling, seductive tale of dark mystery and brooding passion."*

WHAT CHILD IS THIS?

"Chilling suspense and snowballing excitement from a master of intrigue."*

*Melinda Helfer, *Romantic Times*
†Debbie Richardson, *Romantic Times*

Dear Reader,

43 LIGHT STREET heroes and heroines become very real to us. We suffer along with them when they're in danger or under emotional stress, and we feel an enormous sense of satisfaction when they claim the happiness they deserve. You'll hear us breathe a sigh or two over Zeke Chambers as he searches for the daughter he never knew he had, and for the woman he secretly loves.

Father and Child is the fifteenth book in the 43 LIGHT STREET series. It's wonderful to see how all the men and women of LIGHT STREET have grown and changed. Some even have families now—and we're delighted with each and every one of them!

We're hard at work on the next 43 LIGHT STREET book, *Nowhere Man*. Check the pages after this story for a sneak preview. Harlequin Intrigue will be bringing it to you in July 1998. We know you're going to love it! And be sure to look for our short story in the special Valentine anthology, *Key to My Heart*, in February.

All our best,

Rebecca

a.k.a. Ruth Glick and Eileen Buckholtz

Rebecca York
FATHER AND CHILD

Harlequin Books

TORONTO • NEW YORK • LONDON
AMSTERDAM • PARIS • SYDNEY • HAMBURG
STOCKHOLM • ATHENS • TOKYO • MILAN
MADRID • WARSAW • BUDAPEST • AUCKLAND

ISBN 0-373-22437-0

FATHER AND CHILD

Printed in U.S.A.

Directory
4 3 L I G H T S T R E E T

	Room
ADVENTURES IN TRAVEL	204
ABIGAIL FRANKLIN, Ph.D.	509
KATHRYN KELLEY, Ph.D.	
Clinical Psychology	
BIRTH DATA, Inc.	322
INNER HARBOR PRODUCTIONS	404
THE LIGHT STREET FOUNDATION	322
KATHRYN MARTIN-McQUADE, M.D.	515
Branch Office, Medizone Labs	
O'MALLEY & LANCER	518
Detective Agency	
LAURA ROSWELL, LL.B.	311
Attorney at Law	
SABRINA'S FANCY	Lobby
STRUCTURAL DESIGN GROUP	407
NOEL ZACHARIAS	311
Paralegal Service	
L. ROSSINI	Lower Level
Superintendent	

CAST OF CHARACTERS

Zeke Chambers—He never thought he'd say the words "Will you marry me?"—or be a father.

Elizabeth Egan—Could she dare believe she'd have a future with Zeke?

Ariadne—All she wanted was a family to love.

Sebastian Demos—Once a friend, now an enemy—an enemy who refused to die.

Aristotle—He was blinded by jealousy.

Sophia—She kept a secret who was now five years old.

Theia Irena—She was making the same mistake again. This time she hoped for better results.

Cyril—Revenge had made him mad.

Chapter One

"Will you marry me?"

It must be a trick of the wind howling through the trees outside. She couldn't possibly have heard correctly. Elizabeth Egan's blue eyes widened as she stared at the man seated across the table. "Pardon me?" she said.

"I said," he repeated, "will you marry me?"

A burst of rain pelted the floor-to-ceiling glass, and a bolt of lightning struck so close to the house that the instant rumble of thunder made the silverware on the rosewood table rattle.

But she barely registered the storm. Her attention was focused on Zeke Chambers. His powerful shoulders were as tense as tree limbs about to snap. Under his deep tan, his skin was pale. One large hand was clenched so tightly around the stem of his water goblet that Elizabeth thought it might shatter.

She blinked a couple of times, then met his gaze, searching. When he'd called her earlier, Zeke had said he was in trouble but couldn't talk about it over the phone. She'd heard the near panic in his voice, and something inside her had melted.

Softly she whispered his name. "Zeke?"

"I'm sorry," he mumbled. "I'm not doing this very well."

Nothing new about that. Verbal communication was definitely not his strong suit. She'd met him a couple of years ago at a faculty party when she'd been finishing her master's degree, and their attraction was instant and mutual. He was a hunk, dark haired, tall and ruggedly handsome. And she'd seen something in his gray eyes—a fiery spark that hinted at excitement and passion, even danger—that stirred her blood and made her heart race. But he kept those inclinations well hidden, and over the course of time she'd come to know a man who was soft-spoken, charming and rather shy in an endearing sort of way.

He was also clearly terrified of getting close. Every time she'd thought Zeke was about to lower his defenses, he'd backed off. And finally, before they became intimate, she'd backed off, too, disappointed and only half convinced that it was best to quit while she was ahead. She hadn't thought he'd call again. But very quickly they'd fallen into a friendship that seemed to make Zeke more comfortable. Sometimes she didn't see him for months at a time. Then he'd come back, and her heart would leap. While the relationship left her mildly frustrated, she'd tried to tamp down the arousal she invariably felt when she was around him, telling herself that what he needed was a friend. Lord knows what she needed. She should have gotten serious with somebody else, yet other men always suffered in comparison to Zeke.

"Let me get this straight," she said. "You're asking me to *marry* you?"

He nodded.

Elizabeth looked at him, baffled.

His eyes held the same combination of panic and turmoil she'd heard in his voice that afternoon when he'd called. Worried but strangely elated that he'd reached out toward her, she'd left the office early and come straight to his starkly modern stone-and-glass house—where she'd been astonished to find the table in his elegant dining room set with china and silver and starched linen, as if his request for her presence had been nothing more than a simple dinner invitation.

"I've got to have a wife by tomorrow night," he said, his voice strangled. "I didn't know who else to ask."

The world tipped so sharply that she felt as if she were going to fall off her chair. But she refused to let her turmoil show. Sitting up straighter, she tucked a strand of brown hair behind her ear. "That isn't exactly a declaration of undying love."

He looked confused. "But you don't want a declaration of love."

Don't I? she almost shouted, stunned by her own reaction and the sudden knowledge of how badly he could hurt her.

He shook his head a little. "I thought you'd be the perfect choice. You won't get emotionally involved. And when it's over, we can each go our separate ways and there won't be any problem."

Her mouth dropped open.

"It wouldn't be for very long," he hurried to add.

She was trying to frame a reply, when the wind gave the house an ear-shattering blast that rocked the very foundations. The lights flickered and went out, pitching the room into inky darkness.

Zeke swore, and she heard his chair scrape the slate floor as he rose. A second later he was at her side, gently but urgently pulling her to her feet. His hands were strong, sure as he drew her to his side. "I think we'd better get away from the windows, just in case," he said.

She might have argued, but another blast reverberated, rattling the giant panes.

The room was absolutely dark, and he was Elizabeth's only point of reference as he began to lead her toward the interior of the house. She wanted to pull away, wanted to put as much distance as she could between the two of them, but the blackness and the strong grip of his hand on her arm gave her no alternative.

He opened a door, led her through, and she judged they

were in the hall. More thunder rumbled, and Elizabeth trembled. Not because of the storm, though.

"Elizabeth, you *have* to marry me," he whispered.

Outrage bubbled inside her, but she tamped it down, gritting her teeth as she muttered, "I don't have to do anything."

When he turned her toward him, she tried to resist, but he anchored her against his body.

"I thought...I thought we were friends," he said.

She heard the strain in his voice, realized at some level that he didn't have a clue how tactless, how hurtful he was being. Still, she couldn't help the defensiveness that colored her tone as she spoke.

"That's not exactly enough for marriage."

She heard him sigh. "I guess it isn't, is it? I'm sorry. I'm not thinking straight. But I do need you. I need you because—"

"You don't *need* anyone," she shot back, unable to control her wounded feelings. Taking advantage of the cloak of darkness, she gave voice to thoughts she'd kept hidden for some time because she'd been afraid she'd drive him away. "Zeke, you never let anyone get close to you. Oh, you're charming and friendly, and you're very good at making everyone around you feel completely comfortable. But I think you have secrets—things you don't want anyone to find out—so you keep people at arms' length."

He sucked in a sharp breath. "I'm that transparent?"

Shaking, she gave a little shrug. "I don't know. Probably not to everyone. I guess I got close enough to you to figure out that much," she added in a whisper.

He muttered an oath.

She had nothing left to lose, so she continued. "Zeke, I realize you haven't had much practice being straight with people... But, well, you can't ask a woman to marry you and in the next breath tell her that you don't love her."

She heard him swallow. "I'm sorry. You're right, but things have happened—"

"What *things?*"

He drew a ragged breath. "I'm...I'm trying to save a life."

Stunned, she lifted her face toward him, wishing she could read his expression, but she couldn't penetrate the blackness surrounding them. Still, she felt the urgency in the hands that gripped her shoulders, and she heard the desperation in his voice as he continued in a rush.

"My daughter. I just found out about her," he said. "She's five years old. Honest to God, if you won't help me, I don't know what—" He broke off, his hands tightening their grip. "Please, Elizabeth. Please, help me save my child."

A galaxy of emotions swept over her. She'd thought he had done his worst with the outlandish marriage proposal. Now she knew he'd been involved with someone else. At least involved enough to father a child. The jagged edges of shattered assumptions stabbed her. Lord, he'd played to her gullibility, all right. Yet her own wounded feelings receded into the background when she imagined the little girl. He'd said she was in danger, that he was trying to save her life. The thought of a five-year-old frightened and alone tore at her heart as nothing else could. Once, she had been abandoned and terrified, and Sam and Donna had been her only salvation. Zeke was giving her yet another chance to repay a debt she could never fully discharge.

"I—I'll help you," she answered in a shaky voice.

"Thank God." The words rushed out, and she felt some of the terrible tension in his body ease. Quietly, she waited for him to explain.

When he volunteered nothing, she prompted, "If I'm going to—to be effective, you'll have to tell me what's going on."

She sensed his hands moving in the darkness. "I don't know where to start."

Her mouth was so dry she could barely continue. "I suppose with her mother. Was she your wife? Are you di-

vorced?'' *Did you love her?* The last question went un-
asked. She knew she was too much of a coward to hear the
answer.

"She's dead," he clipped out.

"I'm sorry."

"She wasn't my wife," he added gruffly.

Profound sadness seeped into his voice, answering her
unspoken question: he had loved the woman who had borne
his child. Elizabeth felt the world drop out from under her
feet. All along she had concocted a logical explanation for
his behavior toward her, convincing herself that he was
incapable of commitment. Now she knew he had been capable of love—only he'd loved someone else. "Why didn't
you marry her?" she blurted.

"She married somebody else."

"You—you had an affair with a married woman," she
asked, unsure of how to cope with this new revelation.

His denial came out like a small explosion. "No. That's
not what I mean. She married Aristotle after we—we were
together—" He broke off and sucked in a gulp of air, then
let it out in a harsh exclamation. "I had a job to do. I'd
given my word—don't you see? I thought I was only going
to be away for a couple of days. When I got back, her
family had pushed her into the marriage."

It was the longest speech about himself that she'd ever
heard him deliver. It ended as abruptly as it had begun.

"Hell, I shouldn't be telling you any of this," he said.

She squeezed her eyes shut in frustration, then opened
them again. She wanted to shake him—shake the truth out
of him instead of getting it in tiny portions that hardly made
any sense. Then she wanted to run away from him, as fast
and as far as she could get before he hurt her any more.
But when he didn't volunteer any additional information,
she sighed, wondering what it would take to get through to
him. Could either one of them deal with honesty? "Zeke,
I feel like you've socked me in the stomach. Maybe I'd
better quit while I'm ahead."

"No, please."

"Then explain what's going on. I can't be much help to you unless you tell me everything you know."

"I understand. But I can't go into certain things. Not about—" He stopped again.

"Damn you, Zeke. Stop playing games with me." She realized she had reached out and grabbed his shoulder; that she was in fact trying to shake him. He stood immobile, towering over her. When she discovered she was the one flailing back and forth, she made a strangled sound and stilled.

"I—Elizabeth, please—"

He sounded like a man trapped in a pit—calling out for help. He also sounded as if he were on the verge of cracking. His arm muscles were tied into knots, and Elizabeth imagined that his fists must be clenched at his sides. The hands that clutched his shoulders gentled. What had he gotten himself into that he couldn't talk about? Something so serious that he'd left the woman he loved for—what did he call it—a job?

"Did you do something illegal?" she murmured.

"Yes."

She swallowed hard, trying to digest that. In the space of a few minutes, Zeke Chambers had swept away all the naive assumptions she'd ever made about him. No, not every one. She'd caught the hint of danger in the depths of his eyes. She hadn't guessed how close she'd come to the mark.

"Illegal but not criminal," he clarified quickly, his voice shaking with emotions he was obviously trying to suppress. "I mean, not in the sense that you're probably thinking."

She blinked, feeling like she'd stepped into an alternate universe where black was white and white was a strange shade of gray. She needed more answers, yet she sensed that the man standing in front of her like a statue about to shatter couldn't handle any more questions. On a soft sigh, she cupped her hands around his shoulders, stroking, kneading the muscles that were as tense as coiled springs.

For a long moment nothing changed. Then he let out a shuddering breath. Some of his stiffness dissolved, and he laid his cheek against the top of her head in a gesture of surrender.

Her fingers moved upward, winnowing into the thick hair at the back of his head, holding him to her the way a mother might hold a child. They stood that way in the darkness for long moments as she listened to the sound of his harsh breathing. She should be angry with him, but somehow the knowledge that he needed her made all the difference.

"It's all right," she whispered.

He shook his head. "No. I'm asking too much of you. Too much of anyone."

"Not of me." Eyes closed, she slid her hands around his back and clasped him to her. It seemed more right than anything else that had ever passed between them. He was trembling now, and she wondered if he was as undone by tenderness as he was by the secrets gnawing at him. She'd been so sure that he didn't want to open up with her. Now she knew he'd been lugging around terrible burdens no man should have to carry; and he didn't know how to share them.

The storm had receded into the background. In the darkened hallway, the only thing that mattered was her silent offer of aid and comfort.

At first his arms stayed at his sides, then slowly they pulled her to him, and she felt something in her chest expand as she realized he was reaching out to her in new way. It wasn't on a verbal level. But it was a start—a good start.

"It's going to be all right," she said again.

"You make me think it will be."

She closed her eyes and let her head rest on his shoulder, pretending a calm she didn't feel. In the space of a few seconds, he'd changed her whole life. She would never be the same again, no matter what happened next. But one thing she had learned, communication was going to be her responsibility.

"How did you find out about the child?" she asked.

"A letter. Can you believe it? Her name is Ariadne, of all things," he added quickly, his voice bemused.

"It's pretty," she answered.

"Yes, from Greek mythology."

"Princess Ariadne helped Theseus escape from the Minotaur," she said.

"You've heard the story?" It sounded as if he were clinging to the name, as if the mere fact of knowing it gave his daughter a reality he hadn't expected.

"Who sent the letter?" she prompted gently.

"Her aunt. She didn't give me much information."

Before he had a chance to elaborate, a wayward bolt of lightning struck so close to the house that everything around them seemed to shake. Then, above the sound of the thunder, a glass-shattering explosion made her cringe against Zeke. "What was that?" she gasped.

"I don't know. We'd better go and have a look." In the darkness he found her hand, his grasp firm and steady as he led her back through the door into the dining room, moving confidently like a man with the eyes of a cat.

She could make out very little. But her other senses told her that something was very wrong. The slate floor was slick with water, and she would have slipped if she hadn't been holding on to Zeke. He clasped her hand more tightly, keeping her still. An odd pinging noise rang in her ears. Then a blast of wind sent a sudden spray of cold droplets across her face.

Instinctively she turned toward the long windows that enclosed one side of the living room. Another jagged bolt of lightning split the sky, and in that moment she clearly saw a gaping hole in one of the panes. Rain streamed into the room, dousing the furniture and the rug. Along with the water, pellets of glass clattered to the floor.

"I'd better have a look." Zeke let go of her hand and crossed to the window.

She snatched at his sleeve. "No. You'll get cut."

"It's okay. It's safety glass."

Reluctantly she let go of his shirt. Moments later she saw his silhouette moving steadily along the edge of the room, till he stooped and began to search along the floor. Did he expect to find something else besides water and glass?

She was getting wet from the driving rain, but she stayed where she was, watching him intensely until he returned.

"We need a light before we do anything else," he said. His hair and clothes were dripping. "I don't want you to get hurt, so don't try to move around. I'll be right back."

She understood the wisdom of remaining where she was. Still, as soon as he left her side, her back felt exposed, and a little tremor traveled up her spine. Moving so that her shoulders were pressed against the wall between the dining room and the kitchen, she listened intently. All she could hear were the sounds of the rain and wind lashing the house, like predators seeking additional access points. She could hear Zeke rummaging in a cabinet or a drawer as she edged nearer to the kitchen. Then a wide shaft of yellow light pierced the darkness. Some of the illumination shone upward, accentuating the harsh lines of his face. *He must have one of those camping flashlights,* Elizabeth thought, as she watched him set it on the counter and swipe his wet hair off his forehead with both hands.

The light was like a ray of safety piercing the gloom. She was about to utter an exclamation of relief and bolt through the doorway when she caught a flicker of movement at the far end of the room. The next seconds flashed by so quickly that she barely had time to register what was happening—beyond the fact that she saw a vaguely human outline detach itself from the darkness.

As the apparition advanced quickly toward Zeke, it took on form and substance. It was no ghost but a short, muscular man. His face was hidden by the darkness. Later she wondered which ancient god had stopped her from calling out a warning to Zeke. Perhaps she was too shocked. Or perhaps providence was watching out for their welfare.

The stranger moved toward the light. But his steps must have been audible on the tile floor, because Zeke whirled to face him.

The intruder stopped a few feet away, his posture tense. The beam of illumination from the flashlight on the counter was like a line of demarcation between himself and Zeke. She could see a little of his face now—not enough to describe the features but enough to make out the rigid planes of anger or hate—or perhaps both. He didn't spare a glance in her direction, and she assumed he must think Zeke was alone. Automatically, she pressed herself against the wall, barely breathing as she tried to think of what she could do to help.

Zeke was the one who spoke first. "Sebastian Demos, what are you doing here?" he asked in a voice that rang out loudly above the pounding of the rain. She realized immediately he was trying to warn her that they had unexpected company, dangerous company.

The words hung between the two men like a gauntlet tossed to the ground by a combatant.

"I take it you weren't expecting me," the intruder clipped out in heavily accented English. His voice was arrogant, but tinged with fear. The combination probably made him more dangerous, Elizabeth decided.

"Why have you come here now? You could have found me any time," Zeke challenged, subtly shifting his weight to the balls of his feet like a fighter getting ready to strike.

"Sophia's dead," the intruder spat out. "Do you know? Do you care?"

"Irena wrote me. Of course I care."

The man named Sebastian Demos ignored the answer—and the anguish in Zeke's voice. "You got her pregnant when she was betrothed to another."

Zeke winced, but his expression didn't change.

"Do you deny you seduced her?"

"That's not true. We—"

The other man cut him off with a harsh sound deep in his throat. "You can't pretend you didn't leave her stranded with your baby."

"I didn't know about the baby!"

"Couldn't your sight-seeing trip to Athens have waited a few days?"

Unable to do more than stand by the door and listen, Elizabeth saw Zeke's hands clench into fists. "It wasn't a sight-seeing trip. I—I had no choice."

The other man shook his head in a dismissive gesture. "I don't have to listen to any more of your lying words. It will be much more gratifying to kill you."

Chapter Two

Now. He means he's going to do it now, Elizabeth thought wildly, snapping out of her trance as the man advanced on Zeke. He raised his hand, and Elizabeth saw the blade of a knife glinting in the flashlight's beam.

A terrible sick feeling rose in her throat. Teeth clamped around her lip to keep her from screaming; she looked frantically around for some weapon—anything to even the odds. Before she could act, the whole scene shifted. The hand with the knife came up, but Zeke was obviously prepared. He didn't give the attacker a chance to land a solid strike, as he jumped backward.

With a wide sweeping motion, his arms drove the flashlight off the counter, and it clattered to the floor with a deafening thud. Neither man took any notice. Demos moved in rapid pursuit of his quarry. Zeke feigned to the right, then astonished Elizabeth by shifting directions in midstride and springing forward like a jungle cat on the attack.

A millisecond later, Sebastian's arm came up, the knife slashing toward Zeke. For a terrible moment, she thought the blade had struck him on the shoulder. But he didn't falter. Without missing a beat, he twisted Sebastian around and wrestled him onto the tile floor with the ease of a seasoned street fighter.

For a moment Sebastian lay still, and Elizabeth dared to

hope the battle was over. When he sprang up again, she gasped.

She couldn't simply stand in the doorway watching. She had to do something to shift the odds. Turning, she darted across the wet rug toward the fireplace, where she remembered seeing Zeke poke up the fire one evening the previous winter. Thank God the tools were still there, she thought, as she detached the poker and hefted it, testing its weight. At a run she started back toward the kitchen, swinging her weapon experimentally. When she returned, everything had changed. Now the men were rolling across the floor, first one way and then the other. Neither seemed to have a clear advantage. Zeke was larger, heavier, and he'd demonstrated that he knew something about hand-to-hand combat. But apparently so did Sebastian. And he was armed.

With no thought for her own safety, she rushed into the fray and smashed the metal bar down on Sebastian's shoulder. As he yelped, Zeke used the unexpected opportunity to land a solid blow to his jaw.

Trying to get some leverage, Sebastian lashed out with his left leg. This time Elizabeth got him in the shin. As he pushed himself up on unsteady arms, she brought the weapon down on his back. He yelped and rolled away from Zeke, who fell back onto the floor.

"Zeke," she shouted.

"I'm okay. Watch out for Sebastian."

Her gaze shifted to the other man, who sat with his back against one of the kitchen cabinets. Sucking in gulps of air, he turned his head from side to side—trying to figure out who had come to Zeke's aid, Elizabeth supposed. When Sebastian spotted her still holding the poker, she went cold all over, bracing for him to spring at her with the knife. Then she realized the weapon was no longer in his hand.

"Where did you come from?" he gasped.

"Afraid to take on the two of us?" she challenged, hefting the poker. From the corner of her eye she could see Zeke had made it to a sitting position. Slowly, not entirely steadily, he climbed to his feet and advanced toward the man on the floor.

Sebastian's gaze shifted from her to Zeke. For several heartbeats he didn't move. Then, uttering an exclamation, he scrambled up. For a moment, he swayed on his feet before turning and limping toward the other end of the kitchen.

Zeke followed, hardly more steady in his gait. As he moved into the light, Elizabeth saw to her dismay that a red patch was spreading from under his sports jacket across the front of his white shirt. Sebastian had cut him, but he'd kept fighting like a demon. Now he had to be at the limit of his endurance. Before he could move past her, she grabbed his arm and held tight. "No," she whispered. "You're in no shape to go after him."

The sound of her voice made Sebastian turn and snap his head toward her once more. For an endless moment, the three of them stood motionless. "Don't think it's over," Sebastian growled. "I'll be back to take care of you and your new girlfriend."

"Not if I can help it!" Zeke answered, then turned to Elizabeth. "Let me go." He surged forward, but she kept her death grip on his arm. His strength must be ebbing, she thought with a small corner of her mind, because her grasp held him while the other man limped toward the back door and disappeared into the night.

ZEKE MUTTERED A LOW CURSE. Now that he wasn't fighting like a madman, his damn shoulder was starting to hurt like hell. He tried to ignore the pain. He couldn't ignore the implications of Sebastian's surprise visit. He'd thought his only immediate problem was Aristotle Pappas. Apparently there was someone else who hated him enough to kill him. Or maybe Aristotle had sent Sophia's cousin to do his dirty work. He'd have to consider that as a possibility.

He heard the poker slip from Elizabeth's hand and rattle

to the floor. Immediately his attention snapped to her. "Are you all right?" he asked.

She tried—and failed—to give him a little smile. "Yes."

He stared at her, as comprehension of what she'd done sank in. He'd always thought of her as small and delicate, yet she'd found herself a weapon and waded into the fray like a soldier on a combat mission. "You're either very brave or very reckless," he whispered.

"I couldn't let him kill you." It was such a simple statement, but it said so much.

He closed his eyes for a long moment, struggling for words. All he could manage was a simple "Thank you," which seemed woefully inadequate under the circumstances. He wanted to slip his arm around her and pull her close, but it was all he could do to stay on his feet. He'd turned to her because he trusted her more than any other woman he knew. Now, he was beginning to recognize she had qualities he hadn't even guessed. Or perhaps he hadn't seen them on a conscious level.

"You're hurt," she said. "You've got to sit down."

"I'm fine," he insisted. He had to be, because there were no other options. Wincing, he pushed himself off the countertop he'd been leaning on and was surprised by the sharp stabbing pain in his shoulder.

Elizabeth pulled aside the edge of his jacket, and they both looked at the spreading red stain.

The cut was high up on the left, and Zeke knew with a jolt of alarm that it might involve an artery. *Stupid*, he thought. *Stupid*.

Bending down, Elizabeth snatched up the flashlight and shone it on the wound. To his relief, he saw that the blood was oozing rather than gushing out.

Her reaction wasn't quite so sanguine. "You need an ambulance," she said, in a voice edged with panic.

He moved his arm experimentally and struggled to hold back any sign of pain. *Maybe not*, he thought. He hoped not.

"And we have to call the police," she continued.

The declaration snapped his thoughts into sharp focus. "No police," he cut her off curtly. "No ambulance."

She tipped her head to one side, searching his face.

"No police," he repeated in a firmer voice. Fumbling in his pants pocket, he brought out a handkerchief. One-handed, he unbuttoned his shirt and thrust the cloth against the wound, holding it awkwardly in place. "We have to get out of here. Come on."

He wheeled and started toward the garage door, with what he hoped was reassuring steadiness. The show of strength cost him more than he wanted to admit.

Then he saw something glinting on the ground and felt a little surge of adrenaline. The knife. Sebastian had dropped his knife in the heat of battle. He started to stoop, and wondered if he could make it down to the floor and back up again. When he grimaced, Elizabeth held him back.

"I'll get it."

Gingerly she picked up the weapon. The blade was long, the handle ornate. He couldn't see the details, but he had a good idea what he'd find when he examined the hilt in the light. A museum-quality piece, no doubt. A symbol. But then, like many of his countrymen, Sebastian suffered from a sense of the dramatic. Lucky for Zeke, he hadn't been practical enough to bring a gun.

Snatching a dish towel off the counter, Zeke thrust it into Elizabeth's hand. "Wrap it up."

She looked surprised, but followed directions.

"Put it in your purse."

"My purse. It—it's still in the dining room," she said, looking momentarily confused. No wonder. A lot had happened in the past twenty minutes.

"Then get it. Hurry."

He rested in the doorway, letting the jamb take his weight, angry with himself for not having more energy in reserve. When he heard her coming back, he straightened quickly and started toward the garage. By the time he

reached the Mercedes he'd parked earlier that evening, he
noted absently that his knuckles were white where they
gripped the door handle. He could make himself ignore the
pain burning his shoulder, but not the way his body was
shutting down against his will. Even his vision was blur-
ring. Probably if he tried to drive, he'd pass out and end
up plowed into a tree. And that wouldn't do either one of
them any good.

"Dizzy..." he muttered. "Damn. I'm sorry."

"It's not your fault, Zeke," she answered.

Without bothering to argue the point, he asked, "Can
you drive a stick shift?"

"Yes." She held out her hand, and grimly he dug the
keys out of his pocket. As soon as the door was opened,
he sank heavily into the passenger seat, his head thrown
back, his breath shallow. His shoulder was on fire, and
sweat beaded on his forehead. He concentrated on staying
conscious. If he passed out, Elizabeth would take him to
the hospital, where he'd have to answer too many incon-
venient questions.

When she slipped behind the wheel, he made an effort
to rouse himself.

"Put your head down," she murmured.

"I would. I don't think the shoulder can take it."

"Zeke, are you sure you don't want to see a doctor?
You're hurt, and it could be serious."

"I'll be fine," he grated with as much conviction as he
could muster, then switched his attention to getting out of
the garage. "The door opener's under your sun visor. Press
the button."

When the door opened, he reached out and captured her
small hand in his larger one. "Elizabeth, I'm sorry I got
you into this," he whispered. "I didn't expect Sebastian—or anybody else," he added.

"Why don't you let me take you to the emergency
room?"

He drew in a shuddering breath. "My daughter's life is

at stake. The police could make things worse. I've got to
be free to operate on my own. Do you understand?''

''No.''

Of course she didn't. There was too much she didn't
know. Things he had to tell her. Things he didn't want to
talk about. But he needed her cooperation. ''Promise you'll
keep this between the two of us—for now, at least.''

An eternity passed before she answered. ''All right.''
Turning her palm up, she gave his hand a reassuring
squeeze.

''You'd better start the car and get us out of here—in
case Sebastian decides to come back.''

Her head snapped around and she looked frantically into
the darkness, her gaze zeroing in on the evergreens that
framed the garage door. He hated to frighten her, but he
wasn't going to be caught flat-footed again.

The car bounced as Elizabeth drove over a small tree
branch, and he couldn't hold back a hoarse cry of pain.

''Zeke, I'm sorry.''

''Just go,'' he managed.

The wind was louder outside, and Elizabeth had to steer
around a larger branch farther down the driveway. Some
storm, he thought as she wove her way up the street, avoiding various obstructions. Had a bolt of lightning really broken the window? Or had the tempest given Sebastian the
chance to set things up the way he wanted?

He was too light-headed to sort though the possibilities.
Instead, through half-closed eyes, he watched Elizabeth
concentrate on driving a route that had turned into an ob-
stacle course. Several blocks from the house, the street
lights came on, and she visibly relaxed.

''Make sure we're not being followed,'' he grated, angry
with himself for not thinking of it sooner. It was more proof
that his brain was only functioning on half its neurons. If
that.

Her hands whitened on the wheel as she glanced in the
rearview mirror. ''There's a car in back of me.''

"Turn up a side street. See if he follows."

She took the next turn, then another. "No."

"Good."

He felt his body start to shiver and switched his limited energy to keeping his teeth from chattering. But it was a losing battle. His clothes were soaked through.

"If you won't let me take you to the emergency room, where are we going?" she asked.

With a rueful grimace he realized he hadn't thought that far. "Your house?"

"Okay," she answered without missing a beat.

The promise of a safe haven was enough for him to give up the fight to keep his eyes open. Maybe he even dozed. When the car stopped, he jerked awake.

"Zeke?"

"I'm fine," he repeated. From the look in her eyes, he knew he wasn't fooling either one of them. The sweat on his forehead had turned icy. Making a concerted effort not to wince, he pushed himself up and looked around, recognizing her driveway. Overhanging trees hid the car from the road, and a feathery hemlock blocked the view of the front windows of the comfortable Parkville Victorian he'd visited several times.

"I'm going to open the door," Elizabeth advised him. Slipping out of the car, she climbed the back steps. By the time she turned around, he was standing up and walking slowly to the trunk of the car.

"What are you doing?" she called out in alarm, as she hurried to his side.

"I need my bag." Too bad he hadn't had it in the house, he thought.

"Zeke—"

"I've got to bring it in. Stuff I need."

"You shouldn't be walking around," she countered.

"I feel better."

"Sure."

"We don't have too many options, unless you're plan-

ning to carry me." He laughed hollowly as she glanced up
at his six-foot frame, probably thanking God that he was
still mobile.

By the time she'd retrieved the duffel bag he'd packed
that afternoon, he was already two thirds of the way up the
steps, his hand gripping the banister to keep himself erect.
The damn shivering was getting worse.

"You've got to get out of those wet clothes," she said
as she set down her bag and purse so she could guide him
to the second floor and into the bathroom. Like the rest of
the house, the bathroom was old-fashioned and large. The
black-and-white tile had been in place long enough to have
come back in style.

He sat down heavily on the closed cover of the com-
mode, silently acknowledging that the short journey had
taken more out of him than he cared to admit.

He tried to shrug out of his coat, then winced as fire shot
through his shoulder.

"Let me," Elizabeth offered. Slowly, she pulled his right
arm out of the sleeve, then she switched to the injured side
and eased the fabric down his left arm. With the jacket off,
Zeke took a better look at the dark stain. It covered most
of his shoulder now, but the bleeding had stopped.

He watched her trying not to register alarm. Instead, she
began to slip open the shirt buttons one by one. But he felt
her fingers trembling. They were long and graceful, and he
thought about the times he'd imagined her undressing him.
He closed his eyes for a moment, trying to pretend that she
wasn't bent on tending his wound. As he concentrated on
her gentle touch, it was tempting to let his mind drift into
a fantasy that featured the two of them in a nice, warm bed.
But he couldn't afford the luxury. He couldn't afford to
lose control tonight. Or any time, for that matter.

THE OLD MAN'S FACE was lined beyond his years. But his
mind was still sound. And focused.

"*Yasou*, Walter. To your health," he murmured, as he

raised a glass of ouzo between leathery fingers and sipped the clear liquid, savoring the licorice flavor. During the twenty years he'd been in prison, the potent liquor had been just a memory. Like freedom.

"Ah, how I wish you could be here with me, Walter," he whispered as he walked slowly to the window of the handsome whitewashed villa he'd rented in the mountains. It was evening, and the setting sun painted the rock-strewn vista with soft pink and orange. The air was pure and clean. Symbols of his freedom. Yet freedom was hardly as sweet as he had imagined.

The wardens had released him early for good behavior. But he'd come home to the ruins of his life. His land was gone to pay his debts, because there had been no way to tap the secret stash of money he'd hidden. His lovely Helen had died of shame. His sons had scorned his name and moved from the village of their birth. And he had come to this new place, not to start again, but to settle the unfinished business that had eaten at him for the past twenty years.

He set down the small glass with a thunk on the windowsill. The stark reality of prison—and of his own dishonor—had turned the dreams of his youth to ashes. Once he had thought he'd be the richest man in his village, honored and respected among his peers. Now he had the wealth he'd hidden, but it brought him no joy and no respect. In prison, he'd had nothing left except the one goal that had sustained him during the long bitter years of confinement. He would find Walter Chambers, the man who had come from America with promises of wealth and power. Instead his friend Walter had led him down the path to dishonor. And he would make him pay for his treachery.

But it hadn't worked out the way he'd expected. The son of a whore had cheated him of his revenge, the way he'd cheated him of everything else. Walter was dead. His wife, too. Someone else might have given up, the old man conceded. But the ability to keep old animosities alive had always been a characteristic of his race, like when the city states of old had fought among themselves incessantly. They'd weakened each other, leaving the whole region ripe for conquest. His people had hated the invaders with every drop of blood in their veins. He was simply continuing old traditions on a personal scale.

His dead enemy had a son named Zeke Chambers. He was still within reach. And he would have to pay for the sins of his father.

From the courtyard, the woman softly called his name.

"I'm in here," he answered, schooling the blood lust out of his face. Moving to the bed, he lay down comfortably with his hands behind his head.

"Would you like some company?" she asked, her hips swaying sensually as she approached.

"Yes. I was waiting for you." For a little while, she would ease his body—distract his mind. He smiled. "Take off your clothes for me, the way I like to see you do it."

She nodded, and her hand went to the black scarf that modestly bound her hair in the traditional way. She was no longer young, yet the years had been kind to her.

He hadn't told her of his past disgrace. He let her go on believing he was the best thing that had ever happened to her. No matter how wrong she was.

He was lucky to have made her beholden to him. For as long as he could, he would enjoy the solace she offered. Then he must get rid of her—painful as that would be.

ELIZABETH SLOWLY EASED open the buttons of Zeke's shirt, watching him. This wasn't supposed to be a sensual experience, she reminded herself. Yet the smoldering look in his dark eyes told her he was reacting to the intimacy as much as she was. When she came to the waistband of his slacks, she hesitated, then gingerly pulled the shirttails out.

She cleared her throat. "Lean forward a little."

He obeyed, his face pressing against her shoulder so that she felt his warm breath on her skin as she removed his shirt. When he was naked to the waist, she stepped back and looked at the blood-soaked handkerchief still covering the wound. It was enough to snap her back to reality.

"Zeke, it could start to bleed again if I take it off. You need a doctor"

"I've had some experience with this sort of thing."

"What sort?"

"Knife wounds."

"*Personal* experience?"

"An occupational hazard," he tossed out.

She had little time to take that in, before Zeke plowed on. "If he'd slashed an artery, we'd know it by now."

She was no battlefield nurse, but she conceded the assessment was probably true. Still, she noted that his steely tone contrasted with the tremor shaking his body.

"I just need a little patching up, some rest, and antibiotics to make sure I don't get an infection." He paused for a moment. "And I've got to get warmed up. Do you have a blanket?"

"Yes." Darting out of the bathroom, she opened the door to the linen closet and snatched an old comforter off one of the top shelves. When she returned to the bathroom, she found Zeke fumbling with his belt buckle. But his hands were awkward from the tremors, and after several seconds he swayed dangerously.

Elizabeth tossed the blanket over the side of the claw-footed tub and took over the task of undressing him. Her ability to remain detached lasted only a few seconds. If she had felt awkward removing his shirt, it was even worse lowering his zipper. Willing her hands not to betray her nervousness, she slipped them inside the waistband and pushed downward. But the feel of his thighs against her palms sent a ripple of sensation through her. They were rock hard and muscular. The right one was marred by a long slash that had healed to a thin line. *His previous experience with knife wounds,* she thought.

She realized suddenly that she had been standing still for several seconds staring at his jockey shorts. The damp fabric had molded itself to his body, leaving almost nothing to her imagination. The masculine part of him was as impressive as the rest. He broke the spell by sliding his right foot out of the pant leg. Her cheeks turned rosy as she hastily reached for the comforter, which she managed to drape around his shoulders without making eye contact. It was a relief when he pulled the blanket closed.

"Well, now for the fun part," he muttered in a flat voice. "Too bad you can't kiss it and make it better."

Her gaze rose to his face. His gray eyes were filled with an intensity that sent a shiver through her.

"We could try it," she heard herself say.

Time seemed to stand still, until finally he bent slightly and brushed his lips against hers. It was the merest touch, yet she felt it in every cell of her body.

"Don't I wish," he murmured softly.

Her throat clenched. She wished, too.

Before she could speak, he appeared to deliberately shake himself, and his voice changed from intimate and soft to no-nonsense and practical. "The handkerchief is probably stuck to the wound, so I'd suggest using a clean cloth dipped in boiling water—cooled, of course," he added.

"Um-hum." She tried to match his tone.

"Maybe I should lie down while you get ready."

"In my spare room."

Although she took his arm, he didn't let himself lean on her as she ushered him down the hall to her guest room. Still, his face was drained of blood by the time he lay down, pulled the blanket around himself and closed his eyes. She thought he was going to sleep, until he said, "You should put on some dry clothes, too."

She'd been so focused on him that she'd forgotten about herself. Now she glanced down and realized with chagrin that the light summer dress she'd worn to dinner was plastered to her body. Worse, it had turned transparent, revealing everything underneath in vivid detail. Cold—it must be the cold—had turned her nipples to small, hard points, and the outline of her panties was clearly visible. Horrified, she started to make a quick exit, then heard him chuckle. Her gaze flew to his. He might be wounded and in pain, but a little grin played around his lips as he stared at her.

"The view is good for morale. Too bad I'm temporarily out of commission."

"Zeke!" She sputtered, before turning on her heels.

"Bring the duffel bag, too," he called out. "There's medicine in the first-aid kit."

Once she was in her own bedroom, she studied herself in the mirror as she unbuttoned the front placket of her dress. Her hair was a riot of dark brown curls around her face, her cheeks were flushed and her deep blue eyes shone with a brightness she hardly recognized. Methodically she yanked off the sodden dress and dropped it in a heap on the floor. Then she shucked her slip and panty hose and pulled on a T-shirt and shorts, before heading down the hall. When she looked in on Zeke, he appeared to be dozing, so she tiptoed down the stairs.

Ten minutes later she was back with sterile gauze, adhesive tape, the duffel bag and a number of other supplies she thought she might need.

Zeke's eyes snapped open the moment Elizabeth walked into the room. He visibly relaxed when he saw it was her.

"Expecting company?" she asked.

"I hope not."

She'd only been kidding, but the tone of his voice made goose bumps rise along her arms. "I kept checking in the rearview mirror," she protested. "I'm sure we weren't followed. How would…Sebastian know where to find us?"

"Sebastian is pretty resourceful."

"Well, he was surprised to find a woman attacking him with a poker, and he sure didn't know who I was," she countered. "So he can't look up my address in the phone book."

"That's a point in our favor." Zeke cleared his throat.

"Set the duffel bag over here." With his good arm he gestured toward the floor beside the bed.

She nodded and did as he asked, wondering why he wanted to keep the bag so close to him.

When she glanced up, she found he'd slid the blanket from his shoulder and was peering at the blood-soaked handkerchief. "Let's get it over with."

"Yes," she agreed, as she adjusted the reading light beside the bed. To her relief, there was no more fresh blood on the handkerchief and no immediate redness of the surrounding skin. So far, no infection.

Although she proceeded as gently as possible, she knew she was hurting him as she worked the fabric free from his flesh. Yet when she paused for a moment, he urged her to hurry.

When she finally got a look at the wound, she found a slash that was long but not very deep.

"I thought I deflected the blade," Zeke said with satisfaction. "It could have been a lot worse."

"You still need stitches."

"Why don't we try to get away with butterfly bandages?"

"You're more likely to have a scar," she informed him. "And the cut could pull open."

"I heal fast."

She gave him an exasperated look, but sensed there was no use arguing. It was his funeral, she thought, as she let him tell her what to do, ending with a loose bandage.

"Hand me the duffel bag," he said. "And I'll get some antibiotics."

"You lie still. I'll get them."

"No." He leaned over the side of the bed and made a grab for the bag.

But she had already pulled open the zipper. On top of some neatly folded shirts, glinting in the light from her lamp, was an automatic pistol.

Chapter Three

Zeke watched Elizabeth staring at the gun.

"Is it loaded?" she asked in a strained voice.

"Yes."

She stood very still for several seconds, then sat down in the chair beside the bed and turned deliberately so that she was facing him. Gone was the feeling of intimacy that had been building between them since she'd brought him to her house. "Okay, Zeke, now that we've got you patched up, maybe you'd better fill me in. Were you expecting Sebastian—or someone like him?" she inquired, her voice raspy.

He wasn't exactly at the top of his form, and he wasn't used to answering questions about his private business. He felt his jaw harden, and before he could think about what he was saying, old instincts took over. "You don't have to marry me," he snapped. "I'll figure out a way to solve the problem myself. I just need a good night's sleep, and I'll clear out."

After a moment of silence, she murmured, "I gave you my word."

"Unfortunately, neither one of us knew what we were getting into."

She pinned him with a gaze that was both steady and unnerving. "So the moment I try to find out what I'm facing, you don't want my help. Is that it?"

The challenge in her eyes made him realize he was acting like a jerk. She'd been magnificent tonight. Hell, she'd probably saved his life when she'd attacked Sebastian. Then she'd taken him home, instead of dropping him on his ass at the nearest emergency room. Now she was asking him perfectly reasonable questions, and he was responding like a POW at an interrogation session. He suspected it had as much to do with his attraction to her as with his instinct to play his hand close to his chest. Over the past two years, he'd tried to fool himself into thinking that they could keep up a friendship, when what he really wanted was to take her to bed. Now he was worried about how to be her husband for a little while and not make love to her. He sighed. "I'm sorry. I'm being unreasonable, aren't I?"

She gave him the ghost of a smile. "It's been a stressful couple of hours."

He shifted on the bed, trying and failing to find a more comfortable position. "Starting with my crazy marriage proposal."

"Do you need my help to save your daughter?" she asked.

"Yes."

"Then you have it."

"Why?"

Emotions flickered across her face—emotions that made his pulse race. Yet her answer had nothing specific to do with him. "I know what it's like to be a frightened child with nowhere to turn. I also know what it means to have someone rescue you."

He knew she'd been adopted, though she'd never talked about her life before that. He watched her swallow, knowing he'd stirred up memories.

"I was eight when I was lucky enough to land at the Egans'. Old enough to have had a lot of bad stuff happen."

"I didn't know."

"I don't advertise it," she said.

He knew what that was like, to keep old anger and pain locked away.

"I mean, it doesn't hurt me any more."

He wondered if it was true, and wished he could say the same thing.

"Let's talk about Sebastian Demos," she said.

Zeke sighed. "Once he was my friend. We've been enemies for a long time."

"Because he was in love with Sophia."

His eyes widened. "What?"

"He was in love with her," she said firmly. "When he told you she was dead, I know he was grieving for the woman he loved. And I know he considers you responsible."

He nodded slowly, as the new pattern formed in his mind. All at once a lot of things made better sense. But he would never have thought about them on his own. It had taken an outsider—a woman.

"Demos sounds Greek," Elizabeth said.

"Close enough. He's from Mythos."

"It's in the Aegean?"

"Yes. Near Crete. The island was claimed by both Greece and Turkey. It's nominally part of Greece now, but the local government has a lot of autonomy."

"I know you've been on a number of archaeological expeditions there."

He drew in a breath and let it out slowly. He hadn't talked about Sophia or Sebastian in years—or even thought about them. He'd consigned them to his sordid past, until the letter from Irena had arrived and damn near blown him away. "Sebastian was her cousin. He never could have married her."

"He's the one who introduced you to her," Elizabeth said suddenly. "That's one of the reasons he's so angry. He's angry with himself, not just you."

Zeke's mouth dropped open. He eased his jaw back in

place. "You got all that from overhearing a one-minute conversation?"

She shrugged. "It goes along with the rest of it."

"I guess I'd better tell you about it, before you come up with something worse than what really happened," he muttered, wondering as he said it what that would be. It helped when he felt her hand gently cover his.

He signed out a long breath. "I was, uh, on a dig with a team from Hopkins—translating inscriptions from an ancient library. Sebastian had trained with the university in Athens, and the government had insisted that he work with us. At first I was annoyed. But he turned out to be very knowledgeable in ancient Greek and the perfect liaison to the local population. We got to be friends. He took me into his household, and I betrayed his trust."

He watched her, trying to gauge how she'd taken that. She softly stroked her fingers over the top of his hand and waited for him to elaborate.

He swallowed, then turned his hand up and knit his fingers with hers. When she clasped him more tightly, he felt a little of the constriction ease from his throat. Marshaling his words, he tried to make the rest of the story concise and coherent. "Sophia's father was Sebastian's uncle. There was still guerilla warfare between the Greeks and the Turks on Mythos when she was little. Her parents were killed in a terrorist attack, and her father's people agreed to raise her."

Elizabeth nodded tightly.

"Marrying her off was a way to end their obligation. But it was more than that. The marriage was supposed to cement relations between two important families. But she didn't love Aristotle—her fiancé. He was much older than she was—a widower. I was an outsider, and she started talking to me about things that no one in the household wanted to hear. I didn't plan to get involved. I knew it was a mistake. But we got close, too close. I wanted to talk to her uncle about us—see if he'd agree to let her marry me.

She told me he'd never listen. I guess she thought we could run away together."

He shifted uncomfortably again, his whole body tense once more. He was certain from the way Elizabeth's hand had stiffened that she didn't want to hear the intimate details of his relationship with Sophia.

He didn't need to tell them to her, but there were other things he'd kept hidden, and he knew he'd reached a point where he either had to step over a line he'd never crossed or end the conversation.

Silence hung between them.

"My throat is kind of dry. Would you get me a glass of water?" he said, stalling for time.

She tipped her head to one side, and he knew she understood what he was doing. Still, she made no comment as she got off the chair and exited the room. After she'd left, he shut his eyes for a moment. Either he could trust her, or he couldn't.

When she returned, she handed him the water without saying anything. No pressure.

He took several swallows and set down the glass before continuing. "I had to make a trip to Athens. That's when they married Sophia to Aristotle. I couldn't tell Sophia why I was leaving. I couldn't tell anyone. And I can't tell you about it either…without getting into things I swore I'd keep confidential."

"Either you trust me, or you don't."

The observation was so startlingly close to his own recent thoughts that he was speechless for a moment. Then he found his voice again. "Over the years, I've made myself available to various government agencies. That time it was the CIA. They pulled some strings to put me on the archaeological expedition in Mythos. It was in the hill country where there was still trouble between the Greeks and the Turks. I was keeping tabs on some of the groups, and I found out that one of them was going to plant a bomb on a U.S. plane scheduled to leave the country. The plan was to make it look like the other side had done it. I had to get the information to my contact in Athens. There wasn't anybody else who could deliver the message."

Her eyes widened. "You were working as a spy?"

He shrugged.

"You've done it more than once."

He gave a tiny nod.

"Is that how you got wounded before?"

"Yeah."

There was a new look of respect in her eyes.

He hadn't told her the story to make himself look good. He'd only been trying to make her understand that he hadn't left Sophia to go on a sight-seeing trip to Athens, as Sebastian had put it.

"Don't start thinking I'm some unsung hero." He'd certainly never thought of himself in those terms. He'd simply been atoning for past sins. "I made my report as quickly as I could. But the weather turned bad, and I couldn't get back for almost a week. When I showed up at Sophia's family compound, I found out she was already married to Aristotle. And I was no longer welcome in the house. I couldn't stand to stay in Mythos any longer, so I arranged for a replacement on the expedition. And the CIA got somebody else to do their spying."

He was all wound up now. Maybe it was partly because Sebastian might have killed him a couple of hours ago— and no one would have known the truth. So he kept speaking, aware that the need to bare his soul had won out over caution. "You heard me tell Sebastian I didn't know Sophia's child was mine. That's true as far as it goes. I didn't know for sure. But I kept track of Sophia for a while—through my government contacts. When she gave birth eight months after her wedding, I had to wonder. Still, there was nothing I could do about it. I didn't have any claims on her or Ariadne. And I knew that if I came back, I'd only make trouble for her. So I got on with my life." He ran a shaky hand through his hair. "Then I got the letter from Sophia's sister Irena, telling me Sophia was dead and Ariadne was in danger.''

"What happened to Sophia?" Elizabeth whispered.

"Irena told me that Sophia's marriage was very unhappy. Aristotle was angry because she didn't get pregnant again—that she didn't give him the son he wanted. He kept—" He swallowed painfully and made himself say it in a rush of words. "He kept forcing himself on her and complaining to his friends that she'd become barren. Finally one of his associates got tired of hearing about it and told him that he might as well leave her alone because he'd never fathered a child. The baby was mine. So he killed her to save face," he added in a flat voice.

"You can't mean that!"

"Morality can be strange by our standards in a place like Mythos—at least in the back country where the people follow customs and traditions thousands of years old. It's a society where a man's honor is one of his most important possessions. It's also a society where he can do almost anything he wants with his property—including his wife and daughters, as long as he's careful. There was no murder investigation. Irena says Aristotle arranged for an accident in the mountains. Thank God, Sophia had sent Ariadne to her before it happened. She's trying to keep her safe until I get there. But she says Aristotle is looking for them. He wants revenge. Not just on his wife. He wants to wipe the slate clean. He doesn't want a child hanging around with his name, who isn't his."

Elizabeth closed her eyes for a moment. "It looks like he wants revenge on you, too. Do you think he sent Sebastian?"

"That occurred to me."

"Can you legally take Ariadne out of the country?"

Once more, Elizabeth had cut right to the heart of the problem.

"Not by myself. I've done some quick research and found out that under Mythosian law, a single man can't adopt a child. Only a married couple, and they're pretty strict about the rules.''

"So that's why you need a wife."

"Yes. And I need someone who can take care of her on the trip home. I don't have a clue about how to...do any of that."

"And what about afterward?" she asked in a breathy voice.

"What do you mean?"

"When you get back to Baltimore, are you planning to raise Ariadne by yourself?"

His gaze turned inward. "I hadn't thought about that. I hadn't thought about anything past getting her out of Mythos. I'm not exactly cut out to be a family man."

"Why do you say that?"

He felt his hands clench. He'd admitted a lot of things tonight, but he drew the line at opening up on that particular subject. The one time he'd broken his own rules and talked about his dysfunctional family was when Sophia had lulled him into sharing confidences—and it had turned out very badly. He wasn't going to make the same mistake again.

Elizabeth's eyes flashed. "What are you thinking—that once you've saved Ariadne's life, you'll give her away or something?"

"I don't know how to be a father," he said hotly. "I didn't ask to be one."

"Fatherhood is usually the last thing on a man's mind when he takes a woman to bed."

He flushed, because she had hit so close to the mark again.

The air between them felt charged with electricity, and he realized once again how quickly things could go wrong when a man and a woman got into an intimate conversation. Now he was sorry he'd let his guard down. "You don't have any right to judge me," he grated.

"Maybe not. But the conversation has stopped being productive." She kept her gaze steady, apparently waiting

for him to say something else. She was going to have a
long wait.

When the silence stretched, she murmured, "If you don't
need anything else, I'm going to bed."

"Fine."

She didn't say good-night, she simply turned on her heel
and left the room.

Zeke watched her leave, relieved yet angry—with himself and with her, too. Yet now, at least, she was giving
him some privacy. His emotions in turmoil, he slipped the
gun under some of the clothes in the duffel bag and rummaged for a pair of sweatpants, which he pulled on gingerly, afraid he might dislodge the butterfly bandage from
his wound. By the time he finished, his shoulder was throbbing. He was searching through the medical kit for aspirin
when his fingers encountered a small jar. He'd gotten the
stuff several months ago from Thorn Devereaux and forgotten all about it. Now he remembered his friend pressing
it on him. It was a wound-healing salve being developed
by Thorn and Mac McQuade, the director of Medizone
Labs. Thorn had described it as a medical breakthrough,
and asked Zeke if he wanted to be a test subject—on the
proviso that he keep the product strictly confidential. He'd
agreed. But he hadn't had any occasion to use the stuff
until tonight.

Lifting the bandage over the knife wound, he winced as
he removed the butterfly tape he'd suspected wouldn't be
very effective. Then he smoothed a generous amount of the
ointment along the length of the slash before replacing the
bandage. Immediately his skin felt hot and tingly.

He was still in pain, so he also took a couple of aspirins
before snapping off the light. As he lay in the dark, Elizabeth's face floated in his mind, her soft lips pressed together, the color high in her cheeks. He'd touched a nerve,
all right, when he'd admitted that he was scared spitless of
being forced into the role of a father. Only now that he
thought about it, he realized he'd felt too intimidated to put

his feelings in those terms. Still, he didn't have to explain himself to her. Damn, he wished he didn't need her or anybody else. If he could have rescued the little girl on his own, he'd be on his way to Mythos already. But he had to bring along a woman. A wife. The authorities would check to make sure it wasn't a sham before they'd let him take his daughter home. And he needed someone he could trust. Elizabeth. As his thoughts came back to her, he found it was impossible to hang on to his anger.

He'd wanted her in his bed. On his own terms. Yet she'd declined his unspoken invitation to what she'd rightly judged would be a dead-end affair. He'd walked away from other women who wouldn't settle for pleasure over commitment. He'd stayed friends with Elizabeth—and stayed obsessed with her. He'd fed his obsession by digging into her background—using some of his old contacts and the considerable power of several data bases that were unavailable to the public. The more he'd learned, the more he'd liked her—and the closer he'd felt to her. And at the same time, the more he'd worried that he might lose control of his emotions and ask for more than he himself could give.

Elizabeth wasn't typical in any way that he'd yet discovered. He'd met her at a party he'd almost skipped and been mesmerized by her face, which was interesting rather than beautiful. Her eyes were slightly slanted and her jaw was a little too strong for the feminine ideal. But her lips and nose were damn near perfect. It was what he'd seen in her blue eyes, though, that had touched his soul—a hidden past. A painful past.

If Zeke had to describe Elizabeth in a few words, they would probably be "too selfless for her own good." Tonight she'd confirmed what he'd suspected, that the years before her adoption had been traumatic. Perhaps that explained why she'd taken care of her father at home in his declining years and why she worked for Birth Data, a charity that helped adoptees find their birth parents. She'd never used their services herself, but she was still working there and going to graduate school part time. "For the intellectual stimulation," she'd told him.

He could spend the whole night thinking about her. He'd done it before. In his mind he changed the fierce expression on her face to a smile. Then he replayed the kiss she'd given him when he was too shaky to take off his own pants. Her lips had hardly brushed his, yet the memory was enough to turn him on. Lazily, he began to imagine undressing her the way she'd undressed him. But he was too worn out to get farther than unbuttoning her shirt before he drifted off to sleep.

He woke hours later, glanced at the lighted dial of his watch and cursed. Almost five in the morning—so much for staying alert. Yet he couldn't deny that he'd needed the sleep. Experimentally he moved his shoulder, and to his surprise, the throbbing pain was only a dull ache.

Sitting up, he threw back the covers, stood and cautiously stretched. The skin over the wound smarted, but nothing more. Tiptoeing down the hall to the bathroom, he closed the door and turned on the light. First he removed the bandage and inspected his shoulder. Astonishingly, it was almost healed. Thorn hadn't been kidding about the power of this stuff, he thought, as he traced the dull red line where the cut had been. He could see why his friend had asked him to keep it confidential.

Elizabeth had hung his soggy pants over the radiator, and they were almost dry. The bloody shirt was stuffed into the trash can. He pulled it out and wrapped it around the bandage he no longer needed before stuffing the whole wad back into the trash. After using the facilities, he washed his face and peered at his reflection. His color was a lot better, he decided. Back in his room, he slathered on another application of the miracle ointment and pulled a knit shirt from the duffel bag.

After shrugging into it and donning a pair of sweat pants, he headed for the stairs, intent on having a look at the knife that Sebastian had used to carve him up. It was still in

Elizabeth's purse, which he remembered her setting down in the front hall. Hopefully, it was still there.

The old steps creaked a couple of times on the way down. So did the floorboards in the hall. He stopped, afraid that he might have awakened Elizabeth. But he didn't hear any movement from the upper floor.

Her purse was right where she'd dropped it. Picking it up, he carried it through an archway into the living room. From old habit, he closed the blinds before turning on a lamp and sitting on the couch. In the weak circle of light, he unwrapped the knife. The blade was smeared with dried blood, his blood, he noted with a grimace. And maybe Demos's. In the fight, he'd driven the weapon toward Sebastian's side. He didn't know if he'd done any damage.

Grasping the blade in the towel, he held the gold hilt under the light. Either it was an authentic fifteen-hundred-year-old piece from the Roman occupation of the island or a very good copy. More than a weapon, it was a work of art, the kind of masterpiece that would generate high excitement at an archaeological dig and command hundreds of thousands of dollars if it was smuggled out of Mythos and offered to the right collector. The observation made him think about his father. Old news, he told himself.

Sebastian must have chosen the weapon for the symbolism, he decided, as he ran his thumb over the delicate work. An expert craftsman had depicted a miniature scene from mythology. On one side of the hilt was the beautiful Persephone, who had been abducted by Hades, the god of the underworld. He was on the opposite side, a dark, ugly presence waiting to swoop down on the fragile young girl and drag her off to his bed. Odds were that was how Sebastian had seen his relationship with Sophia, Zeke thought. What Sebastian didn't know was that Sophia had been the seducer, not he.

In the silent living room, Zeke turned the knife in his hand, remembering Sebastian's attack and the events leading up to it. His thoughts were so intently focused inward that it took several minutes before he heard an intermittent squeak.

When the noise finally registered, the hairs on the back of his neck prickled in reaction. Raising his head, he listened intently. The sound came again, and he realized what it was—the same clandestine creaking his own feet had made on the old floorboards when he'd been trying to move silently.

He swiveled his head, appraising his options. There were two entrances into the room—the archway through which he'd come and the doorway to the dining room. All he saw in either direction was darkness. Every muscle tense, he waited. The squeak came again. Stealthy. Closer. From the hallway.

Sebastian. He'd appeared out of nowhere yesterday evening. Now he was back, as if Zeke's very thoughts had drawn another attack from his old enemy. He had only seconds to react. In one fluid motion he sprang off the sofa and pressed into the shadows at the side of the archway. Whipping the towel from the knife blade, he raised the weapon in his right hand, ready to strike.

Chapter Four

A figure glided into the archway—a figure holding a baseball bat. A split second after Zeke brought the knife down, he realized with horror that it wasn't Sebastian. Somehow he changed the angle of the blow even as he gasped her name. "Elizabeth."

She leaped back, and he wasn't sure in the dim light whether the blade had missed her neck. Overbalancing, she landed heavily on a braided rug. He dropped the knife as if it had suddenly turned red hot in his hand and went down after her.

"Elizabeth, are you all right?" he shouted as he scrambled over her and turned her head. When he ran his hand along her neck, he felt smooth, warm skin, and thanked God that he had missed.

"Zeke," she breathed, staring up at him with large, rounded eyes. "I heard someone down here. I didn't know who it was."

"Why didn't you check in my room?"

She looked confused and slightly abashed. "I did. I stuck my head in your door. It was dark, and all I could see was the comforter on the bed. I thought you were still there. Sleeping. After last night, you needed to sleep," she added in a small voice.

"Elizabeth, if you thought someone was in the house, you should have gotten me up, not tried to handle it on

your own. It wasn't very smart coming down here by yourself.''

"But you were wiped out. You needed—"

He cut her off with a sharp exclamation. "Don't you
understand that I could have killed you just now? And what
if it hadn't been me? Did you think you were going to beat
off Sebastian with a baseball bat?''

"Why not? I beat him off with a poker," she said de-
fensively, but some of the strength had gone out of her
voice. Probably she had come down here without thinking
clearly—the way she'd reacted when she'd grabbed the
poker. Now she was starting to realize she could have made
a fatal mistake.

A roiling mixture of anger and fear made his voice harsh.
"You could get in a couple of licks with the poker because
he was fighting me, too," he choked out, still grappling
with what had almost happened.

"You didn't hurt me, Zeke," she whispered.

"I could have killed you. God help me, I could have
killed you," he said in a strangled voice.

She lay there on the rug staring up at him, her hands on
his shoulders. His right hand was still pressed to her neck
where he'd been afraid he'd struck her. Without conscious
thought, he stroked a path down to her collarbone and back
up to the tender skin just behind her ear, awestruck that her
body was so delicately made. So fragile. So vulnerable.

Under the slight pressure of his fingers he felt her pulse
accelerate, and he was suddenly filled with a primal need
to make her understand how much she meant to him, and
how thankful he was that he hadn't harmed her.

Her lips parted. So did his as they touched down on hers
and brushed back and forth over soft, warm flesh.

When she made a tiny incoherent sound, feelings he'd
struggled to hold in check spiraled through him. They were
fueled by his previous anger, by her misguided heroics and
by his fears for her. The kiss changed from gentle to urgent
in the space of a heartbeat. His mouth pressed hard against

hers, greedy for the taste of her. He kissed her until they were both trembling and breathless in the darkened hallway.

He hadn't meant to lose control like that. When he started to pull away, he felt her hand in his hair, pulling him to her, urging him closer. Unable to turn away, he feasted on her, first with his lips, then with his tongue. It was impossible to deny himself the sweet pleasure of her mouth. He wanted her——had wanted her for too long. Now she was soft and pliant under him, telling him wordlessly that she craved this as much as he did.

With his tongue, he traced the outline of her lips, feeling her shivering reaction like an electric charge through his body, jolting his heart.

She was still wearing the T-shirt she'd put on earlier. But not her bra. Through the knit fabric he felt her breasts strained upward against his chest. Her nipples were hard points that tantalized him almost beyond endurance.

"Ah, Elizabeth," he breathed. He wanted more, needed more.

Shifting to one side, he propped himself on his elbow. Their eyes locked. Hers were large and bright, following the movement of his hand as he slowly pushed up her shirt. She went very still as he gazed down at her breasts, mesmerized by the way the dark tips crowned her rounded curves. They seemed to beg for his touch. Gladly he obliged, brushing his fingers back and forth across one and then the other, feeling them bud even more tightly. His own body tightened in response——even as she sighed in pleasure.

She didn't speak, and he wondered if she was afraid to break the spell. He stopped thinking clearly, as he felt her fingers on the hem of his shirt. A smile played around her lips as she slipped her hands inside and slid them upward, winnowing through his chest hair. She did what he had done, only with both hands, gliding her fingers across his hardened nipples until he groaned softly. He lowered his head again, giving her small kisses that sipped at her lips.

Gradually they deepened, until he was taking hot, greedy drafts of her. When he lifted his head, she gave him a bemused look. He had imagined making love to her many times, but this was so much sweeter that he could hardly breathe.

"I wanted to do that before," she whispered.

"Yes."

"In the bathroom. When——" She stopped short and gasped. "Zeke!"

He knew from her indrawn breath and the alarm on her face that she'd suddenly remembered why they'd come to her house in the first place. It wasn't so strange that she'd forgotten. He'd been suffering from the same memory loss.

"I'm sorry. I—I forgot all about your shoulder."

"It doesn't matter." He tried to gather her close, but she was no longer pliant in his arms.

She looked down at her front, her cheeks reddening. Quickly she tugged at her shirt, covering her breasts. "We can't. You can't do this."

"Want to bet?" he murmured, shifting so that his erection was pressed into the cleft between her thighs.

She shook her head, the color in her face deepening. "I mean you shouldn't."

Right, he thought, giving himself a mental shake. But his reasons were different from hers. He'd promised himself he wouldn't take advantage of her, and the first chance he got, he was doing just that.

"I'm sorry," he said in a gruff voice. With a sigh, he rolled onto his back, his breath uneven as he tried to remember all the reasons making love with her was a bad idea.

She followed him over, reversing their positions. "I should have remembered," she said in a small voice.

He tangled his fingers in her silky hair, pressing her cheek against his chest, needing to hold her.

"When you kissed me," she whispered, "my head started spinning."

His, too, he thought. But he wasn't going to admit it. Besides, he had another problem. He could either break his promise to Thorn or lie to Elizabeth. He didn't like either alternative. But he forced himself to choose.

"You stopped…" he caught his breath "…making love with me because you were worried about my shoulder. It's…healed."

"It couldn't be!"

"Remember when your friends at 43 Light Street helped Thorn and Cassie Devereaux?" he asked.

"Of course."

"Thorn and I have a number of mutual interests, so we've stayed in touch. He knew I was going places where I might not have access to medical facilities, and he gave me some drugs he's developing with Medizone Labs, stuff that's a long way from FDA approval. I forgot some of it was in my first-aid kit. There's a salve to heal wounds. I used it before I went to sleep last night."

She listened impassively but still looked skeptical. "Let me see your shoulder."

He sat up and tugged at his shirt, pulling it upward until the shoulder was exposed. Her eyes widened as she peered at the place where the slash should have been. With her finger, she traced the red line that was the only marker of where he'd been cut. Her touch was light, yet it was enough to start his pulse racing again.

"I wouldn't have believed it unless I'd seen it," she said, her gaze focused on the knit flesh. Then her eyes met his before flicking away. She didn't say what they were both thinking. There had been no medical reason to stop what they were doing.

"I'm lucky to have the stuff," he said in a thick voice. "I agreed not to tell anyone about it until it's on the market. But I told you."

She held his gaze for several heartbeats. "A man can tell his wife things he can't tell anyone else," she whispered. "So pretend we're already married."

He looked away, thinking about what else a man might share with his wife. "And when the marriage is over?" he asked, reminding them both that it wasn't for keeps.

Her eyes turned guarded.

He climbed to his feet. When he held out his hand, she declined the offer and pushed herself up.

He knew from the way she turned her head away that he'd hurt her again. This time it had been deliberate, and he felt a fist-sized knot constrict within his chest. It took a great deal of willpower to keep himself from reaching out, dragging her into his arms and telling her that he was only trying to protect her. Instead he cleared his throat and said in an almost normal voice, "You get dressed, and I'll fix breakfast. What do you want?"

"Surprise me," she whispered, before turning toward the stairs.

QUICKLY ELIZABETH CLIMBED the steps, feeling Zeke's gaze drilling into her back. She kept her shoulders straight and her head high as long as she thought he was watching her. But as soon as she knew she was out of his line of sight, she started to shake. She'd done a pretty good job of holding herself together while she was with him. Now she wrapped her arms around her shoulders and leaned against the wall, wondering if her legs would support her weight.

A rush of color came into her face. He'd almost made love to her. He would have if she hadn't stopped him. She pressed her fist against her lips. At least one of her questions had been answered. She knew that Zeke wanted her. That was something she could hang on to. The sexual attraction wasn't one-sided.

She drew in a quivering breath and let it out slowly, trying to find the calm center of herself that had eluded her since Zeke's outrageous marriage proposal. She rarely lost her cool or got angry. And she'd certainly never thrown herself at a man like that. But she'd been on an emotional roller coaster since the previous evening—alternately angry or frightened or turned on. Now she was upset that Zeke was pushing her away again. Yet she knew he was trying to grapple with his own emotions.

He'd never been married. He'd never been a father. In fact, he'd never been responsible for anyone except himself. He was alarmed at the prospect of raising a child—particularly a child who legally belonged to another man. Even so, he was going to Mythos to rescue his daughter and bring her home. He was so panicked in the process that he'd broken what appeared to be one of his most unbreakable rules. He'd let another human being see his vulnerabilities.

Her face softened. Last night she'd lain awake for a long time thinking about how to help him—and Ariadne. Inevitably, her thoughts had drifted to a picture of herself, Zeke and a little girl who looked a lot like him, all happily sitting around a breakfast table. Or on the way to school in the morning. Or at the beach. All the things a family did together. Only they weren't a family and might never be.

She squeezed her eyes closed, trying to blot out the tantalizing images. It was simply a fantasy, like making love with Zeke or imagining a future for the two of them. And fantasy was a luxury until they brought Ariadne safely home.

In the bedroom, she turned on the intercom she'd installed when her father was sick. Downstairs in the kitchen, she could hear Zeke open the refrigerator and various cabinets and wondered what he was going to fix.

Her mind still on him, she started to pull up her T-shirt. She went very still, her breath hissing out, as she remembered the feel of his hands on her breasts and his lips on hers—and the warm look in his eyes. Well, she could lecture herself about fantasies all day, but it didn't change the fact that something powerful was building between them, something that could easily explode out of control again. If she had any sense, she'd run in the other direction. Yet she couldn't. She'd given him her word that she'd help him. Quickly she pulled off the shirt and threw it on the chair. Grabbing a robe, she headed for the shower. A cold shower.

IRENA TIPTOED INTO THE tiny room where the little girl was sleeping. Ariadne was lying on a low cot, curled on her side, one chubby hand clutching the quilt that covered her. Irena's chest tightened as she gazed at the child's dark lashes and features that were so like Sophia's. "You remind me of your mother when she was your age," she whispered. "Peaceful. Innocent. Before disaster struck."

Irena sighed. Life was a series of disasters. She'd done her best to cope, but sometimes that wasn't enough.

The child didn't stir. She had no inkling of the trouble she'd caused simply by existing. She knew nothing of Zeke Chambers. All she knew was that her mother had gone away on a long trip, and *Theia* Irena was taking care of her. And everything would be all right.

The trusting naïveté made Irena's heart squeeze. The child was too young to know that things didn't always work out the way you wanted.

Irena had been twelve and Sophia had been six, when their parents had been killed by terrorists. They'd been taken in by relatives who resented the responsibility of two more girls to raise; girls who would need dowries if they were going to make a good marriage. Sophia had been so sad and afraid, and Irena had made herself the strong one. She had to give her sister special care. She had to make things right for her, because there was no one else to do it.

By the time Sophia began to mature, Irena could see that she'd made a terrible mistake. She'd made her sister selfish, taught her to want more than she should expect. Irena married and was obedient to her husband, but little by little her sister had crossed a line into territory where no woman should tread. No woman of Mythos, at any rate. Perhaps in America it was all right for a woman to make love before her marriage. Or to choose her own husband. Or to think of ways to hurt the man she married. But not in a land where she was supposed to take care of her home and obey the men in her family.

Ariadne stirred, cried out in her sleep, and Irena was instantly at her side. Coming down beside the bed, she stroked the dark head and whispered soft words. The little girl's lids blinked open. For a moment panic filled her eyes. Then she focused on her aunt and quieted.

"Go back to sleep," Irena crooned.

"Where's Mama, *Theitsa* Irena?"

"I told you. On a trip."

Ariadne looked down at her chubby little hands. "Did she send me away because I was bad?" she asked in a small voice.

Irena took the child in her arms, rocking her. "Oh, no. Of course not. Something wonderful is going to happen. You're going to have a new father," Irena whispered. "A man named Zeke Chambers."

Ariadne lifted her head and blinked. "You can't get a new father."

"Your mother and I did, when she was just a little older than you are now."

"Was he nicer?" the child asked in a quavery voice. She had never been treated very well by Aristotle, who had wanted a son and probably always had secret doubts about her paternity, anyway.

"Much nicer," Irena lied.

"He and Mama will take care of me."

"Maybe just him. But don't talk to anyone else about him. He's our secret."

The little girl's face clouded. "I want Mama."

"I know," Irena answered. "But promise you won't say anything about your new papa."

Ariadne regarded her gravely. "All right." Then she yawned and pulled the covers up.

Irena stroked her hair, the rhythm soothing her nerves as it calmed her niece. She knew she was doing it again, making the same mistakes she'd made with Sophia, trying to force life into a better pattern. But she acknowledged the truth. It could go either way. If Aristotle found them, she and the child would die. And if Chambers got there first, then the daughter would live the fairy-tale life her mother had always craved.

And what about herself, Irena wondered, her thoughts turning to the man who sheltered her and the little girl. Although she'd warned herself to be cautious, her feelings for him were growing stronger. Yet she sensed that he had been hurt terribly in the past. He was closed and bitter. He needed someone to love him. But trying to break through the wall he'd built around his heart might only bring her grief.

ZEKE CHECKED THE LARDER. He could fix them bowls of cornflakes, he supposed. Yet his nose wrinkled at the idea. He'd never liked cold cereal for breakfast. Besides, pouring out two bowls of the stuff wouldn't serve the purpose of diverting his mind from the real issues plaguing him—like the ethics of making love to a woman you intended to abandon as soon as she'd helped you save your daughter's life.

He grimaced. He didn't want to abandon her. He'd fantasized for a long time about what it would be like to settle down with Elizabeth Egan, really settle down and stop traveling the world. But he knew deep in his heart that he could only hurt her, the way he'd hurt Sophia. Unfortunately, that was his heritage. Before Sophia, he'd hoped that maybe he could change the pattern of his life. He'd been wrong. Making love with Sebastian's cousin had been one of his major mistakes. And he hadn't even known the magnitude back then. They'd made a baby, a little girl he'd done his best to pretend wasn't his responsibility. Yet now that he knew she was his and that she was in trouble, he had to rescue her.

And then what? He hadn't been thinking very far ahead. But Elizabeth's question had made him realize that he'd have to come up with a plan for after the rescue operation. He clenched his hand on the edge of the counter, thinking about his own childhood. The birthdays he'd spent with his aunt and uncle. The school plays nobody had attended. The boarding schools.

His parents had been out of the country for months at a stretch. And when he'd spent time with them, they'd been like polite strangers. No wonder he didn't know how to be a father, especially to a little girl he'd never met. But from everything he knew, Elizabeth had bonded with her stepparents. Maybe she could give him some pointers.

He stopped short, realizing he'd been staring into the open refrigerator for several minutes. The direction his thoughts were taking astonished him—and frightened him, he silently admitted. He couldn't cope with the sudden constriction in his chest, so he forced his mind back to the designated task—cooking breakfast.

He felt his blood pressure returning to normal as he pulled milk and eggs from the refrigerator and bread from the pantry. Elizabeth liked French toast, he remembered from a brunch Katie and Mac McQuade had given.

The kitchen was old-fashioned, he noted as he settled down to the business at hand. The sink featured a real drain board. The controls for the stove were in the front. Dangerous if you had small children, he mused, then wondered why he was worrying about something like that.

Bending, he searched the lower cabinets and found a skillet. Nice and heavy, he thought appreciatively. Then he combined the egg and milk in a flat-bottomed casserole, so it would be easy to soak the slices of bread.

As he stopped beating the mixture, he thought he heard the floor squeak out in the hall again. The fork raised in his hand, he stopped and turned his head sidewise, listening intently. Nothing else drifted toward him besides the sound of the shower upstairs, so he went back to work. Long seconds passed, during which he tried to convince his tense muscles to relax. The attempt was only partly successful.

He couldn't entirely shake the feeling of uneasiness. Angry with himself for inventing enemies where none existed, he poured oil into the skillet, added two slices of the bread and adjusted the heat.

Then deliberately he looked up, and his hand froze on the pan's handle. It couldn't be. But it was. Sebastian Demos was standing in the doorway, one arm held awkwardly across his chest. This time the intruder was better prepared. He was armed with a gun instead of a ritual knife. Still, he couldn't hide the shock on his face as he stared at Zeke's shoulder. "I thought I cut you, too," he growled.

"I guess you were mistaken," Zeke replied in a quiet voice, even as his mind scrambled for a way out. He wanted to shout a warning to Elizabeth. He knew he'd only get shot, and then she would be on her own. Instead he inquired politely, "Does your arm hurt? Or is it your side?"

Sebastian growled a curse.

Pretending to cower against the stove, Zeke bent his elbow in back of his body, moving his hand slowly up, reaching for the control knob. "How did you find us?" he asked, partly to distract Sebastian and partly because, despite the evidence of his own eyes, he still couldn't believe the man had trailed them to Elizabeth's house.

Sebastian gave him a smile that turned up his lips in an artificial grimace. "I thought you spies were taught all the tricks."

Zeke struggled to keep his expression neutral as he moved slowly to the side, away from the pan sitting on the left front burner. Demos had called him a spy, but his undercover activities in Mythos had been well camouflaged. He couldn't have known at the time, could he?

"There's no point in lying. Why don't we be honest with each other?" the man in the doorway continued.

"All right. Did Aristotle send you?" Zeke asked, forcing himself not to glance at the pan of French toast. Soon it would be hot enough to burn, unless he'd made a mistake, he thought in sudden panic, unless he'd turned the knob the wrong way. Damn, now what was he going to do?

"No. Aristotle isn't the only one who hates you, or the only one with the power to thwart you."

Is that true? Zeke wondered.

"I propose an exchange of information," Demos went on. "I'll tell you where to find your daughter, if you tell me where your father hid the treasure he stole from my people."

Again Zeke tried not to react. His father's thievery had been a central motivating force in his own life. Yet how could his father's criminal activities be connected to the present situation? "Why should I trust you?" he countered, trying to buy some time. "Last night you tried to kill me."

Sebastian gave a little shrug. "I'm sorry about that. I thought that I could handle my feelings. But when I saw you standing in the kitchen, in the middle of your rich and comfortable life in America, I lost my head for little while. I'm okay now."

Sure, Zeke thought. *And you're so friendly that we can't have this conversation without a gun in your hand.*

"So tell me about the treasure," Sebastian suggested mildly.

"My father didn't reveal his plans to me."

"So you say." Sebastian raised the gun threateningly.

Then several things happened almost simultaneously. The pan on the burner began to hiss and pop.

When Sebastian's attention shifted to the fire, Zeke reached for the handle of the skillet and threw the pan and its contents at him—just as the sound of a gunshot split the air.

Chapter Five

Zeke ducked, even as he braced for the impact of the bullet in his chest.

To his astonishment, it was Sebastian who groaned and clutched his arm. Behind him, Elizabeth shouted, "Next time, I'll aim for the middle of your back. Move over by the refrigerator."

Sebastian half turned.

"Move!" Elizabeth ground out.

The intruder complied, his steps shaky.

Stunned, Zeke took in Elizabeth's policeman's stance, her arms braced in firing position. Slowly she advanced into the room.

Casting aside his astonishment, Zeke crossed to her side and gave her a quick, grateful look before taking the gun from her hand. It was the one he'd packed in his duffel bag, the one he hadn't wanted her to see.

"Sit," he ordered Sebastian, pulling out one of the kitchen chairs.

The other man complied, his face pasty. As he sat there with his eyes closed, he looked like all the fight had gone out of him, Zeke thought. But it could be an act. He could be getting ready to strike.

"Do you have any rope?" he asked Elizabeth. She looked a sight—her hair was wet, she was shoeless, and her T-shirt stuck in patches to her skin. Clearly, she'd thrown on her clothes and come charging downstairs.

"Rope," he repeated, when she didn't answer.

"For what?"

He gestured with the gun toward the man in the chair. "To tie him up."

"But he's hurt. I—I shot him," she added in a strained voice, as if she'd just realized the magnitude of what she'd done.

"It's only a flesh wound. He'll live."

She didn't seem to hear him. "He was going to kill you. I had to do it," she whispered, her eyes pleading for understanding.

"You had to shoot him," he repeated. "And now we have to tie him up so he can't hurt us."

Her head bobbed. Then, moving like a sleepwalker, she stumbled toward the pantry. When she returned, she was holding a plastic bucket with several coils of hemp inside.

Zeke eyed the rope. He didn't trust Elizabeth to do a good job of tying Sebastian up. On the other hand, he wasn't sure he liked the idea of her taking charge of the gun again, either. She looked too spacy.

"Can you cover him?" he asked.

"I—" He saw her make an effort to pull herself back together. "Yes," she answered in a stronger voice.

"Good." He thrust the weapon back into her grasp and knelt beside the chair. "Hands behind your back."

ELIZABETH KEPT THE GUN from shaking in her grasp as she watched Zeke tie Sebastian. The man winced when Zeke pulled his wrists into position and efficiently secured them to the sides of the chair. Next he tied his ankles to the chair legs.

After checking that the bonds were tight, he took Sebastian's chin in his hand, forcing him to make eye contact. "You say Aristotle didn't send you. Then who was it?" he growled.

"Nobody." The denial was issued through gritted teeth.

"Don't bother lying," Zeke said in a deceptively mild voice, his fingers tightening.

Sebastian's jaw clenched, probably from equal measures of pain and determination.

"I can make you talk," Zeke growled.

"You could try, but you don't want your girlfriend to see what a bastard you are," Sebastian countered. His face was gray, and beads of sweat stood out on his forehead. Elizabeth knew he must be suffering. She had to clamp down on her lip with her teeth to keep from screaming.

Zeke must have read her mind, because he shot her a quick glance. "You may feel sorry for him now, but don't forget he tried to kill us—twice," he muttered. "It's lucky we were up early."

She nodded tightly. He was right. Yet she'd never been in a situation like this, a situation where the enemy wasn't playing by civilized rules, and you might have to sink to his level to survive.

Zeke's hand squeezed into a fist and opened again. "I have to know who I'm up against," he said, his eyes asking for understanding.

"I know," she whispered. She did. Truly. But she didn't have to like it.

"Go and get dressed," Zeke ordered in a strangled voice.

She hesitated. As he shifted his gaze back to Sebastian, his look was murderous.

"Go on. Pack a bag with a couple changes of clothing. Comfortable stuff. Slacks and pullovers. The weather's unpredictable in Mythos at this time of year. Take a slicker if you have one." He paused. "And bring down my shoes and my duffel bag. We have to get out of here as soon as I'm finished."

She didn't want to leave the two of them alone, but she didn't want to stay, either. Stiff legged, she exited the room. Her fingers sweaty on the banister, she climbed the stairs, wondering what interrogation techniques Zeke might have learned in the CIA. The intercom was still on in her room, and Zeke's voice came to her hard and ruthless. ''Now that we're alone, you're going to talk.''

Before she could hear Sebastian's response, she crossed the floor and turned the monitor off. When she caught a glimpse of herself in the mirror, she was shocked to see her hair was wet. She'd forgotten all about it, when she'd heard Zeke and Sebastian talking.

It took her but a few minutes to dry her hair, pull on new clothes, throw some items in a carry-on bag and bring the things Zeke had requested. The whole time, she tried not to think about what was happening in the kitchen, but she had to keep gulping in air to counteract the iron bands that were tightening around her chest.

When she came down the stairs again, Sebastian was sitting with his eyes closed and his head bowed. Elizabeth could see a couple of red marks on his face where Zeke might have slapped him.

Zeke stood with his back to her, his shoulders rigid. With an angry jerk, he picked up the shoes she'd brought and shoved them on his feet. Then he pulled on a light jacket and slid the gun underneath, tucking it into the waistband of his slacks. Elizabeth and Sebastian listened intently as Zeke picked up the telephone receiver and called in a terse message to 911. Without giving his name, he stated that a burglar had been apprehended in the Egan household and gave the address. Declining to answer any questions, he hung up. ''Let's go,'' he said to Elizabeth.

She trod gingerly around Sebastian's chair. When his foot twitched, she practically threw herself through the open door.

Zeke turned to give the man in the kitchen one last look. ''I'd love to hear what you tell the police about that bullet wound,'' he growled. ''And the knife slash, too.''

Sebastian stared silently back, and Elizabeth felt the tension crackling between them like heat lightning.

With a low curse, Zeke broke the eye contact first. Eliz-

abeth followed him onto the porch. Feeling as if she had
emerged from the depths of the earth, she dragged in a
lungful of the early morning air, but said nothing until they
were in Zeke's car and several blocks from the house.

"Did he tell you anything?" she whispered.

He gave a short, derisive laugh. "He told me plenty. But
nothing that's going to help us."

"I thought...I thought you were going to beat the truth
out of him," Elizabeth finally said.

"I wanted to. But when I looked into his eyes, I
couldn't," he said in a tight voice. "He believes he has
reason to hate me. Maybe he's right."

"And that governs your behavior?" she asked with a
catch in her voice.

"Yes."

Based on his confession that he'd been a spy, she'd made
assumptions about Zeke But now he'd just proved he was
more complicated than she had thought.

"At least he won't tell the police any more than he told
me," Zeke growled. "He's in the country illegally. That
gives us some advantage."

She stared at his rigid profile, knowing now that he was
acting on some personal code of honor—even if it was
against his best interests.

"You didn't harm him...because you seduced his
cousin," she clarified.

"I didn't seduce her. But I shouldn't have let her climb
into my bed. And I should have been smart enough not to
get her pregnant."

"*She* climbed into *your* bed?" It was the first time she'd
heard that version of events.

"Let's drop the subject," he snapped. "She's dead, and
I'm not going to say anything I'll be sorry about later."

Elizabeth compressed her lips. She longed to know what
had happened between Sophia and Zeke six years ago, or
between Zeke and Sebastian just now. But she could see

from his stern expression that this wasn't the time to hound him for information.

When she silently looked down at her hands, he let out a little sigh. Then he reached for the phone on the console and punched in a number. In response to a voice on the other end of the line, he pressed more digits and listened.

"Your answering service?" she asked when he hung up.

"Yes. There's a package at my house." He made a sharp left turn.

She clenched her hands together tightly. "We can't go back there. It could be a trap."

"I know, but the package is from Irena, Ariadne's aunt. She may have some information about Sebastian." Again the silence between them stretched. This time she sensed that he wanted to say something more.

"A penny for your thoughts," she offered.

He kept his gaze on the road. "Things aren't working out the way I planned. I never dreamed I'd be putting you in so much danger—even before leaving the country. Maybe I should go to Mythos alone."

Her fingers tightened painfully. More than ever, she was convinced that Zeke needed her—and not simply in the next few days. But she was willing to bet he wasn't ready to hear that. She'd have to offer a more compelling reason why they shouldn't dissolve the partnership. "Leaving me behind won't help," she said in a steady voice. "Unless, of course, you go back and kill Sebastian before the police arrive. He knows I'm involved. If you abandon me here," she added, choosing her words carefully, "Aristotle or whoever Sebastian's working for, could come after me."

Zeke's response was a low curse. "You're right. I'm not thinking clearly."

She reached over and covered his hand with hers. "I didn't say it to make you feel bad. Only so you'll realize that we have to see this through together."

His knuckles whitened on the steering wheel. "I should have pulped Sebastian."

"I'm glad you didn't. My shooting him was bad enough."

His lips quirked. "We make a fine pair of undercover operatives."

"Actually, we do."

"When you came downstairs with the gun, how did you know I needed help?" he suddenly asked.

"After my father got sick, I installed an intercom. I turned it on before I took my shower."

"Oh." There was a wealth of implication in the syllable.

He must know she'd heard the cryptic exchange about his father, but he didn't offer any information. Well, she hadn't expected him to tell her everything, had she? She'd known all along that he kept his own counsel. If she wanted him to confide in her, she had to bolster his sense of trust. "I turned the intercom monitor off when I went back upstairs," she murmured.

"I appreciate that," he said but to her disappointment didn't volunteer anything else.

A few minutes later, they reached the vicinity of his home. He pulled to the curb a block and a half away, instead of driving the rest of the distance. "Your job is to guard the car," he announced as he reached for the door handle.

"The car doesn't need guarding," she muttered.

"I don't want you near my place. If I'm not back in twenty minutes, drive to the nearest police station and tell them everything that's happened."

"But after Sebastian cut you, you said you couldn't call the police," she answered in surprise. "And we left my house just now before they could get there and ask us any questions."

"That's right, but if something happens to me, you don't have any alternative. You'll have to explain what's going on." Her face must have registered her alarm, because he went on quickly. "But nothing's going to happen. I'll be right back."

*There's not much I can tell them, beyond the fact that
Sebastian keeps attacking us. Give me some more dribs and
drabs of information. Like what does this have to do with
your father, and where will I find Ariadne?* She wanted to
shout a barrage of questions at him. But she suspected he
didn't have all the answers. Moreover, reaction to questions
would divert his attention from making sure he got in and
out of the house safely. So she contented herself with a
reassuring squeeze of his hand.

Zeke left the keys in the ignition. After climbing out of
the car he reached back inside, fished a baseball cap out of
the back seat and plopped it onto Elizabeth's head. It was
several sizes too big and slid down over her forehead.
"Good," he approved. "And slouch in your seat."

She complied, giving him as much of a smile as she
could muster. When he turned his back and started rapidly
down the block, she checked her watch, then closed her
eyes. They snapped open immediately, because she wanted
to watch him as long as she could. It was then that a chilling realization hit her. Every time she'd let him out of her
sight, something bad had happened. She reached for the
door handle, ready to bolt after him. At the last second, she
stopped herself. He was right. She had to stay out of danger
in case he needed a witness. But he wouldn't. *Not this time,*
she told herself. This time everything was going to be okay.

Sitting up a little straighter, she looked around. The
morning was overcast, and a light fog rose from the pavement. Under the circumstances, she counted that a good
omen. At least the mist gave Zeke a little bit of obscurity.

Still, when he disappeared around the corner, she felt
utterly alone. She managed to keep from looking at her
watch for five whole minutes. After that she found she was
checking it every minute and a half. She might as well
watch the second hand go around, she thought with a
self-accusing little snort.

Seventeen minutes… Eighteen… Time was almost up.
She felt her heart thumping inside her chest. Only a minute

to go. Sitting forward, she strained her eyes for the first
sight of him as he turned the corner.

Twenty minutes.

He didn't appear. Lord, had she been right the first time?
Had someone been waiting for him to pick up the package?
Silently she began to pray for his safe return. The prayer
kept her from railing at him for being so reckless.

Her fingers clutched the door handle as she tried to keep
from leaping out of the car and charging up the block. But
that was a bad idea, she told herself. What if he was coming
back a different way? Or what if somebody hiding in the
house had taken him captive? They'd get her, too.

She was almost ready to slide into the driver's seat, when
he came trotting down the sidewalk.

Her eyes traveled eagerly over his tall frame as he came
toward her. She'd expected to see a package in his hands,
but they were empty. Before he could see what kind of
state she was in, she wiped her sweaty palms on her slacks
and tried to bring her breathing under control.

"Zeke! What happened?" she demanded. So much for
appearing cool, she thought as her voice rose on a frantic
note. He opened the door and slid into the driver's seat like
a man who had come back from a long journey, not a trip
down the block.

His expression was a mixture of caution and exasperation. "I'm sorry. A neighbor came outside. He wanted to
commiserate about the broken window, and I couldn't get
away without looking like something strange was going
on."

"The window," Elizabeth repeated. With everything
else that had transpired, she'd forgotten all about that. "My
God, your whole living room must be a mess."

"Yeah. Maybe I should call the insurance company before we leave." The way he said it made her think that he
was stalling.

"What about the package from Irena?" she asked quietly.

His face softened, took on a look she'd never seen before. "She sent me pictures," he said in a low voice. "Of Ariadne. And her mother."

He didn't move, yet Elizabeth could sense an almost charged intensity in the air around him. She hesitated, not wishing to intrude. But she wanted to see his daughter—and get him talking about her. That might come naturally, if they looked at the picture together. Sophia was a different matter. Elizabeth was curious about the mother of his child. *More than curious,* she silently admitted, though she dreaded what she might find out.

"Can I look at them?" she asked in a halting voice.

He reached into the pocket of his jacket and produced a folded brown envelope. For several seconds he held it loosely between his two hands, like something of great value that might be damaged by exposure to the light. Then gingerly he removed three photographs, being careful not to smudge the image on the top one as he handed them across the console.

Elizabeth held them in her palm. The first was of a stunning young woman, slim and lithe. Wild, dark hair framed her narrow face. She smiled at the camera in a way that made her look like she had just rendezvoused with her lover.

"Sophia," Elizabeth breathed.

"Yes."

"She's very…attractive," Elizabeth murmured, unable to suppress a stab of jealousy. She might have said "breathtakingly beautiful," if the words hadn't stuck in her throat.

"She was," Zeke corrected.

Elizabeth felt a wave of relief followed immediately by guilt. Never in her life had she been glad that someone was dead, and the admission shocked her. Yet she could see from the photograph that she paled in comparison to this woman who had borne Zeke's child. What did he feel for Sophia now? Elizabeth wanted more than anything to know, but she was unable to ask the question for fear that

the answer would be too hard to bear. Instead she shuffled
the picture to the back of the pile.

Underneath was the photo of a small girl, about four or
five, sitting at the foot of a gnarled tree with feathery
leaves. Her features were delicate like her mother's, but her
face was more rounded and her dark hair was cut straight
across her forehead. Her huge dark eyes stared solemnly at
the camera. Elizabeth drew in a little breath as she absorbed
the total effect. Then she switched to the third photo. This
time the girl was standing with her knees locked and her
arms straight at her sides. She looked small and spindly,
yet somehow defiant.

"Your daughter's beautiful," she said. "Like her
mother."

When Zeke didn't comment, she continued, "You've
never seen her before?"

"No. I told myself it was none of my business, that she
was better off if I stayed the hell out of her life." He swallowed hard. "Now…she looks sad."

Elizabeth studied the picture, striving for some other in-
terpretation. "Maybe not. Maybe she's being thoughtful."
Her free hand fluttered in the air. "Or…or the picture could
have been taken on a bad day."

"Stop making excuses," Zeke snapped. "She's under-
nourished. And I get the feeling she hasn't had a very
happy life. I should have come back and claimed her," he
concluded.

"You said that was impossible," she reminded him.

His voice shook. "I used to think it would have been
better if she'd never been born. Now I realize that was just
a cop-out. I should have tried to make sure she had a decent
break."

Elizabeth slid him a sidewise glance. His eyes were
misty, and it was obvious the pictures had affected him
powerfully. Up until now, his daughter had been an abstrac-
tion. The photographs had given him a brief but telling
glimpse into her life. Coupled with that was the shock of

seeing Sophia, the mother of his child. He hadn't had any contact with her in years, and he'd said he'd tried to forget about her. But he must have started remembering their liaison as soon as he'd learned about the little girl, and the vibrantly beautiful photograph had reinforced the memories. The speculations tore at Elizabeth.

She sat quietly in her seat as Zeke started the car engine with a decisive twist of the ignition key, and they lurched away from the curb. "Ariadne needs me," he said in a low voice.

She found her voice. No matter what she was feeling, she had to help Zeke understand that he hadn't already failed. "And now that you know what's happened, you're going to be there for her," she reassured him.

"If it's not already too late."

Chapter Six

Zeke drove down York Road, then onto the Beltway, his face tight and closed.

"Where are we going?" Elizabeth asked.

He lifted his hand from the wheel with an exasperated gesture. "I wish to hell I knew. Before Sebastian showed up I was thinking we could take a commercial airliner to Greece and a charter flight to Mythos. Now I've got to make other arrangements—figure out a way to slip onto the island and get to Ariadne without Aristotle finding out I've entered the country."

"Zeke, I know you want to keep this confidential, but we need help."

He sighed. "I hate to ask a favor of the CIA. But maybe they'll figure they owe me one..."

She ran her fingers along the edge of the leather seat, wondering how to phrase her next remark. "I have another suggestion. We were talking about Thorn and Cassie Devereaux."

"Um-hum."

"Remember my friends down at Light Street got together to help Thorn when he was in trouble? I'm sure they could do the same thing for us."

Zeke's eyes didn't leave the road, but Elizabeth saw from the change in his expression that he was seriously considering the suggestion. "I have a lot of respect for the Light Street irregulars," he said.

"Jason's a security expert," Elizabeth reminded him. "So is Cam. Jed is an ex-spy. Steve has his own air transport company. Jo and Mike are PI's," she ticked off some of the qualifications of her friends. "Collectively, they've had a lot of experience dealing with crises. They can tap into government intelligence information, and we won't have to worry about anybody leaking our plans."

Zeke swung his head toward her. "Jason told me to call him if I ever needed a favor." He grimaced. "But this is a pretty damn big favor."

"You could have blown the whole operation with Thorn. You didn't. And I think they consider they owe you for that. So what do you have to lose by asking?" she pressed.

"Nothing, I guess."

"Do you want me to call?" she asked, gesturing toward the phone on the console. "I've got the number in my address book."

Zeke shook his head. "Thanks, but I'll do it. And not from a cell phone where the conversation can be monitored."

He exited the Beltway and found a fast-food restaurant with an outside phone that faced a quiet side street.

"But first," he said, pulling into the drive-through line. "I promised you breakfast. I'm sorry you missed my French toast. What about a biscuit and some eggs?"

She dredged up a grin. If he was thinking about food, he must be feeling better. "A biscuit and coffee sound good," she allowed, wondering if she could choke anything down.

He gave the order to the speaker, along with a breakfast ham sandwich and coffee for himself. When her stomach rumbled, he changed her order to the same as his.

The need to fuel the body was a powerful force, she thought, as she sat with him in the car working her way through the sandwich and coffee. Neither of them tried to carry on a conversation while they ate. Long before she was finished, Zeke wadded up his sandwich wrapper and took his coffee to the pay phone.

THE OLD MAN WADDED UP the fax transmission from Baltimore. So much for the wonders of modern technology. The world had shrunk considerably while he was locked away in prison, but remote control devices like the fax were only tools. You still needed a physical presence to give you power over people. *People like Sebastian Demos,* he thought with an angry growl. He'd paid the son of a shepherd well and sent him to America to keep an eye on Zeke Chambers. It seemed he had his own agenda.

Out in the hall he heard soft feminine steps approaching.

"Cyril? Are you all right, Cyril?"

Quickly he hid the transmission under a pile of papers.

The footsteps stopped, and he looked up to see the woman standing in the doorway, studying his face.

"I told you not to disturb me while I'm in my office," he said curtly.

"I'm sorry," she murmured, her fingers plucking at the coarse black fabric of her skirt. She didn't look him directly in the eye now. She was well trained. Of the old school. A woman who recognized that men were the ones who made the big decisions.

"You should be resting in the heat of the day," he said.

"I was on my way to my room. But I heard your voice. You sounded upset."

"It's nothing. A business deal that I thought was running smoothly. It appears to need my personal attention."

She hesitated several seconds before moving away from the door. Was she going to turn into a problem, too, he wondered. It would be a shame for their relationship to end so abruptly—the way his relationship with Sebastian was about to end.

As ZEKE RETURNED from the phone, Elizabeth anxiously

studied him for clues about how the conversation had gone. She was glad to see his step was lighter and his features were more relaxed.

"Good news?" she asked.

"Yes," he said, glancing down at a sheet of paper on which he'd written directions. "As it turns out, Jason and Thorn are testing some new equipment up at Whispering Pines, the Randolph Electronics secure facility near Camp David."

"Oh, right. In the Catoctin Mountains. I used to go camping in the state park with my Girl Scout troop. Sometimes my mother was a chaperone, even though she hated sleeping in a tent. But we didn't do it this late in the season..." Her voice trailed off when she realized that nerves were making her prattle on about things that would be of no interest to Zeke.

"Whispering Pines has the standard Randolph Electronics communications equipment," he said as he started the engine. "While we're driving up, Jason is going to check out some of the information I need on Mythos."

"Good."

"They may be able to get specific information on the Pappas family," he added. "Sophia's husband's family."

"Um-hum."

As they headed north, Zeke fell silent. Casting him a sidewise glance, Elizabeth decided he looked like there was something eating at him. However, she had also discovered that it was a mistake to push him.

She kept from asking questions by turning toward the window and watching the urban sprawl slowly give way to countryside. She hadn't been up here in years, and it made her a little sad to see how far the new housing developments had stretched from the city. In the distance she could see a line of hazy blue mountains. Soon the relatively flat landscape turned to rolling hills.

From time to time Elizabeth stole a look at Zeke. His expression was brooding. He waited almost half an hour before clearing his throat. What he said was so out of context that she blinked. "You—and your Girl Scout troop went camping up here."

Why was that—of all things—on his mind? "Yes."

"And, uh, your mother went along, even though she hated sleeping in a tent."

She nodded.

"So she was like a regular mother—even if you weren't a baby when you came to live with the Egans."

So that was it! All at once, she understood the logical flow of his thinking. "She was a regular mother," Elizabeth said thickly. "Donna and Sam Egan were the best things that ever happened to me."

"How old were you when they adopted you?"

"Ten."

"But you formed a bond with them," he said in a low voice.

"Yes. I did." She almost never talked about her early life, even with her closest friends, but she realized what Zeke's questions represented. She'd made him start contemplating life with Ariadne after this rescue mission, and he was trying to figure out if he had a chance to be a real father to his child after being totally unknown to her for so long. She wanted to reassure him, but she had to tread lightly. If she mentioned Ariadne, he might accuse her of pushing him into something. At the same time, she had to paint a realistic picture. If Ariadne had been badly traumatized, getting her to trust a stranger wouldn't be easy. So, hesitantly, she began to talk about herself. "My birth mother kept me until I was three. She and my father were never married. I assume he had some exotic genes in his background. Maybe Native American."

Zeke nodded.

"I don't remember much about my mother, but I suspect it would have been better for me if she'd turned her unwanted kid over to the welfare people right away."

Zeke made a low sound, but she plowed on.

"By the time I landed with Donna and Sam Egan, I'd been in more than a dozen crummy homes. The Egans were the foster parents who ended up with kids that were difficult—the ones that weren't considered normal."

He shot her a questioning look. "What do you mean by that?"

"At the age of ten, I was a hard case. I was angry. Withdrawn. Destructive. A lot of bad things had happened to me, and I didn't have any reason to believe life would get better."

"Why?" he asked, his voice so low she could barely hear.

"Different reasons." She swallowed painfully. "There was one couple who didn't feed me much. When I was bad, which was pretty often, they locked me in a closet."

He swore loudly.

"There were others who beat up on me or made me do housework all day. And one guy..." she stopped and took several breaths "...who climbed into bed with me one night after I'd been with him about two weeks."

"No!"

"He touched me—with his hands," she whispered, her own hands twisting in her lap. This was so hard to reveal. She'd only told three other people in her life. Mom and Dad, and the therapist they'd sent her to when they realized she needed help they couldn't provide. She probably wouldn't have told Zeke, at least not at this stage in their relationship. But now that she'd spoken, she wanted him to understand that it could have been a lot worse. "It only happened once. The next day, I—uh—made sure I was caught stealing money from his wife's purse. She called the welfare department, while he just stood there looking at me. He knew why I'd done it, but neither one of us told. I was sure nobody would believe me about the abuse. He was probably sweating bullets over whether I'd keep my mouth shut."

"My God," Zeke gasped, his face thunderous. "I didn't know about any of that."

"Hardly anybody does." She gave a little shrug. "But the story ends okay. Even if a child has a really rough start, the right parents can make a tremendous difference," she said. "At first I didn't believe anyone really cared about me or would treat me like a...human being," she gasped, astonished that even after all these years, the emotions were like fresh knife wounds.

She hadn't been sure how he'd react to her revelations. When he reached over and covered one of her hands, she breathed a little sigh and unclasped her own fingers, turned her palm up and grasped his. For several heartbeats, she simply held on to him. "The Egans were very patient with me. Donna was a natural-born mother. She'd straightened out a lot of messed-up foster kids before she got me. At first I fell back on my defensive behavior—lying, hiding, refusing to do any chores. I kept challenging them, but they understood where I was coming from. They didn't get angry or beat up on me, the way I expected, or threaten to send me away. They were firm but patient. Gradually, when they didn't meet my expectations, I started to feel safe enough to let my guard down. I'd find myself smiling—or carrying my plate to the sink when I was finished eating. And I remember what a revelation it was, when I realized I actually enjoyed some of the subjects in school. Reading. History."

Zeke nodded.

"I was with Mom and Dad for nine months before they asked me how I'd feel about adoption."

"How did you feel?"

"Scared spitless." Her fingers tightened around his. "I'd never lived with anyone like them. Things were going better than they ever had, and I was afraid to jinx it. But I wanted to belong to them more than I was afraid to take the chance." She paused for several seconds, staring out the window as she tried to phrase the next part right.

"There are so many good memories. The first time I ever had a birthday party and got to invite kids from school. The garden Sam and I planted and tended together. The proud look in Donna's eyes when I came home with all A's and B's on my report card. Or when I graduated from college. I know they loved me and that they didn't do any of the things they did for me because they felt obligated, or because I was born to them. They loved me because having a child of their own completed their lives—and because I needed somebody to care about me."

"It sounds...wonderful," Zeke said wistfully.

"Better than if I had been their flesh and blood, I think, because I knew how differently things could have turned out. We were a strong family for eleven years. Mom died of a heart attack right after I finished college. Dad was never quite the same after that."

"You took care of him when he got sick."

Elizabeth's vision had turned inward. "He'd done so much for me, and I knew it would tear him up to leave his house. He had a good disability insurance policy, and he owned a part interest in a farm with his brother. He sold that out to his nephew so I could afford to work part-time for a few years."

"Some people would say you put your life on hold."

"Well, I never cared much about what anybody said. That's one of the legacies I carried over from the bad, old days." She shook her head. "I know a lot of people think I was making a big sacrifice by keeping Dad at home instead of sending him to a nursing home. For me, it was a chance to spend a little more time with him."

Zeke nodded. Being a man, he was probably wondering how living with her aging father into her late twenties had affected her love life. Then Elizabeth flushed when she realized she was jumping to conclusions. Probably he wasn't thinking about anything like that at all. Probably he was still worrying about his own role as a father. She was the one thinking about making love—because they'd come so close to doing it.

When the car slowed, she saw that they were leaving the highway. A few minutes later, they turned onto a winding road that followed the course of a fast-running mountain stream. "Almost there?" she asked.

"Yeah." He said nothing further, and Elizabeth hoped she'd offered him a more constructive way to think about his relationship with Ariadne. Sitting back in her seat, she tried to relax in preparation for the meeting with Jason. But she couldn't. She'd revealed more about herself than she'd liked, and she wanted to know what Zeke thought about her now that he knew her rocky beginnings. He wasn't saying. And he wasn't talking about his own background, either, she noted, although she'd given him the perfect opportunity to explain to her how his father was involved in their present problems. But he'd fallen back on silence.

They had entered an area of dense woods, ablaze with yellow and orange foliage. A few houses were visible from the road. Elizabeth imagined that more were hidden by the trees.

Zeke didn't say anything until he'd consulted the piece of paper on which he'd written the directions. "Start looking for a mailbox with a kitschy little Dutch windmill," he instructed. "The address is 44002."

"A windmill? You're kidding."

"That's what Jason told me they use to identify the turnoff—instead of a big sign advertising the research facility."

She watched the rural boxes that came up at odd intervals, sometimes in clusters at the ends of long driveways leading into the woods, sometimes alone.

After a relatively straight stretch, she spotted the windmill and pointed. "Over there."

Zeke checked the address before turning in.

"Wait a minute," Elizabeth said. She'd been wrapped up with her past, but now that they were here, she realized that she and Zeke hadn't talked about a rather important subject.

Zeke braked the car and looked at her inquiringly.

"I gather you told Jason about the rescue mission. But what did you say to him about…us?" she asked, hearing her voice rise at the end of the sentence.

It gave her a little frisson of satisfaction to see color bloom in his cheeks. "Well, I guess everybody down at Light Street already knew we were good friends. I didn't say it in so many words, but I…uh…let Jason think we were already engaged when you agreed to help me."

"They know we're getting married?" she clarified, wanting to be sure of the situation she was walking into.

"Yes. It seemed less awkward," he added. "For you."

"Oh," she managed. *And how awkward is it going to be when you dump me afterward,* she wondered, wishing she hadn't spent so much time with her mouth shut and her gaze on the scenery. She'd thought she was giving Zeke the space he needed, but she realized she'd been avoiding important issues. And now there was no time to discuss their relationship.

He started the engine again, and the car jerked forward. The first part of the narrow road was gravel, like most of its neighbors. But as it curved up a hill into the woods, the surface changed to asphalt. Rounding a bend, they came to a double chain-link fence with barbed wire on top.

"After the cute little windmill, that doesn't look very friendly," Elizabeth murmured.

"Cam Randolph got tired of coping with industrial espionage in Baltimore. They've moved a lot of their most sensitive projects up here where the security is tighter— and only people actually working on a particular project have access to it. Also, Thorn feels more comfortable away from the city."

Elizabeth nodded.

Zeke pulled up at the gate and spoke into an intercom. It was attached to a video camera and a machine that looked like something from a drive-in bank. In fact, he was instructed by a mechanical voice to insert his driver's license into the slot. After half a minute, the machine gave back the card and the gates swung smoothly open.

"You may proceed to the main facility," the same stilted voice advised.

"Well, the security measures make sense, but I'm not sure I'd want to work here," Elizabeth said as they headed for a low wood-and-stone building that looked as if it might have been a hunting lodge in former days.

"You can get used to this kind of security," Zeke told her.

"Are you speaking from personal experience?" she asked.

"I've been at training centers like this," he clipped out.

"With the CIA?"

"With various government agencies. Once I spent a month in the country—at a complex hidden under a tobacco field. I didn't see the sun for a month. But they had a very nice gym at level B-4."

The conversation ended when they pulled into a paved area where three vans, a couple of four-wheel-drive vehicles and a sports car were parked. Before Zeke cut the engine, Jason and Thorn came striding through the front door. Both of them were tall, rugged looking, and similar in bearing. Jason had been a secret agent before joining Randolph. Thorn was a man without a past, who was glad to have found a group of colleagues who appreciated his talents and could market his inventions without his having to worry about nosy people questioning his identity.

Zeke climbed out of the car. The three men shook hands and spoke for a few minutes. Then Jason turned to her. "So you're engaged," he said. "Congratulations."

She nodded, fighting not to blurt a disclaimer. Jason and Thorn were married to two of her best friends, and anything she said to them would get back to Noel and Cassie. Although her silence now might mean a lot of explaining later, she decided to postpone the pain.

"I hear you're in a bit of a hurry to get on with the wedding," another voice said. It wasn't one of the men.

Elizabeth blinked. Somehow agreeing to marry Zeke hadn't translated into an actual wedding in her mind. The oversight said a lot about her emotional state, she supposed. You didn't get married by remote control. You stood up in front of a judge or a minister and exchanged vows. She'd always pictured herself getting married in a church. She was pretty sure that wasn't going to be the case.

Turning, she found herself facing Kathryn Kelley, a psychologist who had begun working several months earlier with another of her friends, Abby Franklin. The look in Kathryn's green eyes said that she wasn't as willing as the guys to take Zeke's story on faith.

"What are you doing here?" Elizabeth asked.

"Randolph Electronics is planning to station some personnel at this location for several weeks at a time. I was hired to evaluate the facilities for long-term use and make some recommendations."

Elizabeth gave her a weak smile, wishing she hadn't run into someone so insightful at this particular time in her life. The last thing she wanted to do was answer questions about her personal relationship with Zeke—or to have another woman making a silent assessment.

"I've been working on your request," Jason remarked to Zeke as he led the way into the building. "Irena is no longer at the address from which she mailed you the initial letter."

"How did you find that out so fast?"

"You can get quite a lot of information from databases. The apartment she took in the port town of Kalana has been listed for rent since the Thursday before last. She and the little girl checked into a small hotel in Delvia a couple of days later."

"Delvia's in the mountains," Zeke said.

"She was only at the hotel one night, but she's still in the area. She signed for a package from UPS a couple of days ago—at a rented villa."

"That's consistent with what she told me. She gave me a number to call and leave a message when I arrived in the country. Then she'd let me know where to meet her."

"Do you want to look at some maps I've pulled up on the computer?" Jason asked. "You can get a small plane from the mainland to Kalana. Then get transportation to Delvia."

Kathryn put her hand on Elizabeth's arm. "Since I'm here, Jason asked if I'd take care of some wedding arrangements while the men discuss strategy."

"Is that how they divide up the duties between the men and the women?" she shot back.

Kathryn gave a little shrug. "Well, both jobs need to get done, and I don't have much experience with covert operations. Do you?"

Elizabeth shook her head. *Not until the past couple of days,* she thought.

"Zeke said you need to be married before you leave for Mythos," Kathryn continued. "Usually there's a waiting period for the license, but Jason showed us how to backdate that in the computer files. I've pulled up the pertinent information on Zeke through his employee record at Johns Hopkins University. But I need some personal information from you. Date of birth. Address. Stuff like that."

"That would be in my Birth Data records," Elizabeth said crisply.

"Those files aren't accessible to us," Kathryn replied, brushing back a lock of red hair that had fallen across her face.

Elizabeth stared at her. Irrationally, she wanted to come back with a sharp reply, even though she knew this woman was trying to help her.

"Lucky they don't require a blood test in Maryland," Kathryn murmured.

"I'm sorry. I'm a bit tense," Elizabeth answered.

Kathryn gave her an encouraging smile. "I understand. I would be, too."

Elizabeth summoned an answering smile, as she followed the psychologist into a comfortable lounge and settled onto one of the couches.

"Do you want something to drink?" Kathryn asked, pausing beside a table with a coffeepot and a pitcher of water.

"I'm fine, thanks," Elizabeth answered, although it wasn't true. She was far from fine, and she was pretty sure Kathryn could read the signs—in her voice, on her face, in her body language.

The psychologist sat down at a desk with a computer terminal and pulled up the marriage license form that she'd already partially filled out. "When I finish this, we'll transmit it to the Frederick County records department," she explained.

"Why Frederick?"

"I believe that's where the airport is located. The ceremony's going to be held there."

Elizabeth's eyebrows arched in amazement at the amount of work that must have been done while she and Zeke were on the road. Lord, people here had been running around like crazy, and all she could think about was how miserable she felt and how embarrassed she was going to be later.

Trying to stop her insides from churning, she provided data Kathryn requested. Full name. Date of birth. Place of birth. Address. Occupation.

"So how do you feel about entering into a marriage you don't think will last?" Kathryn quietly slipped in at the end of the list.

"Sad," Elizabeth answered before she realized the import of what she was saying.

Kathryn turned from the keyboard and gave her a penetrating look. "I thought so."

Elizabeth sat like an ice sculpture someone had placed on the couch. If she moved she would shatter.

"Do you want to tell me about it?" Kathryn asked gently, "or should I go make myself busy with the survey Cam ordered."

All at once, Elizabeth's control slipped, and she felt hot tears fill her eyes.

Silently, Kathryn pulled a tissue from the box on the desk and handed it to her. Elizabeth pressed it against her eyes, as much to hide her face as anything else. She knew she'd been adroitly tricked into revealing more than she'd intended. In a way she was angry, yet at the same time she was relieved that she didn't have to keep acting so damn cool and collected when her insides were raw.

She knew she couldn't hide forever. Wiping away the tears, she raised her face to the other woman. Still not sure of her voice, she gave a little shrug.

"Jason said Zeke's child is in danger," Kathryn prompted.

Elizabeth cleared her throat. "Yes. And…uh…he needs a wife to get her legally out of Mythos."

"I gather a lot has happened in a short time."

Elizabeth nodded. "Zeke called me—" she stopped short and blinked as she realized the time frame "—yesterday in a panic. When I came over to his house, he asked me to marry him. Then he told me why—sort of." The explanation broke the dam, and words began to tumble out of her as she told Kathryn most of what had occurred since Zeke's desperate proposal.

"That's a lot to cope with," the psychologist said, when Elizabeth finally wound down.

She sighed. "Yes. Sebastian Demos bursting into the kitchen was pretty frightening. Both times!"

"I'll bet."

"But what I keep coming back to is that Zeke said he asked me to marry him because he didn't want any emotional involvement.'' Elizabeth's hands fluttered. "That doesn't make me feel very good."

"Because he's wrong?"

She nodded tightly.

"He could have asked somebody else."

"He could have said he cared about me!" Elizabeth shot back.

"So he's been acting cold and impersonal since you agreed to his plan?" Kathryn asked.

"Not exactly," she admitted in a small voice, thinking about his reaction when she'd undressed him, and then when he'd been afraid he'd cut her. It had been very physical, very intense. She didn't know what to say about that, so she switched the subject. "The worst part is that I keep thinking about the woman who bore his child. He was in love with her, and now she's dead. But I still see her as a rival. Pretty immature, isn't that?"

Kathryn gave her a little smile. "I know you're going off on a dangerous assignment, which doesn't give us weeks to work through your feelings. So I'll cut to the chase and tell you that your reactions are pretty normal— for a woman who cares about her relationship with a man. And from what I read between the lines, I'd guess Zeke cares, too."

"Thank you," she whispered.

"He turned to you at one of the worst moments of his life. That means something."

"Because I've never demanded anything of him," Elizabeth couldn't stop herself from blurting.

"And that upsets you?"

She turned her hands palm up. "I knew Zeke was afraid of letting anyone see his vulnerabilities. I thought he was so walled up he couldn't get close to anyone. Then I found out he got close enough to Sophia to get her pregnant."

"That doesn't mean he'd made a commitment. You don't know the circumstances. Perhaps she turned to him at a bad time in her life, and the relationship got out of hand.''

Elizabeth sighed. ''You're only guessing.''

''We both are.''

''All I can think is that he loved her, and he was so hurt by her marriage that he's been afraid to take a chance on another meaningful relationship,'' she finished in a rush, astonished that she'd revealed so much.

''It may be difficult for him to talk about painful subjects. That's often true of men who feel things deeply. They've been taught to keep emotions to themselves. Besides, you may be misinterpreting his relationship with Sophia. Perhaps he can't talk about it because he feels guilty that he left her. Or even guilty that he didn't love her and he got her pregnant.''

Elizabeth gave a little nod, clutching at the new insights Kathryn had offered.

''What do you want to happen?'' Kathryn asked.

''I want it to be a real marriage,'' she admitted, saying it out loud for the first time.

''Then you can't expect him to guess at your feelings. You have to let him know what's going on with you.''

''But what if he...he rejects me?'' she asked in a strangled voice.

''You're the only one who can decide if it's worth the risk,'' Kathryn answered.

Elizabeth was trying to absorb that, when a loud honking horn made her jump. It sounded like the dive signal in a submarine movie.

The women looked at each other, then rose in unison and hurried into the hall. Apparently, everyone else had the same idea, because the corridor was full of people. She saw Zeke, Jason, Thorn and several other men she assumed must be technicians, all running toward the lobby.

Elizabeth and Kathryn followed.

Outside, a loudspeaker was blaring. ''Reduce speed now. Reduce speed now.''

Kathryn looked from Thorn to Jason. "What's happening?"

"A truck is coming up the road at sixty miles an hour," Jason shouted over his shoulder as he headed for the entrance. He'd opened the door a crack, when Zeke slammed it shut again. "Better wait and see what we've got," he cautioned.

Jason gestured toward the scene through the window. "Yeah, well, if that truck doesn't stop in about thirty seconds, it's going to plow right into the main gate."

Chapter Seven

"He won't get through that gate," Thorn muttered. "Not unless the vehicle is armor plated."

Zeke moved to Elizabeth's side, putting his body between her and the window. She pressed against him, glad for the contact with his solid frame as she moved her head a few inches so that she could see what was happening.

"Warning. Electrified Fence. Warning. Electrified Fence," the loudspeaker blared.

The admonition appeared to have no effect on the driver of the truck. The speeding vehicle was still heading directly toward the automatic sentry where she and Zeke had halted. Elizabeth squinted at the windshield, but the reflection of the sun prevented her from determining who was behind the wheel. So she switched her attention to the outside of the truck. All she could see was a large, heavy green pickup that didn't slow or waver on its course. When it reached the barrier, a collective gasp rose from the watchers inside the building as it struck the heavy wire mesh, setting off a shower of sparks that was accompanied by a loud sizzling noise, like a giant bug flying into an outdoor zapper. Only the zapping went on and on, as everyone stood paralyzed, watching in frozen fascination.

It seemed like hours later, but it was probably only a few seconds before Thorn bolted from the paralyzed group of people, ran down the hall, and pulled open an electrical panel where he flipped several circuit breakers. As he did, the shower of sparks stopped. He'd cut the power to the fence.

Deathly quiet hung around them.

"Good thinking," Zeke muttered. "Stay here," he told Elizabeth firmly as he detached himself from her and drew the gun she'd forgotten he was still wearing under his shirt.

"Where are you going?"

"Out."

She tried to hang on to his arm, but he shrugged out of her grasp, opened the door and slipped outside.

Jason strode to a large keypad in the wall, where he began to punch in a series of numbers. When the light flashed from red to green, he yanked open a door concealed behind a metal panel that looked much like the access to the circuit breakers. But this compartment was for weapon storage. Elizabeth's eyes widened as Jason pulled out a small machine gun, which he passed to Thorn. Then he brought out an identical weapon for himself.

"What kind of trouble are you expecting?" Elizabeth managed.

"Just making sure we're prepared," he snapped.

Without saying more, he and Thorn quickly followed Zeke toward the truck.

Elizabeth and Kathryn exchanged glances. "Did you know about the arsenal?" Elizabeth asked.

Kathryn shook her head as they turned toward the window.

Outside, the men scanned the road, weapons at the ready. Jason slipped through a small gate beside the guardhouse and opened the passenger door of the truck.

"The driver's dead," he called out to the other men, as he lowered his weapon. Their posture became more relaxed. Only Zeke still looked shocked as he peered inside the gaping door. Leaning toward Jason, he said something that made the other man's expression tighten.

Elizabeth strained to see what was happening. Since it

didn't look like an armed convoy was roaring up the road to attack the installation, she slipped outside and strode toward the group gathered around the truck. Kathryn was only a couple of steps behind.

"So who's the driver?" she demanded.

Zeke grabbed her arm before she reached the vehicle. "You don't need to look inside. It's Sebastian."

She goggled at him in disbelief. "Sebastian? It can't be Sebastian. We left him tied up on my kitchen floor and...and called the police."

Zeke nodded grimly.

"How did he get away? And how did he know where we were?"

"Good questions." Zeke looked as dumbfounded as she.

Jason gave orders to the technicians. Two of them trotted back into the facility and returned almost at once with a rolling stretcher.

Zeke turned the two women away. "Let's not watch this," he said in a low voice.

Elizabeth nodded, and the three of them returned slowly to the building. Once inside, Kathryn led the way to the lounge where she and Elizabeth had talked.

"We didn't have a clue that he was following us," Elizabeth murmured, fighting the sick feeling that rose in her throat. "It's like this morning—when he showed up again."

"Whatever happened, he didn't do it by himself this time," Zeke observed. "In the first place, he couldn't have untied himself—not with the techniques I used. And he wasn't behind us. I would have seen him."

"Maybe the police untied him, and then he escaped," Elizabeth offered.

"I doubt it. But even if they're completely incompetent, that still doesn't explain how he got here," Zeke snapped, his voice and expression reflecting both alarm and exasperation. "He wouldn't have had any idea where to pick up our trail."

"Good point," Jason answered from the hallway.

Zeke gave his friend a strained look. "I'm sorry. I never should have used the phone lines to contact you," he grated. "The only thing I can figure is that he traced the call."

"I don't think so," Jason answered as he stepped into the room. "Randolph Security uses privacy technology that isn't on the market. But just as a precaution I'm having one of the men check that out now."

There was nothing they could do at the moment, besides wait tensely for word from the communications room. Elizabeth sat still as a stone on the couch. Zeke paced back and forth across the gray tile floor. Jason stood with his arms folded, looking impatiently toward the hall. His technician came back in less than five minutes and announced that the lines were as secure as a priority military communications channel.

"Great. But we still don't know how Sebastian tracked us here." Zeke pounded his fist into his palm in frustration.

"And why he tried to crash through the gate, when that warning was blaring," Elizabeth added. As she finished speaking, she saw that Thorn was standing quietly in the doorway, his expression thoughtful.

"Find anything in the truck?" Jason asked.

"Nothing definitive," he answered. "But I'd like to hear about your previous contact with Sebastian."

Zeke looked grim as he gave him a quick description of the two previous encounters—at his house and then Elizabeth's.

"So your last confrontation followed a similar pattern," Thorn mused. "You left him, assuming he couldn't figure out where you had gone. Then he made an unexpected appearance."

Zeke nodded tightly.

"That leads to only one logical assumption..." Thorn let the sentence trail off.

Zeke's eyes narrowed as he followed the reasoning. "Sebastian planted some sort of tracking device on us, so he didn't need to keep us in sight," he muttered.

Elizabeth's gaze was riveted to the luggage they'd brought from her house. One of the technicians had set it in the lounge. What else had they carried here besides their clothing and equipment?

"A tracking device is the most likely explanation," Thorn agreed. "If you're correct in your assumption that he couldn't have freed himself, then you must consider the possibility that he is working with an accomplice who has access to the same telemetry and can duplicate his results. The fact that I didn't find any receivers in the truck supports that hypothesis."

As the implications of Thorn's deductions sank in, Elizabeth felt goose bumps pop out on her arms. She rubbed her palms against the prickly flesh. "He's dead. But someone else can find us and keep coming after us? Here and in Mythos?"

She looked from Thorn to Zeke, whose face was stark and angry. "What are we going to do?" she asked in an unsteady voice.

Zeke's expression suddenly brightened as he turned to Thorn. "Wait a minute, last time you briefed me on your new projects, didn't you mention that you were working on a detector to locate clandestine electronics?" he asked.

Thorn nodded. "Yes. That's one of the contracts I have under development up here. I guess your friend Sebastian wanted to conduct a field test."

"Then you can scan everything we brought with us," Zeke pronounced, his voice taking on a note of excitement.

"Yes. Your luggage. The clothes you're wearing. The transponder could be anywhere. But I'm afraid the radiation we're using is damaging to human flesh."

"Then how—?" Elizabeth broke off, as she realized the solution to that particular problem. They'd have to get undressed.

"So do you have something we can wear?" Zeke asked.

"I'll see what I can find," Kathryn volunteered and left the room.

"Hurry," Thorn called after her then turned back to Zeke and Elizabeth. "Better yet, start taking your clothes off while I power up the equipment."

She fought to make her voice sound normal. "You can't mean all my clothes. How would Sebastian have hidden something in my underwear?" The last part came out as a hoarse croak.

"I don't know," Zeke muttered. "I also don't know how long he was in the house. He could have had time to plant something in your dresser drawers, for all we know."

That sounded highly unlikely, yet the stakes were too high to discount the possibility, Elizabeth silently acknowledged. The man kept showing up, and it was a miracle that he hadn't killed Zeke. What's more, she'd come to this group of people for help, and she was putting all of them in danger.

Thorn touched her shoulder, and she flinched. "Why don't you go down the hall to the rest room, where you can have some privacy."

"Fine," she murmured, walking stiffly out of the room. She wasn't going to refuse, but she also wasn't going to pretend that she liked the idea. The light was off in the bathroom and she had to fumble along the wall to find the switch. Then she pulled the door shut and tried to gather her equanimity. She was in a little bathroom that opened directly onto the hallway. There wasn't even a stall where she could retreat for a little extra screening.

Well, she might as well get it over with. Grimacing, she locked the door and pulled her knit shirt over her head. She was reaching for the hook on her bra when a knock sounded on the door, and she jumped half a foot in the air.

"It's me," Kathryn called out. "I've found something for you to wear. Crack the door and I'll hand it in. When you're ready, you can give me your clothes."

Elizabeth could hear the sympathetic tone in the other

woman's voice. Maybe Kathryn was imagining how she'd feel if the shoe were on the other foot, so to speak. Only the shoes were already off, Elizabeth thought with a grim laugh.

Snapping the lock, she pushed open the door a fraction, and Kathryn stuffed a bundle of stiff fabric into her hand. When she unwadded it, she found she was holding a white lab coat. Well, that was better than trying to wrap herself in a sheet, she guessed. With a sigh, she pulled off her remaining clothes and folded them.

"Here," she called, as she passed everything outside to Kathryn's waiting hands.

"Thanks."

As the other woman's footsteps rapidly receded, she tried to get comfortable in the borrowed coat. It was several sizes too big, which was probably good, she decided as she rolled up the sleeves. At least the hem came below her knees. But one of the buttons was missing—the one right below her breasts.

She was tempted to stay in the bathroom until Thorn had finished his scan. But it was hardly an inviting environment. There was nowhere to sit besides the toilet—which was of the institutional variety and didn't even have a seat cover. The ceramic tile floor was painfully cold beneath her bare feet, and the dimensions of the room were smaller than a jail cell.

Pulling the door open, she looked into the hall. No one was in sight. Arms tightly folded across the embarrassing gap in the front of her coat, she stepped outside and followed the sound of voices drifting toward her.

They led to a room about thirty yards down the corridor. Inside, Thorn was standing in front of a console that had a keyboard and two screens—one like an ordinary computer and the other like the luggage scanners at an airport security check. Most of the technicians she'd met earlier were ranged around him, looking alternately at Thorn and a long metal table shielded behind a thick floor-to-ceiling glass panel.

She caught a glimpse of Zeke's head up at the front of the crowd. But she didn't want to get any closer than she was, thank you very much. Not when everyone in the room knew she was naked under this lab coat. When she'd put it on, the fabric had felt thick. Now she imagined it revealed every curve of her body. Struggling to change the focus of her thoughts, she craned her neck toward the work area and saw that the table was illuminated by a misty purple light. Next to the unpacked luggage she and Zeke had brought was the clothing they'd been wearing. Only now the items were spread out like merchandise being offered at a yard sale. Her bra and panties were right next to Zeke's jockey shorts—like they belonged together.

Zeke must have been listening for her. He quickly detached himself from the crowd, zeroed in on her position by the door and started toward her. He looked perfectly at ease, although he was wearing only a pair of well-washed jeans.

She, on the other hand, was a mass of exposed, vulnerable nerves. If a trapdoor had opened in the floor under her feet, she would have been profoundly grateful. However, she stopped thinking about herself as she caught a better view of Zeke. Naked to the waist, tanned and muscular, he looked like Mr. July in the Hunk of the Month calendar. In fact, the effect couldn't have been more blatantly masculine if he'd been buck naked. The broad expanse of his hair-covered chest drew her eyes like a magnet. Her fingers had vivid memories of touching that chest.

It didn't help that she saw him taking in the way she looked in the lab coat. His piercing gaze made her skin prickle and her heart start to dance around inside her chest.

From the corner of her eye, she saw Kathryn swivel around and look at them, then quickly turn back to the table like a kid who'd walked into her parents' room when they were having sex.

Before Elizabeth had time to react to Kathryn's appraisal, Zeke was at her side shielding her from the view of the others in the room. His arm slipped around her shoulder and drew her against him. "Are you okay?" he asked in a low voice.

"No." The syllable came out high and reedy. She wished she were anywhere else in the world.

His hand stroked her arm in a gesture she assumed was meant to be comforting. It made her feel both better and worse at the same time. Then she saw his eyes lower, and realized that she'd forgotten to hold her arm against her front, allowing the place with the missing button to gap open. The skin underneath had never been exposed in public, except when she'd worn a two-piece bathing suit when she was a teenager.

Zeke's hand seemed to move in slow motion as he reached to touch that vulnerable patch of flesh just below her breasts.

A small gasp escaped from her lips, and a forest of goose bumps bloomed as the tip of his finger came in contact with her body.

"You need to close that gap."

"I know," she managed to say, just before his finger started moving inside the recess, delicately stroking, sending darts of sensation across her skin—darts that radiated upward to her breasts, and downward, as well. His touch made her forget about everything else but him. She closed her eyes and turned her face against his shoulder, struggling to catch her breath, as his lips brushed against the tender line at the edge of her hair.

When he nuzzled his face there, she turned automatically toward him, sighing.

She raised her hand, pressing it against his chest, her fingers combing through the hair. She could feel the rapid beating of his heart. It matched the throbbing rhythm of hers.

"Lizbeth."

The raspy way he said her name drew her deeper into their web of intimacy. The focus of her attention became the hand on her hip, which slid downward, finding the bottom edge of the lab coat and reaching under so that he could caress her thigh.

She clung to Zeke as he moved, propelling them both toward the door, to some place in this building where they could be alone.

Then, at the other end of the room, Thorn said something she didn't catch, and she remembered where they were and that a crowd of people was standing only a few yards away. A little exclamation welled in her throat.

Zeke's hand jerked away from her leg. Straightening, he stood very still, staring down at her with a bemused expression.

"I'm sorry," he muttered.

She drew in a ragged breath, trying to gather the shreds of her shattered composure.

"I've got a safety pin," he added.

"What?" She tried to put the words into some kind of meaningful context.

"Somebody thought I might need one for these jeans." He gestured toward the gap just below his navel where the waistband was too tight to snap. Reaching in the right front pocket of the pants, he pulled out a large pin and held it up for her inspection. "Hold still."

She obeyed orders, her heart still pounding as he carefully inserted the sharp end through the fabric of her coat, pulling the gap together as he snapped the pin closed. Then his expression became businesslike. Turning, he looked toward the computer console, as if he'd come over to give her a guided tour of the experiment. "It won't take much longer," he said. "Thorn's getting ready to make a scan."

In fact, the equipment didn't seem to be functioning quite the way Thorn expected, and it took him several more agonizing minutes before he began getting any readings.

Zeke stayed at Elizabeth's side, and from time to time

she was aware of the others glancing covertly at them.
Lord, had someone turned around at the wrong time and
seen what they were doing? At least no one was rude
enough to stare openly. Standing rigid, Elizabeth tried to
pretend that there was another glass wall in the room—one
that separated her and Zeke from everybody else. Her
nerves were jumping. "What's taking so long?" she mumbled under her breath.

Zeke's arm tightened around her. "Hang in there," he
whispered.

She lifted the corners of her lips in a parody of a smile.

After an eternity, Thorn gestured toward the monitor and
announced, "I'm reading something." Elizabeth stood up
straighter. Zeke gave a little tug on her arm. She wanted to
stay where she was at the periphery of the action, but she
knew that didn't suit Zeke. And although she might be
embarrassed by her attire, she was anxious to see what
Thorn had discovered. So she let herself be guided a few
steps closer.

She could feel tension mounting in the room, as Thorn
typed in commands that made the image on the monitor
screen fade to light green—all but the upper right-hand corner. He enlarged that portion of the picture, and Elizabeth
drew in a quick breath as she realized what she was looking
at. Glowing red like a stop sign, was the knife Sebastian
had used to cut Zeke.

"The transmitter's in there." Thorn gestured toward the
weapon. "Where did you get it?"

Zeke cursed. "It's Sebastian's. He attacked me with it.
But it's an early Greek artifact."

Thorn typed in more commands, and the lights illumi-
nating the table faded and snapped off. After checking the
console readings, he strode around the glass barrier and
reached for the knife. Zeke was only a step behind him.
"Let me see it," he growled.

Elizabeth stayed in the background, watching the little
drama.

Thorn deferred, and Zeke snatched up the weapon. Turning it over in his hands, he examined the elaborate design on the hilt, then began to run his fingers over the figures. Now that he knew he was looking for something out of the ordinary, it didn't take long to release a hidden catch near the bottom of the hilt. He made a low noise as the leering head of Hades moved aside, revealing a hidden compartment. With his fingernail, he pried out a small metallic disk, which he held up to the light. His face darkened and he uttered a heartfelt obscenity as his fingers closed around the disk.

"Don't destroy it," Thorn said quickly. "I want to study the design."

"There's a better reason for keeping it operational," Jason said as he joined the other two men and held out his hand. "I want a volunteer who will take this thing to the vault at Randolph Electronics, but not by a direct route. Use the back roads, so it looks like Zeke and Elizabeth are on the run again. That should catch the attention of anyone monitoring the signal." He turned to Zeke. "And before they find out we're wise to the transponder, the two of you will be in a plane on the way to Mythos."

"Maybe we should just take the damn thing and leave," Zeke said, every word coming hard and distinct. "I'm causing a hell of a lot more trouble than I intended. We shouldn't have come here in the first place."

Thorn clapped him on the back. "I would have been insulted, if you hadn't asked me for help."

"But I've jeopardized your security," Zeke said in a low voice.

"Sometimes things happen that are beyond your control," Thorn said in an even voice. "Look at it in a positive light. I've had a chance to test this equipment under actual field conditions."

Zeke met his eyes. After a few seconds, he nodded.

At that moment, one of the technicians who had been absent during the proceedings stepped into the room and brushed rapidly past Elizabeth. He had a strained look on his face, and she wondered what new development he'd come to report. Nothing good, she judged from his expression.

"Jason," he said, the urgency in his voice carrying across the lab so that everybody turned in his direction. "The man who crashed into the gate...you're not going to believe this...but the electricity isn't what killed him. He was already dead when his truck plowed into the fence."

Chapter Eight

"Are you sure?" Jason demanded.

"Yes. It's pretty obvious when you know what to look for. Whoever killed him tried to disguise the murder, but he was smothered—not electrocuted."

"But that's impossible. He was driving the truck," Zeke objected.

"He looked like he was driving. Someone must have wedged his foot onto the accelerator and clamped his hands on the wheel."

Zeke kept his arm around Elizabeth, but his head swiveled toward the parking lot at the front of the building. "Then taking the knife to the Randolph Electronics safe in Baltimore is an exercise in futility. Whoever pulled off that trick is already here."

"Maybe they were. But not now," the technician said. "I've already done a heat scan of the immediate area. The only warm bodies I'm reading in the woods are a herd of deer down by the creek, and some miscellaneous squirrels and birds."

Jason nodded. "Glad to hear it. But we're still going to break up this particular party." He turned to Zeke, "I'm sorry, there won't be time for the kind of intelligence on Mythos you requested."

"Understood," Zeke clipped out.

Jason gestured toward the clothes on the table. "You'd better get dressed, while I arrange some transportation."

Feeling shell-shocked, Elizabeth retrieved her clothing. A few minutes ago she'd been mortified by her lack of attire. She'd gotten so caught up in the discussion about Sebastian, she'd forgotten all about what she was wearing. In the bathroom, she dressed as quickly as possible. As she caught herself staring critically into the mirror and patting her hair back into place, she grimaced. Her coiffeur was the last thing she needed to worry about.

When she emerged, the hall was full of people bound on various missions. Some were carrying portable files toward the back of the building. Others had laptop computers and boxes of floppy disks.

Kathryn, who must have been waiting for her to reappear, stepped out of a nearby doorway.

"It looks like you're evacuating the facility," Elizabeth said.

"Temporarily. Until we get a better handle on the situation."

"We're causing a lot of trouble," Elizabeth echoed Zeke's assessment. "If I'd known about the transponder, I never would have suggested to Zeke that we ask for your help."

Kathryn squeezed her shoulder. "It's not as bad as you think. The guys here get tired of routine real fast. They like functioning in crisis mode, and you've given them an excuse for action."

Elizabeth made a low sound, but she knew these men well enough to realize that Kathryn was speaking the truth.

A beating noise from high above made them both glance up. "Helicopters?" she questioned.

"Yes," Kathryn confirmed. "Jason is moving us out by air—to make it harder for anyone to follow, in case the killer is waiting down the road."

"Where are we going?"

"Luckily, we've already set up a transfer at the municipal airfield in Frederick County. You're on the first chopper." She gestured toward the back door.

When Elizabeth stepped outside, she discovered there was a landing pad several hundred feet from the rear of the building. Zeke was waiting for her, still looking grim. She wanted to tell him nobody blamed him for the invasion of the compound. She suspected he wouldn't believe her. What's more, it was impossible to talk above the noise. All she could do was give his hand a quick squeeze.

They lifted off almost at once, and Elizabeth had a nervous moment as the ground receded. She gripped Zeke's arm, then tried to sit back and pretend the ride was some kind of unique sight-seeing trip. But relaxation was out of the question.

Zeke's features were stony. She knew he was upset about the knife. Had it made him think about abandoning her again? She shivered, knowing there was nothing she could do if he made the decision to go to Mythos alone.

Probably it was only a short direct flight to their destination, but the pilot headed toward Baltimore before circling back toward his intended destination. A half hour after they'd taken off, they landed at a rural airfield.

As she followed Zeke toward a hangar, a small plane with two rear jet engines approached the runway and came in for a landing.

"That's your transportation to Greece," Jason told her, stuffing a portable phone in his pocket and gesturing toward the sleek craft that streaked down the runway. "A Gulf Stream II. It can make Athens without refueling. Steve Claiborne is going to fly you there."

"Um," was all Elizabeth managed to say, wishing she could stop in one place long enough for her emotions to catch up with her body. Jason gave her a pat on the shoulder, then hurried to speak with Zeke. "I'm still trying to get a line on that communications equipment you requested. Unfortunately, it's out in the field, and it could take several hours to get here."

Zeke nodded and looked at his watch before resuming his course toward the hangar. Inside, near the service desk in the hangar, a small man in a gray business suit was standing, looking expectantly toward them. He was only a little taller than Elizabeth, but she guessed he outweighed her by fifty pounds. His wispy gray hair formed a wreath on the top of his balding head, and his gray eyes followed her and Zeke with interest as they approached the counter. He didn't look like a reservations clerk.

Kathryn came trotting from behind them. "I'd like to introduce you to Wesley J. Brenner," she said. "He's the justice of the peace who's going to marry you."

Elizabeth blinked. "Oh, uh… Nice to meet you…" she mumbled, feeling like a tongue-tied idiot.

"Likewise, I'm sure," Mr. Brenner replied.

He and Zeke shook hands stiffly, and Elizabeth wondered if Zeke had forgotten about the requisite ceremony. He looked like a man who'd been struck by the reality with the force of a car crashing into a concrete wall. Tension knotted the muscles in Elizabeth's neck as she waited to hear him say he'd changed his mind.

"I assume a civil ceremony will be satisfactory," Brenner said, giving Zeke another chance to back out.

Elizabeth steadied herself against the edge of the counter as long seconds stretched out.

"Yes," Zeke asserted hoarsely, and Elizabeth felt some of her terrible tension ease.

Before she could catch her breath, Kathryn drew her aside. "I had to make some decisions before you arrived at Whispering Pines," she murmured. "I called Erin and found out your dress size. There are several here you can pick from. And flowers."

Elizabeth blinked, trying to switch gears again. "I…I wasn't expecting anything like that…." Her voice trailed off.

"The ceremony will mean more to the two of you this way," Kathryn whispered.

"Yes," Elizabeth agreed in a daze. Limply she allowed Kathryn to lead her to the other side of the large building. To her amazement, a square tent with a peaked roof had been set up near the back wall. When she stepped inside, she left the impersonal world of the small commercial airport behind. There was AstroTurf on the floor, a bower of flowers massed all around the walls, and about twenty-five chairs arranged in rows, with an aisle down the center.

"My Lord, what's all this?" Elizabeth gasped.

"I guess you could call it a portable wedding chapel. Cam Randolph can arrange anything—when two of his best friends are getting married," Kathryn replied. "He was making phone calls while we were dealing with—uh—Sebastian." She looked a little flustered. "Sorry I mentioned him. Come on, you have to change."

Still in a daze, Elizabeth followed her escort to another tent set up behind the first. It was outfitted as a dressing room, with a makeup table, a full-length mirror and a rack of gowns. Drifting over to them, Elizabeth began to inspect the assortment. Some were white, others were pastel, in all lengths and a variety of styles. One, in particular, made her exclaim in appreciation. It was off-white lace fitted high under the bodice, with a long, flowing skirt.

"You like that one?" Kathryn asked.

"It's beautiful," Elizabeth answered, with a catch in her voice.

"Then let's try it on," Kathryn suggested, pulling the curtain that served as a door. This was a dream, and she'd wake up before it was over, Elizabeth thought as she shucked off her jeans and shirt and let Kathryn help her into the dress. It fit perfectly, she decided, as she inspected her image in the mirror, except that the hem was a bit high. "There are sandals over with the shoes. Just wear them instead of heels," Kathryn suggested. "Nobody will know." Turning, she took a veil from a hanger. At the crown was a circle of flowers attached to a curved comb.

Tears glistened in Elizabeth's eyes as she adjusted the

veil on her head and gaped at the transformed woman in the mirror. "I don't know what to say," she murmured.

"If you don't like it, we can take off the veil. Or try one of the other dresses."

Elizabeth shook her head. "That's not...not what I mean," she said in a quavering voice. "I feel like I've stepped into wonderland or something... Is this real?" she whispered.

"As real as you want it to be," Kathryn answered.

Elizabeth tried to read her face. She seemed serious. Was it really possible to make dreams come true, if you wanted them enough?

"You look lovely," Kathryn told her. "But why don't you put on a little makeup. That will be the icing on the cake."

Nodding, Elizabeth sat down at the dressing table and looked through the assortment of cosmetics. They were the brand she used, and in the right color. Her friends must have been working like demons, she thought, as she picked up a container of eye shadow. Tears clouded her vision again, and she had to wait several moments before she could get hold of herself. Zeke had agreed to the ceremony, she reminded herself. Surely that meant something. But what would everybody think if the marriage were annulled when the bride and groom got back from Mythos?

"Cam asked to give you away," Kathryn whispered. "If that's okay?"

"Yes."

"I'll leave you alone for a little while," Kathryn said, and exited the tent.

Elizabeth's heart gave a little lurch, as she thought about her father and mother. They had done so much for her, but they wouldn't be at her wedding. Yet maybe that was for the best, she decided, her hands clenching and unclenching. They'd be so hurt, if they knew the marriage wasn't real.

Feeling the sting of tears in her eyes again, she blinked

them back and blotted at the moisture threatening to muss her newly applied eye makeup.

A few moments later, Kathryn came back. "It's time."

Standing, Elizabeth walked a little unsteadily toward the door. Cam was waiting for her, tall and handsome in a dark suit. He gave her a warm hug. "You look lovely."

Elizabeth's hands fluttered. "You shouldn't have done all this."

"Of course I should. You and Zeke are like family to me and Jo. Now come on, we don't want to keep everyone waiting."

Elizabeth took his arm, and they marched to the larger tent. When she stepped inside, she gasped. It was full of smiling people. Her friends from 43 Light Street. Jo O'Malley, Cam's wife, holding their toddler by the hand. Mike and Lisa Lancer. Erin and Travis Stone. Noel and Jason. Jed and Marci Prentiss. Thorn and his wife, Cassie, with their son. Abby Franklin with her husband, Steve Claiborne. Jenny and Ben Brisco. They looked as if they'd been invited to a come-as-you-are party, since they were wearing everything from jogging suits to business dress. As all eyes focused on her, Elizabeth tried to keep some semblance of composure.

Lisa and Mike and Jenny and Ben were the last two couples of the group to have gotten married. Lisa, who held a baby girl in her arms, gave Elizabeth an especially radiant smile, and she wondered if her friend was reliving the joy of her own wedding day.

"How? How did they all get here?" Elizabeth managed

"Well, we made a lot of phone calls," Cam whispered. "Steve and Jed brought everybody we could reach. I'm sorry some of the gang is missing."

Zeke was standing beside Mr. Brenner, looking as dazed as Elizabeth felt. He was wearing a dark suit, a white shirt and an elegantly patterned tie. The whole effect was devastating. When he saw her in the wedding dress, his eyes took on a glittering intensity that sent shivers to the base of her spine. She was glad she was hanging on to Cam, because she wouldn't have been able to stand without help.

There was no music, only the solemn words of Mr. Brenner as he thanked everyone for coming and launched into the marriage ceremony.

Feeling as if she were standing outside herself watching, Elizabeth said what she was supposed to say at the proper times. Zeke did the same, his gaze focused somewhere over Elizabeth's left shoulder. She wanted to grab him by the arm and ask what this exchange of vows was supposed to mean. Instead, she stood with her hands clasped in front of her.

"Who has the rings?" Mr. Brenner asked.

Zeke started to say that they didn't have any, but Cam cut him off. "Right here," he said calmly.

Zeke looked astonished as Cam reached into his right front pocket and pulled out a small velvet-covered box. "What's a ceremony without rings?" he asked, as he handed it to Mr. Brenner, who slowly lifted the lid. Inside were matching gold bands.

"Sorry they're not engraved," Cam whispered. "We couldn't quite manage that on short notice."

When Brenner extended the box toward Zeke, he started to pick up the larger of the two circles.

"No, no, you take the small one," the justice of the peace suggested in a low voice.

Zeke flushed and picked up Elizabeth's.

"Slip the ring on her finger and repeat after me," Brenner said.

Zeke's hands trembled as he obeyed. Since Elizabeth was also shaking, it was difficult to accomplish the simple maneuver. But finally the gold band was in place on her finger. Then it was her turn to perform the same service for Zeke.

As she looked down at their hands, each adorned with a new circle of gold, she felt a wave of intense longing sweep over her. This could be real, if only Zeke wanted it to be. She wished she could ask Mr. Brenner to explain that to him as part of the proceedings. Instead she stood quietly by while he brought the brief exchange to a close.

"You may kiss the bride," he concluded.

Elizabeth looked at Zeke, unsure of what she was seeing in his eyes. Certainly not love. Was he angry that he'd been railroaded into such a public display? Regretful? Unable to move, she stood quietly before him, her heart pounding. After an eternity, he finally lowered his face to hers and their lips touched. It wasn't a long kiss. It certainly wasn't passionate. She might have called it dutiful, if she'd been functioning well enough to make an evaluation.

Then people were clapping and getting out of their seats, the men coming over to congratulate Zeke and the women crowing around her. She felt a stiff smile plaster itself across her face as she accepted the best wishes of her friends.

"Why didn't you tell us?" Jo O'Malley asked.

"There wasn't time," Elizabeth improvised.

She saw Jenny Brisco looking bemused. She and Jenny often ate lunch together and shared confidences. For example, she was one of the few people who knew Jenny was pregnant. So she suspected her friend was wondering exactly what was going on.

Mercifully, Cam's voice cut through the excited chatter. "I'm sorry, but weather conditions over the Atlantic are changing for the worse. The bride and groom will have to leave us now."

All at once the mood switched back to business. Jason and Steve took Zeke aside for a conference. Kathryn came over to whisper in Elizabeth's ear, "You'd better change into travel clothes."

Glad to escape without having to make any further explanations, Elizabeth fled to the tent where she'd donned the beautiful wedding dress. Minutes later, it was back on the hanger where she'd first seen it, and she was dressed in a fresh pair of jeans, running shoes and a sweatshirt.

She glanced around the tent, trying to shake the feeling

of unreality that had enveloped her since Kathryn had led her inside. The ceremony had been so brief, and she'd had almost no preparation. The marriage might have been a daydream, she mused, except that now she was wearing a slender gold ring on her left hand, a band that tied her to Zeke for as long as she wore it.

She stood staring at the ring, until the sound of urgent male voices broke through her trance.

"I don't like your being out of communication," Jason was saying.

"But if we wait for the equipment, with the weather changing, we might not be able to get out of here for a couple of days," Zeke answered.

"You're taking a risk by leaving without proper preparation," Steve Claiborne interjected.

"And I'm taking a risk that I won't get there in time to save my daughter, if we don't get moving in the next half hour," Zeke retorted.

Elizabeth walked to the edge of the tent and saw the three of them and Jed Prentiss, another ex-secret agent, standing in a tight circle.

"Okay, when the comms unit arrives, we'll send it on a later flight," Jason said. "Until then, you'll have to check in with us using commercial phone lines."

"Understood," Zeke clipped out. He turned toward Jed. "You don't have to go along. I can copilot."

"Not a good idea," the other man objected. "You want to be rested when you get there."

Steve seconded the recommendation. After several seconds, Zeke gave a tight nod. Then he looked up, saw Elizabeth listening, and stiffened.

She schooled the disappointment out of her face into a smile as she glided toward him. "So when are we leaving, honey?" she asked, feeling her throat tighten around the endearment.

"As soon as Steve finishes with the preflight check," he said.

Cam gave her a warm smile. "We'll see you when you get back to Baltimore."

"Yes. Thank you for everything," she replied, still amazed at the speed of the preparation.

"I arranged this party, so I'd better go play host," he said. "Too bad you can't stay for the food."

Zeke shifted his weight from one foot to the other. "Thank you," he said stiffly. Cam smiled his understanding.

"Tell everyone how sorry we are to run off like this," Elizabeth murmured.

"Right."

When he'd left them alone, Zeke muttered, "As you may have noticed, I'm not great at thanking people. Cam...or you." He raised his eyes to hers. "But I hope you understand I appreciate what you're doing."

"Yes," she managed to say, as they stood awkwardly confronting each other. She didn't want his gratitude. She'd rather ask him what he thought about getting married in front of so many of their friends, but she didn't want to hear him tell her it had been a total embarrassment or that it made him feel obligated to her. So she slipped away before he could see the anguished look on her face.

THEY HADN'T quite met his departure deadline, Zeke thought as he finished up a final radio conference with Jason. But they were pretty close. Steve was in the pilot's seat. Jed was next to him. Both of them had dropped everything else to help him get to Mythos as soon as possible.

He closed his eyes for a moment, glad they were facing forward and couldn't see his expression. He'd been raised to hide his emotions. He suspected he'd make all three of them uncomfortable if he got profuse in his thanks. But until he'd hooked up with the Light Street crowd, he'd never known what it was to have family or friends who would come to your rescue when you needed them—no questions asked.

"Relax and leave the driving to us," Jed said, half turning in his seat.

"Right," Zeke agreed, wishing he could hang around with them for the rest of the trip. But Elizabeth had already gone back to their private cabin. He wasn't sure how he was going to face her after making such a mess of the last thirty-six hours. An image of the knife leaped into his mind, and he squeezed his eyes shut to block it out. Whoever had sent Sebastian with the damn thing had read Zeke Chambers pretty well. He hadn't been able to leave it behind. Grimacing, he wondered what other nasty surprises were in store for him and Elizabeth. Even now he knew he never should have brought her along. But here she was—waiting for him in a nice private little bedroom.

"See you," he murmured, unbuckling his seat belt and standing up.

His friends chorused their good-byes, as he strode across the small space to the rear cabin. Thank God, neither of them made any jokes about wedding rights.

Opening the door, Zeke stepped into the private compartment that someone had been thoughtful enough to convert into a love nest for the honeymoon couple. Only they weren't exactly going on a honeymoon. And they weren't exactly a "couple" in the usual sense of the word, he reminded himself as he closed the door.

There was nowhere else to sit in the small cabin besides the bed. Elizabeth was gingerly perched on one edge, as if she thought the surface might go up in flames at any moment. She looked nervous and vulnerable, and so desirable that Zeke felt a rush of blood to the lower part of his body.

Elizabeth gave him a quick glance, then dropped her gaze to the hands clasped in her lap. His own gaze followed, zeroing in on the band of gold on her finger. It matched the ring that felt so thick and heavy on his own finger. They were man and wife. They had a piece of paper and a whole slew of witnesses to prove it.

His mind flashed back to the ceremony. He'd never

thought of Elizabeth as beautiful. But she'd looked beautiful in that wedding dress. She looked just as beautiful in her travel outfit, her jeans hugging the slender curves of her thighs and legs. He ached to take her into his arms. But he didn't have the right to make love to her, not when the marriage wasn't real. The best thing would be to back right out of the cabin. But he couldn't do that. Not with the guys out front. And he couldn't simply stand there for the rest of the twelve-hour trip. So, being careful not to bump into her, he moved to the other side of the bed and gingerly sat down.

A bottle of expensive champagne sat in a bucket of ice on the floor. The attached note said that it was from their good friends Thorn and Cassie, who hoped he and Elizabeth would be as happy as they were. Very thoughtful of them. He folded the card and stuffed it in his pocket before Elizabeth could get a look at it. Then to give himself something else to do, he picked up the bottle and began to fiddle with the wires at the top, untwisting and pulling them off. Automatically, he began to work at the cork. When he pulled it out, the loud pop made him jump. Damn, he hadn't meant to do that. It had just happened.

"Now that it's open, I guess we might as well have a drink," Elizabeth murmured.

"Yeah." Maybe it would make a good anesthetic.

Two regulation airline plastic glasses were in a small box beside the bucket. He poured them each a good belt.

He was raising the glass to his lips when Elizabeth cleared her throat.

"We should have a toast."

Zeke went very still.

"To finding Ariadne," she said, holding out her hand.

"Yes," he agreed in a low voice as the glasses touched. His fingers brushed hers. For a long moment neither one of them moved. He had to hold tightly to the glass to keep from pulling her toward him. Somehow he managed.

Silence fell again, as they sat sipping the bubbly wine.

"It's been a hell of a day," he finally said to the room in general. "Getting some sleep is probably a good idea." Setting down his glass on the floor, he slipped off his shoes, then started to unbutton his shirt, before stopping suddenly and glancing at her.

"Don't mind me," she muttered. "I'm just your wife."

He swallowed hard. "That was for appearance's sake."

She made a noncommittal sound.

"I'm sorry Cam went to so damn much trouble," he blurted. "I didn't ask him to."

"He thought he was doing us a favor. I gather you'd rather have snuck out of the country with two dozen less witnesses."

He spread his hands in a helpless gesture. There were things he should say, but given his recent track record, he was pretty sure he'd make a mess of them.

He saw Elizabeth lick her lips nervously. "You've had plenty of field experience pretending to be something you're not," she said. "Like a married man."

"Um-hum."

"But I haven't. I might need a little bit of…uh…role-playing with you, to get into the proper frame of mind."

He gave her a wary look. "Like what?"

Her tongue flicked, drawing his gaze to her lips and then her face. Her cheeks were slightly flushed. Her eyes were bright. She dragged in a deep breath, then let it out slowly. "There's a problem I think you haven't anticipated."

His eyes narrowed. "Oh yeah? Like what?"

"Well, you know, it might be dangerous traveling with a woman who's supposed to be your wife, when it turns out she's a virgin."

Chapter Nine

Zeke choked on the swallow of champagne he'd just taken.

"You can't be," he said when he was breathing normally again.

"Why not?"

"You're too desirable," he answered, then flushed when he realized what he'd said.

"I'll take that as a compliment," she answered, her face serene.

The conversation wasn't going quite the way he'd expected. "You can't be," he said again.

She raised her chin slightly. "I wouldn't lie to you."

Silence hung between them.

Getting off the bed, Zeke glanced toward the door, but he couldn't get very far away from her at three thousand feet in the air. Instead, he moved to the bulkhead, propping himself against the curved wall, and folded his arms across his chest. "What do you want me to do?" he asked, then silently cursed the question. He wasn't stupid. He was simply trying to be responsible.

She took the opportunity he'd offered. "Make sure I have a better idea of what it's like to be a wife," she said. "What if we had to convince someone we knew each other intimately? I wouldn't know how to behave. I'm not sure you would either—with me."

He made a strangled noise. "Elizabeth, we can't just—"

"Why not? I promise to respect you in the morning."

Their gazes connected and held for endless moments before he found the breath to say, "That's not the point."

"What is? I'll be gentle with you," she quipped, the slight quiver in her voice setting up a vibration inside him.

He was running out of rejoinders. He dredged up one more. "It's not fair to you."

"I'm a better judge of that than you."

He scrambled for reasons, and came up with one she couldn't dispute. "We can't do anything. I'm not prepared to protect you from pregnancy."

She gave him a little smile that made his insides melt. "The champagne wasn't the only wedding present from our friends. There was an overnight bag with a number of necessities—things I guess they figured we didn't have time to pack." She reached under the bed, pulled out a leather carry-on bag. "For example, there are thousands of Greek drachmas. Too bad they're worth so little on the dollar, or we'd be quite rich. And—" She fumbled inside, before holding up a length of foil-wrapped packets that she held steady so he could clearly see the labels. Then she set them on the tiny stand beside the bed.

"So who do you think bought these?" she wondered aloud. "My friends or yours?"

Zeke muttered an imprecation. The plane hit a patch of rough air and he let himself slide down the wall a couple of inches, bracing his legs to remain steady. The stance tilted his hips slightly forward. Really, he'd be better off lying down. But not on that bed with Elizabeth, because if he lay down beside her now, he was going to do things he regretted.

ELIZABETH STARED AT Zeke as he folded his arms across his chest and braced himself for mortal combat. The lights in the cabin were dim, and he was standing in the shadows where she couldn't get a good look at his face. She'd backed him against the wall. Literally. If she were smart, she'd quit while she still had some dignity. He'd made it clear he didn't consider the marriage real—or the wedding night. Yet she was betting he was acting from a sense of honor, not distaste. He wanted to be fair to her, he said. Well, all was fair in love and war. And she wasn't going to back off. Kathryn had made her realize there was nothing wrong with getting something out of this, something she wanted very much. She loved Zeke. She'd been trying to deny it was true. But she couldn't turn off her feelings. Not after standing up with him in front of their friends and saying wedding vows. She would make the vows real—at least for tonight. If he divorced her as soon as they returned to the U.S., then at least she'd have sweet memories to keep her warm at night.

Before she could lose her nerve, she stood. Heart pounding, she circled the end of the bed, putting herself on Zeke's side. He didn't move, didn't give her any encouragement. Yet she saw him swallow hard. At least she knew he was nervous.

She'd never played the seductress. She wasn't sure she knew how. But she was going to give it her best shot.

The pit of her stomach quivered as she took a step closer. Still, he didn't move, didn't speak, didn't offer a clue about what he was thinking. Suddenly she was seized with the awful thought that he might not want this—that his excuses were given to spare her feelings. Well, better to find that out now, so she could spend the rest of the flight regaining her composure.

Her throat dry, she forced herself to keep walking forward, one step at a time, until her running shoes were between his boots.

Now what?

The question had barely formed in her mind, when the plane pitched again, and she fought to keep her footing. His arms uncrossed so suddenly that she was barely aware of the movement. One second she was standing on her own, trying not to topple over; the next, she was tightly enfolded in his embrace. He held her to him, uttering a low sound that might have been a curse—or a plea. Then his head moved, and his mouth came down on hers.

His lips were warm, hard, challenging, and the thought flashed in Elizabeth's mind that perhaps Zeke was trying to scare her off by giving her a tiny taste of his unleashed ardor. In truth, she was frightened—not by the demand he infused into the kiss, but by the intensity of her own response to him. But she had no intention of backing off. To prove that to both of them, she moved in closer to him and angled her head to one side, so that he could kiss her more deeply.

Zeke made a low, hungry sound in his throat as he accepted the invitation. That was the last thing Elizabeth heard above the pounding of the blood in her ears. He tasted her again and again, deeply, roughly, then more gently, and she felt rather than heard her own soft cries of pleasure. When he finally lifted his head, her body was plastered against his and his palms were under her shirt, splayed against her back. They were both struggling for breath.

With Zeke's legs braced in front of him, they were hip to hip, and Elizabeth felt the unmistakable hardness of his erection pressed to her center. It made her heart skip a beat, to know she had turned him on. Yet she sensed he was struggling for detachment. "You can still change your mind," he whispered.

"Not a chance."

"Lizbeth, Lizbeth, what am I going to do with you?"

She gave him the only answer that she could. "Make love with me."

He swore again, even as the hands against her back moved to find the catch of her bra. He had no trouble unhooking it. Then, with one smooth motion, he pulled her loose-fitting sweatshirt over her head, taking her bra with it, and tossed them on the floor. She gasped as cool air hit her flesh, gasped as she realized she was standing in front of him naked to the waist. If he was trying again to make her think about the reckless course she'd set, he was doing a mighty fine job. She had never felt more exposed, more vulnerable, more shyly uncertain than at that moment. Suppose he hated what he saw?

She wanted to hide her face against his shoulder. Yet she summoned the courage to raise her eyes to his. What she discovered stole her breath away. His gaze was dark, superheated, and—vulnerable. And she knew, with sudden joy, that everything was going to be all right, at least for this night.

"You're beautiful. You're so beautiful." His husky voice made her shiver. Then his hand reached to slowly, slowly stroke one breast. "Perfect."

Elizabeth caught her breath as Zeke's fingertips caressed her curves, then grazed across the hard distention of her nipple.

"I want—" The rest of his sentence was swallowed as he yanked his own shirt over his head and tossed it on top of hers before his hands reached for her and gathered her to him. They both gave a little cry as the softness of her breasts made contact with the hard planes of his chest. For a long moment, he held her still against him, and she savored the warmth of the contact. Then he began to shift her body from side to side, sliding her breasts against the springy hair of his chest, bringing glad little cries to her lips. She felt her knees buckle, yet she didn't fall because he was supporting her weight.

Her breath came in little gasps as he eased her back, his hands moving inward to play with her breasts, cup them, reshape them to his grasp, tease her nipples into unbelievable magnets of sensitivity. The pleasure of it was almost more than she could stand.

One hand glided to her hips, urging her more firmly against the hard shaft behind the fly of his pants, rocking her against him. It was only a moment before her own instincts took over and she began to move on her own, pressing, stroking against him, her need becoming more frantic as his hands did wildly erotic things to her breasts.

The heat built relentlessly beyond endurance as he said her name over and over, telling her how much he wanted her to come undone for him. And she did, swept away by a hot, pulsing surge of gratification that brought an incoherent shout to her throat. In the aftermath, she sagged weakly against him, gasping, her skin slick with perspiration.

He stroked her back, stringing tiny kisses along the side of her face as she dropped her head to his shoulder. When she shivered, he wrapped his arms around her shoulders.

"That felt so good."

"We don't have to go any farther than this," he said in a gritty voice. His body was rigid, his legs still braced against the floor.

She summoned the strength to raise her face and saw the tension burning in his eyes. He had given her pleasure beyond her imagining. She wasn't going to stop there. Slipping her hand between them, she cupped her fingers around his rigid flesh, stroking his hardness through the fabric of his jeans. "I need to feel this inside me."

The breath gasped out of him. "No, you don't."

"Zeke, don't deny me the pleasure of satisfying you. Let me see *you* come undone in my arms. Or are you afraid to let me watch you lose control?"

"I'm not afraid of anything—except hurting you."

"You won't."

"Ah, Elizabeth." His mouth came down on hers for a long, greedy kiss. Yet when it was over, he fell back on his old tactics. First he stripped off her jeans and panties so that she stood naked before him. Then he quickly unbuckled his pants and kicked them away, straightening so that he towered over her, formidable and erect. She felt a moment of sudden panic. Could he really fit inside her?

Then she reminded herself that men and women had been managing it since the beginning of time. Grasping his hand, she silently backed up toward the bed. She didn't have far to travel, but by the time she reached her destination she felt him trembling.

"Remember, I promised I'd be gentle with you," she whispered, before turning away so he couldn't see the skin stretched tight across her face. Luckily, the covers needed to be turned down. By the time she finished, she felt him leaning over her kissing her neck.

"I remember," he murmured. "If I get the same considerations."

She nodded, her face against his shoulder, her eyes squeezed shut as she clung to him.

He helped her into the bed, then turned and gathered her to him. She closed her eyes and held on tight. Despite her bold behavior, she was nervous, and she was sure he knew it. Sure by the way he started with nonthreatening kisses and little touches that skirted strategic areas. Yet soon, simple kisses and cautious touches weren't enough. He seemed to know that, too, seemed to sense when she was ready for him to caress her breasts again and when it was time to glide his fingers over the slick heat of her most sensitive flesh.

She had thought that she had taken her pleasure, and now she was giving it back to him. She soon found there was more than she'd realized for her. Once again, he lifted her higher and higher, until she was twisting against him, begging for him to finish what she'd started.

He reached for the packet she'd left on the bedside table, and tore it open. A few moments later, he moved over her.

"I may hurt you."

"It doesn't matter," she gasped. "Please. Now."

He pressed against her, into her, his breath coming in gasps as he tried to go slowly. She would have none of that. Lifting her hips, she surged against him, surprised at the sharp stab of pain.

"Sweetheart, I—" It seemed he wasn't capable of saying more. Or of stopping. He sank into her, past the broken barrier, past the pain, until he was deeply, fully joined with her, and she accepted him with her body, her mind, her soul.

Her hands soothed over his back, her lips stroked his shoulder. "Show me," she urged. "Show me what it's like."

He kissed her temple, then slowly, carefully began to move inside her. "You feel so good," he gasped out.

"So do you."

He shifted, so he could slip his hand between them to stroke her. Heat leaped at the spot where he touched, heat that grew and spread.

"Ah, Lizbeth."

All her concentration focused on the heat and the friction, and the giving and taking of pleasure. She felt him lose control, felt him drive for completion, felt him taking her with him. For the second time that evening, she cried out her release, even as she heard his hoarse shout of triumph.

He shifted off her and gathered her close.

"Thank you," she murmured.

His lips brushed her eyebrows. "Thank you for insisting," he answered.

For long moments she floated on a cloud of satisfaction, eyes closed as he stroked her shoulder and her arm. He had known how to make it wonderful for her. He had cared enough to do that. She wanted to tell him how much she loved him. And she wanted to know what he was feeling, yet she wasn't quite secure enough to get into either of those areas.

As he held her, the fatigue of the past day caught up with her, and she drifted off to sleep. She woke sometime later when the plane hit another air pocket. Her eyes blinked open, and for several seconds she didn't know where she was. Then she remembered—and with the sense of place came the memory of making love with Zeke. Her first time. With her husband, she thought with a little catch in her throat, at least for now. She reached to touch him, and her hand brushed against his thigh. He was sitting up in bed, the covers pulled around his hips and his back resting against several pillows.

When he saw her looking at him, he gently touched her cheek. "We still have a few hours before we reach Athens," he whispered. "You should go back to sleep."

"You're not."

"I had some thinking to do."

The lights were dimmed, but she could make out the harsh line of his profile. When she'd gone to sleep, he'd seemed relaxed. Now he was tense again.

"How are you?" she asked, dragging the covers with her as she sat up and plumped the pillow on her side of the bed.

"That's my line," he answered.

"Well, I feel wonderful." She stretched, then found his hand under the sheet and covered it with hers. "Or I did until I discovered that you're wound tight as a spring."

"I'm sorry I woke you up."

"Probably it was the plane." She inspected the lines of strain around his eyes. "Were you thinking about Ariadne?" she asked gently.

He sighed. "Actually, about my father."

All at once, she wasn't quite so relaxed herself. "Why?"

"He was on Mythos about twenty years ago, excavating the ruins of a temple dedicated to Apollo in the mountains near Delvia."

"And?"

"He was a lying, cheating bastard who put money above everything else in life."

She tipped her head to one side. "I thought he was an archaeologist."

Zeke gave a harsh laugh. "Well, that, too. Actually, I think he could have been pretty good at restoring ancient cities and palaces, if that had been the main focus of his energy. Right up there with Heinrich Schliemann and Sir Arthur Evans,'' he added.

Elizabeth knew that Schliemann had discovered the historical site of Troy and the home of its conqueror, Agamemnon. Evans had used his own fortune to excavate the ancient palace at Knossos, the sanctuary of the Minotaur, and then turned the reconstructed site over to the Greek government. Both men had helped prove that ancient legends had their basis in fact. If Zeke was comparing his father's abilities to theirs, then the man must have been extraordinary.

''Do you want to talk about him?''

He was silent for a short stretch, then sighed. ''Not really. But his history is relevant. And, uh, I owe you some explanations.''

''You mean because I practically forced you to make love with me?'' she asked sharply.

He slipped his arm around her, drawing her closer. ''It wasn't a question of force. I was trying my damnedest to be honorable. I think it must have been obvious how much I wanted you.''

''I—''

He stopped her with a finger pressed to her lips.

''Don't get off the subject. Let me tell you about my father, before I lose my nerve.''

''Okay,'' she whispered. She might want reassurances about his feelings, but she wasn't selfish enough to put her own needs before his. ''You know Sebastian mentioned my father. Now I'm wondering if, somehow, he's involved with what's going on.''

''But he's dead—isn't he?''

''Yeah. He died in prison,'' Zeke answered in a strangely flat voice, his eyes never leaving hers.

She couldn't stop her face from registering shock. But under the covers, she found Zeke's hand again.

His features were so rigid they might have been carved from marble. His eyes stared toward the bulkhead separating their cabin from the front of the plane. "He was from an aristocratic Baltimore family that lost its money in the depression. But he was a top student, so he got a scholarship to the University of Maryland and ended up with a Ph.D. in archaeology. He thought that was his ticket to fame and fortune. It turned out his younger brother did better."

He paused and sucked in a deep breath. As he let it out slowly, Elizabeth sensed that he was giving himself a little more time before the bad part.

Eyes narrowed, he continued. "My father was always jealous of Uncle Henry. Henry was no scholar. He barely finished high school, but he was smart. He went into business for himself. After trying a couple of things, he found a backer and made a fortune selling pipe fittings. My father couldn't stand being outdone. So he figured out a way to get rich himself. He had an excellent reputation in his field. He used it to get assigned to locations where he was likely to find valuable artifacts." Zeke's face contorted, before he began to speak again. "He started holding back some of the pieces he'd discovered, and sold them to connoisseurs who didn't care whether their private collections were obtained illegally. That knife of Sebastian's could have been one of his finds." He made a low noise in his throat. "Sebastian or whoever gave the knife to him knew I'd be obsessed by it—that I wouldn't be able to leave it behind. They used that to trap me. Trap *us!*" he said in a low voice.

Elizabeth twisted her fingers more tightly with Zeke's, although she wasn't sure he noticed. "Don't blame yourself for that," she whispered.

"Who else should I blame?"

"Whoever killed Sebastian."

He was silent for long moments. When he continued speaking, he sounded as if he were recounting a story he'd read in the newspaper. "My mother knew what he was doing, but she was afraid to say anything. Or maybe she liked the life-style his larceny bought. Usually he worked with a local resident who hid his stash—until Dr. Chambers could smuggle it out of the country. The local guy would get part of the profit, but nowhere near half, because the foreign professor never divulged the real value of the artifacts."

"How did you find all this out?" she asked.

"He got caught. Up till then, I only knew that he never wanted me around." Zeke paused for breath.

Elizabeth turned so she was curled against him. His arms came up to gather her close. The bare facts he'd recited were bad enough. Reading between the lines was worse. "I'm so sorry."

"Not shocked?"

"Well, yes," she admitted. "How did he get caught?"

Zeke gave a harsh laugh, his gaze still focused away from her. "Bad luck. A worker at the temple fell over the side of an excavation and died, and there was a police investigation. They stumbled onto the smuggling operation. I got the news when an enterprising reporter from the *New York Times* called me at boarding school to ask what I thought about my father's arrest in Mythos. I was fifteen, but I knew enough to hang up without talking to the press."

"God, no."

"The archaeological community did its best to bury the disgrace, which is why you probably don't remember the incident. My mother came back to the U.S. right after the trial. She was given immunity in exchange for testifying against him. She wanted us to live together like nothing had happened. But I couldn't do that. I—" His voice hitched. "I didn't like her much…or feel comfortable with her. I went to live with Uncle Henry."

Elizabeth's arms tightened around him. "Oh, Zeke."

"So I've got some firsthand experience on why it might not work out to have a kid live with someone he barely knows," he muttered. "Henry did his duty by me. He even left me enough of his money to make my life very comfortable. But he was never very loving. I guess that's a family trait.''

''Well, you didn't inherit it,'' she whispered. ''Every time you hold me, every time you kiss me, I know you're struggling with deep feelings you don't know how to handle.''

Zeke winced, and Elizabeth wondered if she'd said too much. Relief flooded through her when he clasped her more tightly. She closed her eyes and held on to him, trying to tell him without words how much she valued him, how much she loved him. Lord, she'd thought she had a rough start in life. But she'd ended up in a good home. Zeke sounded as if he would have been better off if his mother and father had put him up for adoption. She'd known from her job at Birth Data that some people simply shouldn't have had kids. She hadn't dreamed Zeke's parents were in that group. She clenched her teeth, then made an effort to let go of the tension—in case he misinterpreted her reaction. She'd known all along that he was a man with a past. She simply hadn't had a clue how far back it went. She felt a shudder go through him as he started to speak again.

''I guess there's some special CIA unit that recruits U.S. citizens who might have personal reasons to take on dangerous assignments. They approached me in graduate school and asked if I wanted to make amends for my father's illegal acts by working for them in foreign countries, using my linguistic specialty as a cover. I accepted and took a quick course in spying—with additional training on an as-needed basis. Sometimes I worked for the CIA, sometimes for other agencies like the State Department. That's how I met Thorn, by the way.''

''You still work for the government?'' she asked, trying to absorb everything that he was saying.

He shook his head. ''I almost got killed about a year and a half ago in Bosnia.''

Her hold on him tightened. ''You mean when you were away for a couple of months?''

"Yeah. While I was lying in my hospital bed, I decided I didn't have to give my life for my father's sins. So I quit."

"Good."

"The joke is that the training they gave me may make the difference in getting Ariadne out of Mythos."

She nodded against his chest, her mind reeling as she tried to process the information he'd given her. She was so absorbed that for several seconds she lost the thread of what he was saying. Then a sentence caught her attention.

"Sebastian said Aristotle wasn't my only enemy. Then he offered to tell me where I could find Ariadne, in exchange for information about the location of the artifacts my father stole. I thought they'd been recovered. Now I'm wondering if the knife is one of them and if some of the pieces are still hidden. They could be worth a great deal of money."

"Or maybe Sebastian did some research on you and found out how to jerk your chain. If he knew about your background, he could figure out you'd find any connection between your father and Sophia's death disturbing."

Zeke went very still. Then for the first time the tension around his mouth eased a little. "I didn't think of that. But you're right, it would make sense."

"Sebastian's dead. It doesn't matter what he discovered about you."

"I wish that were true. Unfortunately, we still have to worry about whoever killed him—and why."

"Not right now. Let's not waste any more precious time on him."

Elizabeth felt Zeke sigh out a long breath as she stroked her fingers though his hair. She'd been afraid to take the risk of telling him she loved him, and afraid that the knowledge of her love would only be a burden to him. Yet everything had changed in this bed when he'd made love to her—and when he'd told her things about himself that he hid from everyone else.

"You're ashamed of your family," she murmured.

He went very still.

"You have nothing to be ashamed of!" she added quickly. "Your parents left you with scars. You've proved they didn't crush your spirit or destroy your sense of what's right and what's wrong."

"I'm damaged," he muttered.

"No. You fought against the damage and won. Nobody can understand that better than I can. I must have sensed it from the beginning, and it made me love you."

Lifting her head, she sought his troubled eyes. "Zeke, I love you," she said again in a strong, clear voice.

The breath froze in Zeke's lungs. His whole body went rigid. "Don't say that."

"I can't hide it any longer, from myself or from you," she told him. "It's been true for a long time. That's why it hurt so much when you asked me to marry you and then said in the next breath that you knew I didn't want to get emotionally involved."

She heard him swallow, saw his features contort. "I shouldn't have hurt you like that. I'm not very good at relationships."

"It takes practice. You're getting better," she encouraged. "And I'm not putting any conditions on my love. It's part of me. Whatever happens."

"I may let you down."

"I don't think so." Cupping her hands around the back of his head, she brought his lips down to hers. He made a noise deep in his throat when she began to kiss him. The meeting of their mouths was as urgent and greedy as if they hadn't made love just a few hours before. She returned his passion. It was time to stop talking, time to show this man who had been through so much how deeply she cared for him.

"WHAT ARE YOU DOING?"

Irena's fingers froze on the small white dress she was

folding. Making an effort to compose her face, she turned toward the little girl who was sitting up in bed. "I thought you were sleeping, my little lamb."

"I woke up," Ariadne answered, rubbing her eyes and glancing toward the window where dawn was just beginning to light the sky. "Do we have to get up yet?"

"No. Go back to sleep."

The little girl crawled out from under the covers, so she could get a better look at her aunt where she knelt on the marble floor. "What are you doing?" she repeated.

"I washed and ironed some of your clothes. I'm putting them away."

The child's head turned toward the old-fashioned wardrobe that stood between the room's two double-hung windows. The doors stood open. Half the interior was fitted with drawers, the other side had a rod for hangers. "I thought my clothes were going to stay in there for a long, long time. Why are you putting them into that black bag?"

Irena's mind scrambled for an explanation, even as she glanced guiltily toward the door. It was firmly closed, and no one else was up at this early hour of the morning, she told herself. "There are too many things for the wardrobe. Your clothes will get wrinkled, if they're all wadded together."

"Are we leaving this place?" the child suddenly asked.

"Of course not!" Irena delivered the lie with great conviction.

"Good. Because I'm tired of living in so many different houses," the small voice answered with conviction. "Zeke Chambers is coming here to live with us. And we'll be like a family."

"Zeke Chambers is our secret," Irena answered quickly.

"I remember that."

"Good." Irena hesitated. She hated telling more lies to the little girl. Yet in this case, she knew it was imperative. She'd thought they would be safe here. This morning, she'd discovered evidence that she was wrong. They had to leave as quickly as possible. But not until she was sure they could slip away without being detected. If they were caught, that would be the most dangerous thing of all.

"This will be another secret. Don't tell anyone that I'm keeping our clothing in a bag. They'll think I'm a strange old woman," Irena said.

The little girl climbed off the bed and threw her arms around her aunt. "I don't think you're strange. I love you, *Theitsa* Irena."

"I love you, too, little lamb."

"I'm good about keeping secrets. I won't tell. I promise."

As she kissed Ariadne's sweetly scented cheek, Irena offered a silent prayer to the Virgin Mother that it was true.

Chapter Ten

While Zeke conferred with Steve and Jed, Elizabeth did the best she could to freshen up in the little bathroom, trying to make it seem as if she and Zeke had simply spent the night sleeping in their private stateroom. Still, as she dabbed on a little makeup and inspected herself in the mirror, she felt as if she had the word *ex-virgin* written across her forehead in blazing letters. Not that she was ashamed of her change of status, but she preferred to keep such matters private.

Back in the stateroom, as she began to straighten up the bed, a sudden thought made her hand go still. Stopping in her attempt to smooth the covers, she pulled them aside. Her breath clogged in her throat as she saw the telltale red stain in the middle of the bottom sheet. How embarrassing.

She had just stripped the incriminating evidence off the bed, when Zeke stepped back through the cabin door. Her fingers clenched around the sheets, wadding them into a ball.

There was a long moment of silence, as they stood facing each other across the expanse of the mattress.

"Are you sorry about last night?" she managed.

He kept his gaze steady. "Yes and no."

"What does that mean?" she whispered, her hand tightening on the sheet.

"I don't want you to get hurt."

"I won't."

He gave her a long unreadable look, and she knew that their talk had only partially reassured him.

"Last night was the best night of my life," she confessed in a steady voice.

His face softened, "Mine, too."

"Zeke!" She reached toward him, but he remained where he was.

"I want—" He stopped and swallowed hard, then began again. "I'm not used to asking for what I want."

"I know. But I'm used to giving."

"Lizbeth," Her name was a hoarse sound that welled up from deep inside him. His hands clenched, then he gestured toward the door. "We have to go up front and buckle in."

"As soon as I finish straightening up," she managed.

He turned quickly, and she watched the tightness across his shoulders until the door closed. If they only had a few more minutes alone, she knew she could break through to him again. But she didn't have the luxury of time.

The sheets were still in her hands. Rolling the top one around the bottom, she pushed them both into the corner. If she was lucky, they'd stay that way until they got to the laundry.

Zeke was already buckled in and staring out the window when Elizabeth reached the main cabin. Taking the seat in back of him, she strapped herself in before swinging around toward the fascinating view—which turned out to be no more than a thick layer of cloud. She wanted to lean forward and touch him somewhere—his arm, his shoulder, but some invisible force prevented her from moving.

The jet broke through the clouds, and Elizabeth saw blue water and a mountainous, rocky shoreline. The landscape changed suddenly from rural to urban sprawl. It was startling, even though she'd heard Athens was one of the world's largest cities.

They landed on a modern field hemmed in by low white buildings, some with gardens of brightly flowering vines and other tropical foliage. When the plane finished taxiing to a stop, Steve pushed open the door at the front of the cabin. Elizabeth felt herself flush as his eyes flicked toward her.

"How are you doing?" he asked.

"Fine." She was braced for newlywed jokes, but he didn't look in much of a joking mood, she decided.

Coming into the cabin, he turned to Zeke. "Jed's still on the radio with Mythos customs," he explained. "We got a call an hour ago from Jason. The pilot who agreed to fly you into Kalana has been arrested for smuggling. His plane has been confiscated."

Zeke uttered a vehement curse.

"Can't we get somebody else?" Elizabeth asked.

Steve shook his head. "There's not a lot of air traffic in and out of Mythos. Anyone who flies there needs a special permit."

"And you're not cleared for that?" she clarified.

He looked apologetic. "It would take a couple of days."

Jed appeared in the doorway. "I've started checking around. There are a lot more boats going back and forth than licensed planes. I think your best bet is to go in by water."

Zeke made a low noise, and Elizabeth looked at him questioningly. "I don't travel well by boat," he muttered.

"We could try to locate another pilot who's cleared," Steve suggested.

Zeke shook his head. "I know how that works. It takes time to find someone. Then the deal can fall through at the last minute."

"Jason put me in touch with a local contact en route. He gave me the names of a couple of skippers willing to take passengers who want to slip quietly into Mythos," Jed told him, handing over a piece of paper.

"Then I guess we'd better check them out," Zeke said with a sigh.

"The guys you want aren't right in Piraeus," Jed informed him. "There are a couple of little harbors outside of town, but they shouldn't be hard to find."

"Good."

They exited the plane and walked rapidly toward the two-story terminal. First came passport control, where Zeke informed the inquiring official that they were on vacation and gave their address in Greece as an Athens hotel. Then he led Elizabeth briskly though the green customs line, the one for arriving passengers with nothing to declare. Did that mean he'd left the gun in Maryland, she wondered but didn't ask.

OUTSIDE THE CUSTOMS AREA, a man checked his watch and glanced casually toward the exit door before bending again to the newspaper story he had been pretending to read for the past forty-five minutes. He was a very ordinary man. Medium build. Dark hair and eyes like many of his countrymen. Clean shaven. Wearing a sports coat, white shirt and conservative tie over dark slacks.

No one would look twice at him, he told himself, although they might wonder why he was staring at the same story for so long. Turning the page, he tried to focus on a new column of print.

His face was impassive. Yet his stomach was beginning to knot. His contact in the States had taken care of Sebastian Pappas. This morning the next part of the plan was swinging into operation, and he knew what would happen to him if there were any screwups. That was why he'd arrived early—so there would be no chance of missing Chambers and the woman. Where in the hell were they? Mother of God, what if they'd changed their plans and landed at a different airport?

He could feel sweat trickling down the inside of his collar. Then finally the door opened, and he glanced up in time to see the face he'd memorized from the photographs—Chambers. And the woman. It was his first glimpse of her. Very striking. Too bad she didn't have long to live.

He gave a curt nod, and the boy he'd hired came scurrying up to them and tried to sell them a map of the city—delaying their exit for a few moments. It had better be long enough. Walking quickly, he made for the door to the ground transportation area and signaled to the driver waiting to slip into the front of the line of yellow taxis. The cabbies here were aggressive. Arranging to let a taxi into the front of the queue had taken a hefty payoff. But it wasn't his money.

ELIZABETH STUCK CLOSE TO Zeke as he led the way to the street, with the assurance of a man who had traveled this territory before. "I appreciate what you've done for us," he told Jed and Steve. "We can take it from here."

"You're sure you don't want any company?" Steve asked.

"You've just finished a ten-hour flight. Get some sleep."

"Okay."

The two men each gave Elizabeth a quick hug.

"Thanks, and take care," Zeke said, before stepping into the direction of the taxis. A man in a sports coat and dark slacks waved him toward the first one in line, a Mercedes, as were many of the others, Elizabeth noted. Probably they were cheaper on this side of the Atlantic.

"Right here. Take the first one, please," he said in English, opening the door.

Elizabeth glanced inside. The seats were leather and the interior was spotless. Much plusher than what she'd expect in the States. After waiting until the luggage was stowed in the trunk, Zeke slipped into the back seat.

"Where to?" the driver asked in barely understandable English.

Zeke pulled out the piece of paper he'd gotten from Jed and began to give directions—in Greek. Elizabeth sat tensely beside him, wishing they could finish the conversation they'd started in the plane. But it was obvious, as Zeke continued to speak to the driver, that any personal exchange would still have to wait.

She could sit and stew. Or she could use the time constructively, she told herself, as she tried to get her bearings in this bustling foreign city. It was more modern than she'd expected, and to her surprise, about a third of the advertising signs were in English. With the ones in Greek, she practiced sounding out the words. She'd studied the language, but this was different from reading a textbook and doing exercises in class. It was also different from the rapid-fire conversation of the men.

The morning rush hour should be over, she mused, as she checked the watch she'd reset for a seven-hour time difference. But there was still plenty of traffic. The coast was on their left, and they passed several marinas full of pleasure craft.

When the driver turned off the highway onto a side road that bisected a line of low hills, he and Zeke began to argue.

She understood Zeke's "Are you sure?" and the driver's quick assertion to the affirmative.

In minutes they had left the metropolitan area behind for fields of corn, cotton and cabbages interspersed with white stucco houses. The hills above them were dominated by rocks and scrubby vegetation.

The road changed rapidly from blacktop to gravel, and then to hard-packed dirt. Again Zeke questioned the driver, and again he nodded vigorously.

They were heading toward the blue water of the Aegean. The lane ended abruptly at a little rock-rimmed harbor, where several tiny craft and a couple of larger vessels, perhaps a hundred feet in length, were moored. One appeared to be an old ferry boat, listing dangerously to starboard. The other looked like a luxury yacht that had seen better days.

About fifty yards away on the right, several dozen houses clustered together. On the left, the concrete skeleton of a two-story unfinished building shaded a flock of peacefully grazing sheep.

"Not exactly a bustling port," Zeke observed. After several seconds' hesitation, he opened the door. "The driver's going to wait, in case I can't do business with the skipper of the yacht. I'll be right back," he told Elizabeth.

She felt a clogging sensation in her throat. "You're not going to leave me here," she objected.

The sun had broken through the clouds, and Zeke shaded his eyes as he scanned the harbor. "I think that's safest, until I find out the situation with the boat," he answered. As he started to get out of the taxi, the driver protested loudly. Zeke switched back to Greek. After a heated exchange, he reached in his pocket for some drachmas. "It's only half of what he asked for," Zeke told Elizabeth. "He'll get the rest when I tell him it's okay to leave."

Making for the harbor, Zeke climbed down a set of stone steps to the dock and started talking to a man with a red bandanna tied around his head.

It didn't take too long before Elizabeth began to feel uncomfortable in the cab. The driver kept eyeing her in the rearview mirror. Then he turned and tried to start a conversation in slowly spoken elementary Greek. Telling him she wanted to stretch her legs, she climbed out and made a small circle around the vehicle.

On the dock a lean yellow dog lifted its head, then went back to sleep.

"You not so friendly, huh?" the driver asked through the window.

Elizabeth was startled that he'd finally spoken in English. Still, she didn't want to get drawn into a conversation. Without responding, she took several steps toward Zeke, who was now talking to two men—the one with the red bandanna and another with salt-and-pepper hair and a short scruffy beard. She couldn't hear what they were saying. But the body language and the gestures seemed to indicate bargaining. Watching the exchange absorbed her attention until she heard the driver's door open. He strode around to the back, opened the trunk and dropped their luggage on the dirt road.

"Hey, what do you think you're doing?" she asked.

He gave her a narrow-eyed look before climbing back in the taxi and starting the engine.

"Zeke, come back!" she shouted.

Zeke looked up, saw what was happening and started running toward her. But he was too late. By the time he arrived, the cab had disappeared in a cloud of dust.

"So now what are we going to do?" she asked.

"Take a short cruise to Mythos. At least it's not a fishing boat. We can have a private cabin."

She glanced toward the dock. It now contained three scruffy-looking men. "They look kind of rough," she murmured.

"What do you expect from smugglers?"

"Smugglers?"

"They're smuggling us in—along with some other stuff."

"Like what?"

He shrugged. "I didn't ask."

"You trust them?"

Zeke scowled at her. "They're already going to Mythos. We're just making the run more profitable."

Before Elizabeth could comment, Zeke plowed on, "If you think I like making the trip by boat, you're wrong. It wouldn't take much to persuade me to look for a ride into town and start calling air transport companies. But we'll lose valuable time—time Ariadne can't afford."

Elizabeth wanted to tell him she didn't like the way events were shaping up and that he was letting his anxiety for his daughter override logical thinking. But she couldn't get the words out. In the first place, she wasn't sure her case of the jitters was justified. What if she delayed their departure and the consequences were disastrous?

"Okay?" he asked.

"Okay."

Picking up their bags, Zeke started back to the dock. She followed.

As they drew nearer, she saw the name of the ship written on the bow in Greek letters. Sounding them out, she saw that they would be sailing on the *Amphitrite*. Elizabeth remembered she was the wife of Poseidon, the god of the sea. At least the captain had a fondness for the old Greek myths. Or perhaps he simply hadn't bothered to change the name when he'd acquired the ship from its previous owner.

The men, who had been craning their necks toward her and Zeke, made an effort to appear relaxed as their passengers approached. One slipped his hands into the pockets of his slacks. Another lounged against the stone wall ringing the harbor. Probably they were on edge because they needed the money, she told herself, glancing around the dilapidated dock area.

Still, the sailors were less reassuring up close than they had been from a distance. One had a wicked-looking scar down his right cheek like an old-time pirate. Another was missing two front teeth. And none looked as if they had taken a bath since the last time they'd fallen in the water—whenever that was.

The man Zeke introduced as Captain Icarus was a little older than the other—the one with the salt-and-pepper hair.

She stood back, letting Zeke do the talking, which was in rapid-fire Greek and much too quick for her to follow. Finally, it appeared a satisfactory deal had been struck.

"All set," Zeke announced. "Let's have a look at the cabin."

"How long a trip will it be?" she asked, allowing him to help her down the flight of stone steps onto the deck.

"Six hours."

"*Kalimera*, madame," Captain Icarus politely wished her a good morning.

She answered in halting Greek. If she'd had some advanced warning about this trip, she would have brushed up.

In response to her best effort, he switched to English. "This way."

They climbed down a short set of steps to a corridor with several narrow doors on either side.

The captain stopped at the third one on the right and ceremoniously swung it open as if he were giving a tour of the presidential suite at the Ritz. Stepping inside, Elizabeth found herself in a cramped stateroom. Although the walls were of expensive teak paneling, the only furnishings were two metal bunks, separated by a three-drawer chest bolted to the deck, and a recessed ceiling light. A layer of carpeting on the floor was so worn in places that the deck showed through. In contrast to the salt-tanged wind blowing across the deck, the atmosphere inside the little room was hot and thick and smelled of motor oil.

"Charming," Elizabeth whispered. At least the blankets on the bunks seemed relatively clean. She could have done with pillows. No, cancel that, she thought as she pictured lumpy gray rectangles.

"If you'll excuse me," Icarus said. "I have duties."

When he'd left, Elizabeth sat down on one of the bunks.

Above them, she could hear a rustle of activity. Apparently, now that they had taken on their passengers, the crew was getting ready to cast off.

Zeke eyed the other bed, then turned toward the door. "I'd better go up on deck and look interested—while I can still stand," he muttered.

He'd said he wasn't a good sailor, and she'd assumed he was simply preparing her in case he wasn't at his best. Now she realized his problem might be more serious than she'd thought. "Let's not do this," she whispered.

"I have to."

The finality of the words left no room for argument. She sighed. "Isn't there something you can take for sea sickness?" she asked.

He glanced toward his duffel bag. "There are some tablets in my first-aid kit, but they'll make me groggy, and I don't want to put myself at that kind of disadvantage.''

She stood again. "I'll go up with you."

He escorted her back to the deck. As they made their way along a narrow walkway to the bow, she counted the crew members. Two were casting off ropes and another was lounging against the rail. The captain was at the wheel, which made four in all. Not the best odds, Elizabeth decided, if they had to fight their way out of here. Even as the thought surfaced, she dismissed it as paranoid. Why would they have to fight? She was simply letting her nerves rule her.

The ride was relatively smooth while the boat putted at low power across the rock-rimmed harbor. Once they hit the open sea, however, the craft began to buck against the waves, and Elizabeth had to hold on tight to the rail to stay in one spot. The sea was high, and the sun, which had been shining brightly when they arrived at the little port, had disappeared behind a wall of clouds. In fact, the whole sky to the west seemed to be turning angry.

She glanced at Zeke, and saw that his knuckles were white on the railing and his complexion had gone the color of key lime pie. If he was already feeling bad, he had a pretty grueling six hours ahead of him.

"I'd better lie down," he said, when he caught her looking at him.

"What can I do?" she asked.

"Shoot me," he quipped, in such a way that Elizabeth knew laughing at the joke would be a mistake.

She saw the sailors eyeing them and exchanging a few knowing snickers. Contempt for seasick landlubbers? Or was their attitude toward the passengers frankly malicious?

She ducked her head away and stifled the impulse to grab Zeke's arm, as she followed him back to the cabin. He flopped onto the far bed and lay with one arm across his eyes and the other hand gripping the edge of the metal bunk.

"Sorry," he whispered. "Unfortunately, this is worse than I remember."

"Not your fault. Maybe the waves will get calmer," she added optimistically.

She saw him grit his teeth, as a particularly large swell rolled the boat from side to side. "It looks like a storm is brewing," he muttered.

Her gaze darted toward the dirty porthole. Everything looked darker than when they'd left the deck, but that might only be from the grimy film on the glass. She sat down gingerly on the other bunk, wishing she could do something for Zeke. She wanted to hold him. But from the anguished expression on his face she was sure that he didn't want to be touched by her or anybody else. He lay rigid in the swaying bunk, his eyes closed and his jaw clamped. Apparently the major part of his concentration was going into keeping his breakfast down. Some fresh air would probably help, but the whole cabin would be soaked if she tried to open the porthole.

Hauling her overnight bag up onto the bed, Elizabeth wedged it against the bulkhead and used it for a pillow. She'd promised herself that on the trip to Mythos she and Zeke could rekindle the closeness of the previous night. Zeke wanted to reach out to her; she knew he did. But he hadn't had much practice at intimacy, and he was still afraid of it.

Her heart gave a little tug. All she had to do was make him understand that she'd never let him down, the way everyone else had.

But nothing like that was going to happen now. Flopping back against the makeshift pillow, she closed her eyes and tried to relax. Perhaps the rocking of the boat made her doze off. Some time later, she heard Zeke calling her name and was instantly at his side.

"Are you worse?" she asked anxiously, leaning over him. Beads of moisture wet his brow. Digging a tissue out of her purse, she gently wiped them away.

"Thanks." He made an attempt to smile and failed. "No, I'm not really worse."

"Do you want something? Water?"

He shuddered. "No water. But I don't like the idea of both of us stuck in this cabin. Could you go up on deck and take a look around? See how things look."

She was reminded of a story her father used to tell about her mother asking him to watch a pot roast on the stove while she was out shopping. He kept going into the kitchen and lifting the cover of the pot, looking critically at the meat, but he didn't have a clue what he was supposed to be looking for.

Unless the crew were standing guard with guns at the entrance to the lower deck or unpacking boxes of ammunition, she didn't have any idea what she was looking for either.

As she walked toward the door, she could tell that the sea was rougher than it had been before.

"Take a jacket," Zeke told her.

She dug a windbreaker out of her bag, then looked toward the door. It was definitely the only one in the cabin. "I...uh...suppose there's got to be a bathroom on board," she said to Zeke.

"If we're lucky. Behind one of the doors farther down the passageway." He shook his head. "You probably won't like it much."

"What choice do I have?" She exited the room, trying to move with the swaying of the ship as she looked for the facilities. Zeke was right; the bathroom she found wasn't up to her standards. Trying to hold her breath, she used the toilet—then made a beeline for the fresh air outside.

When she reached the top of the companionway, she was glad she had dressed warmly. The sky was dark, the temperature had dropped and the wind was whipping up spray from the gunmetal waves.

Ducking her head, she stepped onto the deck and grabbed a handhold to steady herself as she got her bearings. When she felt a bit more confident on her feet, she started her tour of the boat. But she found her path was blocked by the sailor with the scar on his cheek. Perhaps he had been assigned to keep an eye on the passengers. Or perhaps he had simply chosen to lurk around the entrance to the cabins.

In response to her apprehensive glance, he smiled at her, showing an expanse of yellow teeth. The smile and the look in his eyes sent a chill through her that sank all the way to her bones. Deliberately, as if she'd simply changed her mind, she pivoted away and started in the other direction along the stern. To her dismay, she realized he was keeping pace behind her.

Chapter Eleven

Elizabeth could feel her heart pounding in time to the echoing footsteps. Spray hit her in the face as she looked out over the water, which had changed from blue to gray to match the clouds overhead. There were no other craft in sight. And no hint of land. The *Amphitrite* pitched as it climbed the trough of a wave, and Elizabeth grabbed at the rail. Inside the wheelhouse, she could see Captain Icarus's salt-and-pepper hair and the darker head of another crewman. They appeared to be watching her progress and that of the man behind her. Yet neither of them made a move to interfere.

Well, if the captain wasn't worried, perhaps she was simply overreacting, she told herself as she reached the bow of the ship and stood facing into the wind. Deliberately, she kept herself from glancing over her shoulder at the man. Maybe he was simply going about his business—and she had the misfortune to be heading in the same direction. That theory evaporated as she made her way back along the other side of the ship, the wind shoving her from behind. Scarface was still there, a few paces in back of her, his footsteps audible above the sound of the sea.

Still, she had no proof that he meant her harm—besides the intuitive knowledge that he was enjoying the silent game of stalking her. She sped up her pace, trying to get back down the companionway stairs to the safety of the cabin. She almost made it. Before she reached the entrance to the lower deck, however, he made his move, pushing past her and blocking the opening with his body. She stopped in her tracks to keep from hurtling into him, clutching at a railing when the treacherous sea came to his aid and tried to deliver her into his grasp.

He grinned and held out his hand, displaying a big ugly ring with a skull with staring eyes. "I'll help you," he said in Greek.

Pretending not to understand, she flattened herself against the exterior bulkhead. A quick glance in either direction told her that he'd waited until they were alone to make his move.

For several seconds they stood regarding each other—his expression predatory, hers as blank as she could make it when her heart was pounding so hard it threatened to crack her ribs.

Scarface licked his lips and took a step toward her. "Nice breasts," he said, his gaze fixed on the front of her jacket. "Don't hide them."

He reached toward her, the ugly ring flashing, his fingers curled toward her chest. Instinctively, she slapped his hand away. As she did, the edge of the dull metal skull dug into her flesh, making her gasp. Her panic—and the sound of her pain—made him grin.

"You can't get away from me. Unless you jump over the side," he told her cheerfully.

She took a step back, wondering if she could make it to the wheelhouse. Not a chance. He'd bring her down before she got more than a few feet away.

He understood all too well that he had the advantage. He was larger and stronger, and he was used to operating on a swaying ship. If she screamed for help, the wind would only carry her shouts away over the gray water.

Her mouth was so dry that she could hardly speak. Yet, with all the coolness she could muster, she raised her head and gave him a frigid stare. "Let me pass."

The confidence in his eyes made her insides twist. "We get to know each other better—you and me," he said.

"I don't think so," another voice answered from below. Zeke. It was Zeke, she realized with a surge of joy. A heartbeat later, Scarface pitched forward, flying through the air and hitting his shoulder against the rail before slipping silently to the deck. He lay stunned for long seconds, then groaned and crawled several feet away before pushing himself to a sitting position.

Elizabeth stood paralyzed, sucking in drafts of air, her legs braced to keep from pitching forward as Zeke came the rest of the way up the stairs and took a menacing step toward the would-be attacker. Zeke's face was drawn. Yet his eyes were fierce, as he focused on the man who had cornered her.

Scarface said something low and urgent in Greek, something that sounded like he was trying to explain that he had meant no harm to Zeke's woman.

Zeke nodded tightly, his hands clenched into fists, yet he held himself in check as the man staggered to his feet and slouched away. When they were alone, Zeke turned and closed the distance between himself and Elizabeth. She went into his arms, burying her face against his neck and trying not to sob as he clasped her to him.

"Are you all right?" he asked in a strangled voice.

"Yes."

The *Amphitrite* climbed down and then up the trough of a wave. Zeke leaned against the railing to keep his footing. Closing her eyes, Elizabeth clung to him, the warmth of his body contrasting with the coldness of the wind playing with her back and hair.

"I heard your voice. And his. What happened?" he asked.

She struggled to compose herself. "I started walking around the deck, and...and Scarface started following me. I tried to get back to the cabin, but he blocked the way. He made a comment about my breasts and grabbed for me."

Zeke cursed. "Where was the captain when that bastard started following you?"

"He saw what was happening. I guess he didn't care."

"God, I'm sorry. I should never have sent you up there by yourself."

"I thought you were too sick to be walking around," she said.

"So did I. But when you asked where to find the bathroom, I decided it wasn't such a bad idea. And when I made it to my feet, I realized I didn't feel as bad as I thought. So I decided to join you on deck. Thank God," he added, cradling her more tightly in his arms.

She nestled her face against his shoulder and murmured her own amen.

"Let's go back down." He started to lead her away, when she heard footsteps coming rapidly toward them along the deck. She and Zeke both went very still.

Low, urgent voices came toward them, two men talking in a language that sounded almost Greek. Although she strained to catch what they were saying, she found it impossible to understand any of the words. Zeke turned his head, listening intently, his eyes narrowing.

The captain and the other man from the wheelhouse stepped into view. They continued their private conversation for several seconds before Icarus raised his head toward Zeke.

"My first mate, Tyrone, and I have reprimanded Crewman Cydon," the captain said in very formal English. "I want to apologize for whatever he did," he continued, turning his palm up in a conciliatory gesture.

Zeke kept his arm protectively around Elizabeth, his eyes cold. "I want him taken into custody. He attacked my wife."

Icarus blanched. "He was drunk."

"That's hardly an excuse," Zeke shot back.

"It's my fault entirely." The captain apologized again, in a strained voice. "I should have left him home to sleep it off. You are absolutely right. He will be locked in the brig for the rest of the trip, and I promise nothing like that will happen again.''

Zeke was silent for several seconds. "It had better not," he snapped.

"You have my word," the captain said, although it looked as if the promise tasted like acid in his mouth.

"That's comforting," Zeke replied, and Elizabeth caught the edge of sarcasm in his voice.

"My men don't always conform to social niceties. Perhaps it would be safer for your wife to stay in your cabin for the remainder of the journey," Icarus said, his tone a little sharper and his face hard.

Elizabeth felt Zeke's arm muscles tense, and she laid a restraining hand on his sleeve. His jaw knotted; he stood staring at the captain for several more seconds. Then he shrugged and turned away. Elizabeth breathed out a little sigh as he steered her toward the companionway. Confrontation averted.

She held tight to his arm, stopping once when the surging movement of the waves threw her off balance. Ushering her into the cabin, Zeke turned and locked the door with a decisive click. Then he drew her down onto the bunk she'd been using, turning so they could both fit. Wrapping his arms around her, he stroked her back and shoulders and kissed the side of her face over and over.

She started to tremble then, as she held tight to him. He was shaking, too, his hands moving over her in sweeping, possessive strokes. She could feel emotions roiling inside him. But long seconds passed before he spoke in a gritty voice.

"I should never have gotten us onto this tub. Never have put you in that kind of danger."

She reached to press her fingers against his cheek. "You didn't know something like that was going to happen."

"Yeah, well, it seems I was in too damn much of a hurry to get off the mainland." He gave a little snort. "And at the same time, I was worrying about how sick I was going to feel. I should have been thinking more clearly, before signing on with these guys.''

She raised her face and looked at him questioningly. ''They aren't all like Cydon, are they?''

He replied with a mirthless laugh. ''They're not all as stupid as he is. The captain's sorry about Crewman Cydon's little lapse, all right. Sorry the bastard was dumb enough to try something before he had permission.''

''Wh—what do you mean?'' she managed.

''Icarus was having a strategy session with the first mate, and he thought I couldn't understand them because they were using a local Mythos dialect that's quite a bit different from standard Greek. But it happens that I've studied it extensively.'' He swallowed. ''They're planning to turn us over to someone else as soon as they get to Mythos. Maybe Aristotle. I'm not sure about who, exactly. Cydon figured that it wouldn't matter if he—''

''Raped me?'' she asked in a strangled voice.

He closed his eyes for a moment and held on to her more tightly. ''Yes.''

She got the shakes again, and Zeke stroked her gently until she felt more in control.

''We've got to talk about it,'' Zeke finally said. ''Are you okay?''

''Yes.''

He turned so he could meet her eyes. ''The way I figure it, when the captain saw his crewman follow you, he thought the guy was just teasing you. Then when Cydon didn't come back, the captain started worrying it might be going farther than that. Whoever hired him wants us to think everything's on the up and up—until we get to Mythos. It's supposed to be a big surprise.''

Elizabeth looked toward the door, remembering the way Zeke had snapped the lock behind them. She was pretty sure the lock wouldn't hold, if the crew decided to attack. ''What are we going to do?'' she whispered.

"We have to take over the ship," he answered in a matter-of-fact voice, glancing at his watch. "In the next couple of hours. Then we'll have to check the charts and land at a port without a reception committee waiting. There are lots of good harbors along the Mythosian coast. That part won't be a problem."

The scheme sounded preposterous, yet he spoke calmly, as if he really did think they had a chance of hijacking the vessel. Her mind made a quick inventory of the rough-looking crew. She'd counted four of them, including the captain. "I assume you have a plan?" she asked, in as steady a voice as she could manage.

He ran a hand through his hair. "Well, not exactly. Give me a couple of minutes to concentrate."

Right, she thought, struggling not to start shaking again. If anybody could figure a way out of this situation, it was Zeke Chambers.

When he stirred, she raised her head questioningly.

He sat up and cast a glance toward the closed door. "First I'm going to check the hatch at the other end of the passage. If it's locked, I'll open it. Will you be okay by yourself for a few minutes?"

She gave the only right answer. "Yes."

As Zeke climbed to his feet, Elizabeth watched him carefully, trying to judge his physical condition. He'd told her he was holding his own in his battle with seasickness. Yet, as he pulled the duffel bag onto the bed, she could see the claim was relative. His skin still had an unhealthy pallor and his forehead was damp. However, she knew he wouldn't appreciate it if she asked him how he was feeling.

Her focus of attention changed as Zeke dug in the duffel and extracted something metallic from a nest of T-shirts. The gun.

She blinked. "Weren't you taking a chance bringing that into the country? We could have been stopped at customs."

"Yeah," he answered laconically. "But I think it's going

to come in handy. You hang on to it while I'm out of the cabin.''

Feeling light-headed, Elizabeth pushed herself up and braced her back against the bulkhead as Zeke handed her the weapon. She automatically wrapped her fingers around the grip.

"Nothing's going to happen while I'm gone," he said quickly, in response to her strained expression. I'll be right back. The gun is just in case.''

Zeke exited quietly. Pressing her shoulders more firmly against the wall, she trained the gun on the door in a two-handed grip. But the pitching of the boat and the quivering of her arm muscles made the position too difficult to maintain. So she lowered her arms and sat with the weapon in her lap, thinking that when Zeke had asked her to marry him, she'd had no idea what she was getting into. Yet she knew with absolute conviction that foreknowledge wouldn't have changed her decision. She still would have agreed to help him—for Ariadne, and because she loved him.

Three endless minutes ticked by. Finally, the door handle turned, and she braced her arms and raised the gun. When Zeke called her name, she relaxed again—as much as she could relax.

"I've unlocked the hatch," he reported as he stepped into the cabin. "And I took a look topside. Our friend Captain Icarus is in the wheelhouse enjoying a glass of retsina—probably to celebrate pulling the wool over our eyes.''

"A glass of what?"

"Retsina. It's a wine flavored with pine resin."

Elizabeth made a face.

"An acquired taste." He crossed to the bunk and sat down beside her. "You can give me the gun now."

"Oh, right." She handed it to him, then pressed her shoulder against his, picturing the two of them barricading themselves in this room and waiting out the rest of the trip.

Yet that fantasy only held the illusion of safety. He'd said they had to take over the ship. "Now what?"

"We've got to shift the odds in our favor. You're going to go up, the way we came down, and start talking to the captain. Speak quickly, in English, so he has trouble understanding you. Act like you're upset. Tell him that walking around and getting angry about Cydon was too much for me. I'm sicker, and you need some medicine or something."

She listened to the directions, wondering if she could pull that off.

He must have read her thoughts. "You can do it."

"I guess I have to," she agreed, marveling at the cool way the words slipped from her mouth.

"Get him to turn, so that his back is to the door of the wheelhouse. I'll come up from behind and get the drop on him. Once we've bagged him, we'll take care of the rest of the crew."

It sounded reasonable.

"I'll leave the cabin two minutes after you do," Zeke said.

He gave her a hug, and she let herself cling for a moment. Then she snatched up her windbreaker, gave Zeke a cocky grin and slipped out of the cabin.

The moment she closed the cabin door, her expression hardened into a mixture of determination and fear. Could she really follow Zeke's directions? And what would she do if she met Cydon again? To her vast relief, he didn't materialize at the top of the companionway. Perhaps the captain hadn't been lying when he'd said he would throw the man in the brig.

Rolling with the motion of the waves, she struggled toward the wheelhouse, noting that the *Amphitrite* was pitching even more than it had earlier. Any hint of blue had vanished from the sky. Spray hit her in the face, as she clutched the rail and fought the wind. It seemed that Poseidon, the god of the sea, was testing her resolve.

Maybe he didn't want her and Zeke to take over a ship named after his wife, she thought with a grim laugh.

With the boat bucking so badly, she couldn't move very quickly, and it took several minutes to make it to the wheelhouse. Peering through the door at the side of the small enclosure, she froze. Ever since she and Zeke had worked out this plan, she'd been picturing Captain Icarus at the helm. But he wasn't anywhere in sight. The man standing at the console in the center of the room was younger. It was Tyrone, the first mate.

Elizabeth gulped. Now what? She'd taken so long to get here that Zeke was probably already on his way up through the hatch.

She was standing in the doorway dithering, when the man at the wheel glanced to the side and spotted her, his face registering surprise that she'd ventured out in the wind and spray. Now that he'd seen her, she straightened her shoulders and forced a little smile. She didn't have to fake uncertainty, as she took a step forward.

He looked her up and down, as if she were a wet rat that had come crawling out of a drainpipe. Yet he kept his voice carefully neutral. "The captain advised to stay below," he said.

"I—" Elizabeth fluttered her hands in a helpless gesture, as she crossed the threshold of the wheelhouse. "You're right. I...uh...hate to cause any trouble again. I know I should be in my...my cabin, but I have a...a problem, a big problem," she said, speaking quickly, as Zeke had advised, and tripping over some of her words. "I guess you know my husband, Mr. Chambers, is feeling sick. He was lying down. Then he got up...when, uh..." She trailed off and started again. "Now he's feeling so much worse. I'm so worried, so worried. We didn't expect to travel by ship, so we're not prepared. I was wondering if you had something he could take." As she spoke, she moved toward the side of the little enclosure. To her relief and satisfaction, Tyrone turned with her, so that his back was to the door.

"Madam, you will have to speak more slowly," he said, obviously struggling to control his exasperation with this damn female passenger who was causing a variety of problems. "What are you trying to tell me about your husband?"

She gave him a wide-eyed helpless look. Let him think she was a stupid twit, she told herself. "My poor husband's sick," she repeated beseechingly. "It's so upsetting—" Her voice gave a little catch, as she spotted Zeke in back of the man, moving quickly but quietly. She willed herself not to look at him. Raising the volume of her voice and using lots of hand gestures, she continued. "He's so miserable. You must have a medical kit on board. You must have some provision for passengers who—"

Zeke was almost on him now. She increased the speed of her monologue, willing the man to keep his attention on her, willing him not to turn around.

It worked. The impassioned speech ended as Zeke stepped up behind the first mate and brought the butt of the gun down on his head. Tyrone made a low grunt and slipped to the floor. Zeke caught the man with his free hand and eased him to the deck where he lay with his eyes closed, breathing heavily.

Zeke looked down at the dark head. "It's not Icarus. Where the hell is he?"

"I don't know."

"He might be taking a break, but I don't think he'll stay away from the wheel for long." He looked thoughtful, then he handed her the gun and knelt beside the man on the floor. Grabbing Tyrone's shirt in both hands, he pulled it up and over his head. The movement was accompanied by the scent of unwashed flesh.

Elizabeth coughed, then watched as Zeke took off his own shirt before pulling on the one from the first mate. With his back to the door, he hunched over the controls and turned his face away from the door. "How do I look?"

"I guess it might work, but you're going to need a bath."

He wrinkled his nose. "Yeah. Well, that's the breaks. Give me the gun."

She started to comply, then froze as a flash of movement tickled the edge of her vision. Zeke must have registered the expression on her face, because his hands tightened on the wheel.

Speak of the devil, Elizabeth thought, as Captain Icarus stepped into view. His gaze was fixed on Zeke. "Tyrone," he called and began to speak rapidly in the dialect he'd used before. She guessed he was asking his first mate what the hell she was doing in the wheelhouse.

She and Zeke hadn't had time to work out a new plan. The best she could do was harden her face as she raised the gun. "Put your hands in the air and step inside, Captain," she requested.

Icarus's jaw went slack when he saw the weapon in her hand.

"I said, come inside," she grated.

His eyes swung rapidly from her to Zeke; then spotting the shirtless man on the floor, Icarus uttered an exclamation that could only have been a foul curse.

"The lady invited you in," Zeke grated as he turned to face the captain.

There was a moment of hesitation when Icarus must have been assessing his chances of escape—or perhaps of taking the weapon from her.

"Don't think I won't shoot," she clipped out, even as she stood there, wondering if she could pull the trigger. "You've already given me enough reason to blow your head off." She'd done it before, she reminded herself with a grimace. She'd shot Sebastian—only he'd been attacking Zeke. He hadn't been facing her with burning eyes and clenched fists.

To her profound relief, the captain raised his hands. With a small shrug, he stepped into the enclosure.

"Thank you for joining us," Zeke said. "Move over

there, please." He gestured toward the other side of the little room. "And sit down."

The captain sat. "What is the meaning of this?" he demanded, anger and fear thickening his English.

"Oh, I imagine you have a pretty good idea," Zeke clipped out, taking the gun from Elizabeth. She felt as if a two-ton weight had been lifted from her hand. With the weapon trained squarely on Icarus, he said to her, "Get the rope I left by the hatch, so I can make the captain and his mate comfortable."

JASON ZACHARIAS CAREFULLY replaced the telephone receiver in its cradle, picked it up again, then slammed it down a second time with a loud thunk. Muttering a curse, he turned away from the desk and ran exasperated fingers through his hair. He'd wanted Zeke to wait until they could hook up special communications equipment, but his friend had been in too much of a hurry to get to Mythos. The equipment had finally arrived, but there was no way to get it to Zeke. He was on his own.

Jason cursed again. He didn't like the way things were shaping up. In the past few hours he'd received two intelligence reports from Mythos that made him want to get on a plane and fly over there. Only it wouldn't do any good, he told himself. Steve and Jed had phoned in to say that they'd last seen their passengers getting into a cab and heading for a small port near Piraeus. Zeke and Elizabeth hadn't checked in after that. Probably they'd already set sail.

He glanced at the phone again, willing it to ring, but it remained silent. Unless he sent a skywriter over the Aegean Sea, the only way he was going to get a message to Zeke was when he decided to call and report his location.

Jason had to resign himself to the fact that there was no way to get in touch with them—no way to let them know that when they arrived on the island, they'd be walking into a trap.

Chapter Twelve

Captain Icarus and First Mate Tyrone sat propped against the bulkhead, their hands tied behind their backs, their feet secured at the ankles. The captain never took his malevolent gaze off Elizabeth. *If looks could kill,* she thought, *I would be at the bottom of the sea by now.* In contrast, Tyrone sat with his eyes closed, probably hoping that ignoring her would make her vanish. His grungy shirt lay beside him on the floor, where Zeke had dropped it after changing back into his own pullover.

Elizabeth stood with her hands fused to the wheel, trying to keep the *Amphitrite* on a straight course as it wallowed and bucked in the rising swells. Her arms ached from the strain of fighting the seething water. Peering through the droplet-splattered window, she kept her eye on an outcropping of rock off to her right. Were more rocks ahead of them, waiting to slam against the hull?

Zeke came back along the deck, his dark hair plastered to his head by the flying spray. A sudden jolt from the waves made him pitch forward just before he reached the wheelhouse, and Elizabeth's heart leaped into her throat as he tumbled toward the rail. Lord, the deck looked as slippery as a frozen pond in winter. Zeke recovered, however, grabbing the door frame to steady himself. He took a moment to catch his breath, his skin pale in the dim light.

Elizabeth knew the violent motion of the boat was getting to him again.

Still, his voice was strong, as he announced, "I've put one more guy out of commission." Moving close to Elizabeth, he brought his mouth to her ear. "But I haven't figured out where Icarus stowed Cydon."

She nodded, keeping her face impassive. No point in letting the captain know they were worried about anything.

Zeke clasped his hand on her shoulder. "You're doing great."

"How long until we reach port?"

Zeke shrugged and looked out the window at the waves beating the rocks. Pitching his voice so that their audience couldn't hear, he said, "Don't know. It's a good bet we've drifted off course."

"Great." She rolled her shoulders. The boat had once possessed an automatic pilot, but it had gotten broken and never been fixed.

"I'm going back to look for Cydon. After I round everybody up, we can put them off in a lifeboat."

She watched him leave, then jumped when Captain Icarus growled, "Stupid girl, keep your eyes on the rocks or we'll all end up at the bottom of the sea."

The captain was right. In the brief time she'd been distracted, the *Amphitrite* had drifted closer to the churning water where jagged rocks met sea. Yanking on the wheel, she turned the bow back toward open water.

Above the howling of the wind, she thought she heard a shout, and the hair on the back of her neck bristled.

Maybe it was nothing, she decided, until she saw the expression on Captain Icarus's face. He had heard it, too, and he was suddenly looking more hopeful.

"Zeke?" she called out.

Nobody answered, but in the next moment she heard a loud thump to her right. Then two figures appeared and came crashing to the deck, slipping and sliding on the wet boards. Her heart leaped into her throat as she saw that it was Zeke and Cydon, trading punches and wrestling with each other. And Zeke no longer had the gun.

She held back a scream that rose in her throat. The last thing Zeke needed was for her to distract him.

Icarus's eyes were bright as he craned his neck to see what was happening. Even Tyrone raised his head and shot her a triumphant look. When he and the captain exchanged glances, she understood that they had been biding their time, waiting for this moment. It seemed Icarus had been lying through his teeth when he'd said he'd confined Cydon. The man must have been on the loose all along—and the captain had been counting on him to take the ship from her and Zeke.

And he was doing a pretty good job, she judged from the progress of the fight. Zeke was too sick to do more than hold his own.

God, now what? Her hands clenched the wheel. She had helped Zeke when Sebastian had attacked him. But she couldn't do it now because she had to steer the ship. Because if she didn't, the *Amphitrite* would end up on the rocks.

A picture of the hull crashing and splintering flashed into her mind. In that moment, realization slammed into her like the boat slamming into the shoreline. Their only hope was for her to steer toward disaster.

She spared Zeke a quick look. He was still locked in mortal combat with Cydon. She murmured a little prayer—for him and for herself. Then, giving a mighty yank, she turned on the wheel, bringing the boat around in the foaming water.

Icarus felt the motion immediately. "No!" he shouted, as he looked up and saw what she was doing.

"If we can't take over the ship, nobody gets it," she screamed. "I'm steering for the rocks."

The captain cried out in anguish and strained upward, trying to see out the window, but the effort was too much and he sank back to the deck. Growling in anger, he kicked out with his legs, almost knocking her off her feet. Elizabeth stayed erect, then danced away, while keeping the boat moving in the wrong direction. "You don't have much time," she called out.

Icarus bellowed with rage. "No. Stop," he commanded. "You'll kill us all."

Above the captain's frantic shouts, Tyrone's voice rose and fell in a loud wail.

"If you want me to stop, call off Cydon now," Elizabeth demanded.

The rocks loomed. Closer. Closer. And she honestly didn't know whether she would lose her nerve.

Then Icarus's shout told her she had won. "Cydon," he bellowed. "Cydon, you've got to do something. The crazy bitch is going to sink the ship."

Cydon raised his head.

"The rocks. She's steering for the rocks," Icarus shrieked above the foaming of the water and the moan of the wind.

The man gave a mighty wrench and broke away from Zeke's grasp.

"*Yasou!*" Icarus shouted, as Cydon pounded toward the console. He raised his hand to knock her away. She ducked, and took only the edge of the blow.

Zeke pushed himself up and sprang after the hurtling figure. Grabbing him by the back of the shirt, he pulled him away from Elizabeth, then flung him against the bulkhead. Cydon went down, and Icarus let out a mighty curse.

But Elizabeth barely registered the man's anguished protest. All her attention was on the gray shapes rushing toward the wildly pitching ship. Water crashed against the window as she fought to keep her footing and yanked on the wheel with all her remaining strength, trying to wrest the *Amphitrite* away from the impending collision.

In counterpoint, the first mate kept up a stream of anguished moans, while the captain shouted orders that finally penetrated her brain.

He was saying, "Slow down, you fool. Slow down."

As the words sank in, she realized she had no idea how to control the speed.

She was aware of Zeke sucking in huge drafts of air as he reached for a set of levers. The sound of the engine changed, but they were still moving toward the rocks.

Zeke's hands came down beside hers on the wheel. She felt his muscles strain as he gave a mighty yank to port. Even with the decreased speed, the boat seemed to be hurtling through the waves toward a gray wall that encompassed the whole field of her vision. She wanted to squeeze her eyes shut. She could only stare ahead in helpless fascination, bracing herself for the bone-jarring collision.

It didn't happen that way. Zeke kept up the steady pressure on the wheel and the ship came about, avoiding total destruction at the last possible moment. Still, they were too close to escape completely unscathed.

A terrible rending noise tore at her ears as the starboard side of the ship shuddered and scraped against the boulders. The whole structure of the vessel shook with the impact, grinding against the rocks before bursting free from the barrier like a cork popping out of a bottle. The rocks slid away to starboard, and the *Amphitrite* bobbed in the waves, rounding a point of land and coming into open water.

Elizabeth blinked. As soon as they passed the end of the towering gray wall, everything altered like a motion picture cutting abruptly to a new scene. Where before the sea had been like a boiling cauldron, it was suddenly almost as calm as a mountain lake on a sunny day. The howling wind fell away to a light breeze. Even the dark clouds parted to reveal a patch of blue sky.

Dazed, Elizabeth raised her face toward Zeke's. "Are we in the same sea?" she asked in an awestruck voice.

"The Aegean can change like this," he answered, straightening. "Are you all right?" he asked, his fingers moving to press over hers.

She turned her palm up. "I think so."

"You were magnificent," he said in a thick voice.

"I—I took a crazy chance."

"It was perfect," he said.

She turned to smile at him and saw that his skin was bloodless. "Are *you* all right?"

"I'm okay. That bastard Cydon was waiting for me at the top of the forward ladder. When I climbed up, he jumped me."

As she lifted her hand to his face, he repeated, "I'm okay."

From the floor, Captain Icarus spat out a dark-sounding curse. "You damn fools. Don't you know we're taking on water?"

Zeke pushed away from Elizabeth and turned toward him. "I guess we'll have to lighten the load."

The two men exchanged a long pregnant look. Zeke broke the contact first, then knelt and used the rest of the rope to secure Cydon's hands and feet, leaving him lying facedown on the deck.

Icarus kept his eyes on Zeke, his face murderous. "You haven't won yet," he growled.

Elizabeth shuddered, but Zeke ignored the threat as he turned off the engine and drew her out of the wheelhouse where they couldn't be overheard.

"What are we going to do?" she asked, glancing toward the side of the ship where the rocks had scraped them. From the deck, she could see no sign of the collision.

"Icarus doesn't know any more than we do about the condition of the hull. He's just yanking my chain. I'm going to inspect the damage. If we're not in immediate danger of sinking, I'm going to drop a lifeboat over the side and escort Icarus and his bunch off the ship. That way we won't have to worry about them attacking us again."

When Zeke turned and strode toward the starboard side of the ship, Elizabeth followed. In the next moment, she had to stifle a gasp as he grasped the outside of the rail and bent far over the side to scrutinize the damage. Crossing to his side, she grabbed a handful of his pant leg. If he started to slip, it probably wouldn't save him, but she felt better for the contact. She held her breath until he hoisted himself back onto the deck.

"Well?"

"There are a couple of long gashes in the boards, close to the waterline, but not below, as far as I can see. Even if the waves pick up, we should be okay for a couple of hours." He strode toward the wheelhouse, and she heard him exaggerate the damage to Icarus before asking how to turn on the pumps. The man gave an answer immediately, and Zeke hurried below.

A motor cut in, as the pumps began to function. When Zeke returned to the deck, he was holding the gun he'd dropped in the struggle with Cydon. After handing it to her, he went below for the fourth crewman he'd tied up and left in one of the compartments. She marveled at his silent efficiency and his ability to keep pushing himself past his obvious fatigue and seasickness. As the captain cursed, Zeke restarted the engine and steered toward open water.

"We'll sink!" Icarus bellowed.

"I'll take the chance," Zeke replied. When he was satisfied that it would take several hours for the crew to row back to shore, he got a lifeboat into the water, then rigged a pulley to lower the captain and Cydon.

"You can't leave us tied up like this," Icarus shouted as he lay awkwardly on his side in the small boat. "We'll drift out to sea and drown."

"That would suit me fine," Zeke growled as he stared down at the man. "But I'm going to give you more of a chance than you were willing to give us."

Taking the gun from Elizabeth, he had her untie the first mate's hands before lowering him over the side. The fourth crewman followed. Then Zeke tossed the mate a knife. While he was freeing the rest of the men, Zeke untied the line and the boat drifted away.

Icarus was still shouting obscenities as Zeke started the engine and they moved rapidly away.

ZEKE MIGHT HATE TO TRAVEL by water, Elizabeth decided, but he knew his way around a ship. She had expected him to head directly for the nearest port. Instead, he prudently bypassed both of the closest fishing villages and set his course for a small port town several miles down the coast. After giving Elizabeth a quick course in reading navigational markers, he left her at the controls for thirty minutes while he searched the ship. Compared to what she'd gone through earlier, steering through the calm water was like sailing a toy boat in a bathtub.

When Zeke returned, he looked grimly pleased.

"Money's not going to be a problem," he said, as he patted his right front pants pocket before taking over the wheel again. "Icarus must have gotten a down payment from Aristotle before he left for Mythos. There were several million drachmas in a locked drawer in his cabin."

She eyed the bulge of bills in his pocket. "How do you know it was from Aristotle?"

Zeke's expression underwent a rapid change. "I—uh— found a piece of jewelry I recognized...." His voice trailed off, and he gestured vaguely with his free hand.

Elizabeth had come to know that wounded look in his eyes. It only surfaced when he was reminded of a certain other woman—the mother of his child.

"Something of Sophia's?" she asked.

"Yeah. A brooch she liked to wear. I guess Aristotle didn't want it any more." Zeke made himself very busy with navigating the ship.

As she watched the muscles bunch under his shirt, she took her lip between her teeth. He didn't volunteer anything more, and his behavior only confirmed her worst suspicions. Whatever he'd wanted her to think, his feelings for Ariadne's mother were still strong.

She began tidying up the wheelhouse, folding charts and

coiling rope that had been used to bind their prisoners. As she worked, she tried to keep her mind from spinning off in unwanted directions. But the frantic activity was only partially successful. She kept picturing the guilty look on Zeke's face when he mentioned the brooch. It was like that every time he thought about Sophia, and each time Elizabeth was reminded of how shallow a claim she herself had on her new husband. He was under a lot of stress. It had been natural for him to turn to her under the pressures of the moment. She wanted to ask if that was the reason he'd made love to her so passionately the previous night. Then she decided she didn't want to know—not if he was going to give her the wrong answer.

She looked up when she heard the sound of the engine cut to half power. They had rounded a little peninsula, and the scene had changed once more. The *Amphitrite* was entering a crescent-shaped natural harbor, guarded by a medieval-looking stone fortress on the right and the few remaining columns of a Doric temple built on a rocky promontory to the left.

"It was dedicated to Poseidon," Zeke said, when he saw her eyeing the delicate classical lines of the temple. "Insurance for the sailors of the island, so the god of the sea would keep them safe."

"I guess he was on our side today. Maybe he even brought the storm."

"It could be."

Nestled between the two arms of the harbor was a sun-drenched town of flat-topped whitewashed houses, rising in tiers above the water. Many were decorated with window boxes filled with flowers blooming brightly. *Not much like fall in Maryland,* Elizabeth mused. The setting was so achingly charming that she felt a lump form inside her chest. If only life were a little different, she and Zeke might be on their honeymoon cruise around Mythos. Just for the fun of it, they'd picked this beautiful little port at random. They were going in to town to have a bite to eat and then find a room where they could be alone together.

She glanced at him. He had picked up a pair of binoculars and was methodically studying a low stone sea wall and the beach next to it, where a number of small boats lay on the sand. *So much for romantic fantasies,* she thought. Zeke was undoubtedly making sure a friendly reception committee wasn't waiting to greet Captain Icarus and hustle away his passengers.

"We're in luck," he said, pointing to a spot where the wall gave way to a low ramp. A small ferry boat was heading toward the docking area. "We're not the only ones arriving."

Zeke cut the engine fifty yards short of the beach.

Elizabeth looked at him questioningly.

"We don't want to make anybody angry by taking their mooring, so I'll drop anchor out here and row us in."

She hadn't thought about their luggage. He'd already brought their bags from the cabin. Unlike the crew, they exited decorously down a ladder to the lowered boat. As the rowboat pulled away, she shaded her eyes and looked back at the *Amphitrite.*

"A boat that large is going to attract some notice," Zeke said. "It won't take long for word to get back to Icarus where we landed. Hopefully, by that time we'll be out of here." He drew up along the beach. Taking off his shoes, he waded through the clear, shallow water to the sand, then pulled the boat up, so she could step onto dry land.

Zeke turned and regarded the damaged ship. "Commit me to a mental institution, if I ever talk about getting on a boat again."

Before she could answer, he hurried her toward the spot where the ferry was unloading passengers. Some of the people getting off looked like local residents returning from a visit to a neighboring island. Others were clearly tourists taking advantage of the waning good weather and probably the reduced prices at the end of the season.

Zeke and Elizabeth were able to mingle with the crowd and follow along up the hill to an open plaza, where several cafés were serving drinks and afternoon snacks.

Men and small boys dispatched to meet the ferry jogged beside the tourists, hawking postcards or trying to steer the crowd toward various restaurants and shops. Zeke spoke to them in Greek, turning them away with ease. Skirting the tourist places, he stopped at a small grocery store where he bought flat loaves of bread, feta cheese, salty black olives and bottled water.

Elizabeth watched the woman behind the counter warm up to him, smiling as she provided him with information. *The old charming Zeke Chambers,* she thought. *The one I fell for in the beginning.* She knew now that he could turn on the magnetism at will, but the knowledge only made her appreciate the performance all the more. The man had been through more in the past eight hours than a character in a Greek tragedy, but you wouldn't know he had a care in the world beyond getting something to eat and finding an inexpensive place to stay.

As they emerged from the shop, he stowed the groceries in his duffel bag and pointed toward one of the narrow streets that wound its way up the hill. "There's a small bed-and-breakfast around the bend. We can get a room for the night."

The pension did indeed have a room—with a private bath, a luxury for which the proprietress demanded quite a bit extra, Elizabeth gathered. Zeke made a show of negotiating the price, probably because he knew it was expected.

Half an hour after they'd arrived in port, they locked the door to the room, which boasted a private flight of stairs leading to the stone-paved street. Elizabeth longingly eyed the comfortable-looking bed.

Zeke pulled out the groceries and set them on the old wooden table by the double-hung window. At home, it would probably be a valuable antique; here it was part of the room's ancient furnishings.

"Eat first. Then sleep."

She joined him at the table, trying to match his hunger, but after their ordeal, she was too tired to hold her eyes open. After a few bites, she crawled into the bed.

It was hours later when she woke. The room was dark, except for a narrow shaft of light coming from the bathroom. For a moment, she didn't know where she was. She quickly decided that didn't matter. The only thing of real importance was the hard male body pressed along the length of her back and the arms that curved around her body.

Zeke, hot and aroused.

She'd fallen asleep in her bra and panties. He'd unhooked the bra and pushed it out of the way. His hands cupped her breasts, his fingers playing back and forth across her nipples, already tight with desire. She'd never imagined awakening like this with the man she loved beside her, silently telling her how much he wanted her.

"You're awake," he whispered thickly, his teeth nibbling at her ear.

She tried to answer. All she managed was a little moan, as he used his thumbs and fingers to drive her wild. She longed to face him, kiss him, touch him. He held her where she was, using his tongue and teeth on her ear and his hands on the front of her body, searching out her most sensitive flesh and making her incandescent with need.

"Zeke...please..." she begged, her body writhing and pitching in his arms. He had shown her pleasure last night, but she hadn't known it could be this sharp, this urgent.

"Lizbeth. Ah, Lizbeth." He turned her then, pulling her against him, his mouth seeking and finding hers in a long, deep kiss that felt like the merging of two souls. It ended when they were both gasping for air.

"I need you," he grated. "I need you now." His body shifted over hers and she opened her legs, bringing him to her.

He surged into her, claimed her, stroked inside her with

quick, rapid movements. On their wedding night, he had been a gentle lover. This time there was no room for tenderness—only the sharp edge of urgency driving him. It was the same for her. She needed this man. Needed to know that he was hers and that she could give him what he craved.

The wild, seeking thrusts of her hips matched his. And when he stiffened in her arms and shouted out his climax, he took her with him over the edge.

His breath came in rapid gasps as he said, "Lizbeth, I'm sorry." Shifting off her, he wrapped her in his arms and buried his face against her neck.

"For what?"

"That was too fast. Too rough."

She laughed. "I think I'm up to speed."

"I didn't hurt you?" he asked, his voice low and full of self-reproach.

She smiled in the darkness and moved her cheek against his shoulder. "Hardly."

He gave a deep, shuddering sigh and held her more tightly. She turned to wedge herself against him. All she wanted was a few minutes of happiness in his arms, yet she was beginning to know him too well to relax. He still hadn't allowed her to engage him in a meaningful conversation about their future. Yet he'd been communicating on quite a different level—and what she'd sensed was an element of desperation, even loss. He'd made love to her like a man getting ready to leave on a long journey—alone.

WHEN ZEKE STIRRED, Elizabeth opened her eyes.

"I have to go out. Go back to sleep," he whispered.

"I'm not asleep." Her fingers tightened on his arm. Gently, he detached them.

Trying not to show her panic, she sat up and thrust the covers back. "I'll go with you."

He shook his head. "The less we're seen in town, the better."

"That goes for you, too," she protested.

"I have to call Jason and see what he found out, then arrange transportation and take care of some things. It's safer now, after dark. But it's better for both of us, if you stay here."

She watched him dress in trousers and a dark shirt that looked like the native attire. "When will you be back?"

"As soon as I can," he answered patiently. "You didn't eat much before, so finish the food I brought, if you like. We can go out to one of the restaurants after I get back."

She relaxed a little, when he left his luggage on the floor with hers. The gun was in his duffel. Surely he'd take the weapon if he was planning to make a run for it now. So she still had a little time to figure out what to do. "I'll take a shower while you're gone," she said, watching his face carefully.

"It's not very hot."

"I'll manage."

HE KEPT HIS GAZE on her until the last possible moment, wanting to store up every precious impression. Then with a sigh he turned and headed for the street, already planning the lies he was going to tell her when he got back.

His first stop was at the public phone booth along the side of the town's main square. He didn't love the exposed location, but there wasn't much choice. Looking at his watch, he calculated that it was pretty early in the morning back home. Still, Jason answered the priority line on the first ring.

"I'm real glad you called," he said. "Where are you?"

"A little town on the coast."

"I thought you were landing in Kalana."

"We had to do some improvising." Zeke described the difficulties they'd encountered with Captain Icarus and his crew.

"Why didn't you call as soon as you got to town?" Jason demanded.

"I needed some food and some sleep before I could hold a coherent conversation." He didn't say how much he'd also needed to make love with Elizabeth.

"Well, as long as you're holed up somewhere safe, it probably doesn't matter," Jason told him. "But there's something you need to know. You were assuming it was Sophia's husband, Aristotle, causing problems. There's another guy who's surfaced—Cyril Agnapopolis."

Zeke swore.

"You know who he is?"

"Yeah." He sucked in a breath, and let it out before answering. "Do you?"

He could hear Jason hesitating on the other end of the line. "He and your father were involved in a smuggling operation. Agnapopolis did about twenty years in prison."

"Right," Zeke conceded. Apparently in his spare time, Jason had checked into the Chamberses' family background.

"He's out now and looking for revenge—from what I heard," Jason continued.

Zeke closed his eyes, as he tried to wrap his mind around this new angle. He hadn't thought about his father's business partner in years. "Do you think he'd want to…uh…take out his anger on me?" he asked.

"Your father's dead, isn't he?"

"Yes."

"So you're all that's left."

Cyril Agnapopolis had been little more than a name to him. Now he conjured up the image of a man rotting in prison, living for the day he could get even with the foreign professor who had put him there. But when he got out he was faced with the crushing disappointment of learning his old enemy was dead.

"Do you think he's angry enough to involve your daughter in his scheme?" Jason asked.

"He could be."

"He may be responsible for sending Sebastian."

"And responsible for killing him?" Zeke asked.

"Maybe. Or the rival factions could have been fighting it out—deciding who gets you."

"What an honor," Zeke growled.

"So you'd better watch your back," Jason advised.

From his phone booth on Mythos, Zeke silently agreed. After thanking Jason for the disturbing information, he hung up and stood staring with unseeing eyes toward a shop selling T-shirts and pottery. Since Sebastian had shown up, he'd had the sense that things were slipping out of his control. Worse, he'd broken one of the cardinal rules of undercover operations. He was acting with too little information, like a blind man in a minefield. He kept stepping on the mines, somehow miraculously managing not to get blown up. Shaking himself, he looked around, as the scene before him snapped back into focus. He couldn't stand here brooding. He had things to do, and he'd better get them done.

As his footsteps echoed down the medieval streets of the old town, he thought about what had almost happened to Elizabeth on the *Amphitrite*. As soon as they'd set foot on Mythos, he'd thanked God that she was unharmed and had started planning how to get her out of the danger zone before it was too late. Then he'd begun to waver, because he couldn't stand the idea of being parted from her. But his conversation with Jason had put things back in perspective. He'd been dragging her through the minefield with him, but she wasn't coming any farther.

Chapter Thirteen

When Zeke came back, Elizabeth was sitting in bed, wearing a T-shirt and studying a guidebook about Mythos that their hostess had supplied for the room. He could see that she was trying to look at ease, although the attempt wasn't entirely successful.

"I was starting to worry," she admitted as her body uncoiled. "What took so long?"

"I went shopping." He handed her one of the packages he'd brought, anxious to watch her face as she unfolded the locally made dress he'd picked out. It was of fine cotton, decorated with several bands of embroidery. The top had a V neck and long bell-shaped sleeves.

He'd never bought a dress for a woman before, so he'd taken a long time over the choice, thinking about how the color would look next to her skin and how the material would drape over her curves. Anxiously, he waited for her reaction. When she smiled, he let out the breath he didn't know he was holding.

"It's...it's beautiful," she whispered, fingering the soft fabric and delicate embroidery.

His grin was only a little forced. "So get dressed, and we'll go out to eat."

She climbed out of bed and gave him a quick glance, before retreating into the bathroom. He'd have liked the pleasure of seeing her take off the T-shirt, but it seemed she was still too modest for that. Below the modesty, though, was a heated sensuality he'd always suspected he'd find. He'd have to—

He cut off the thought before it could fully form, realizing he was making plans for a future that probably didn't exist. A choking surge of melancholy swept over him. Clenching his fists, he forced it from his mind. For years he'd survived by controlling his emotions. Now Elizabeth was making him lose that control. But he couldn't afford the risk. Not now.

When she opened the door again, he'd schooled any hint of sorrow out of his face. He'd wanted very much to see her dressed up tonight, not in the practical travel clothes she'd brought along, and he wasn't going to spoil the evening with her.

She glanced at him shyly, then stood on tiptoes to see herself in the mirror over the chest of drawers. "How do I look?" she asked.

"Beautiful," he replied, trying to speak normally around the constriction in his throat. She had put on a little makeup. The effect took his breath away, and he gave her a warm smile.

"I wanted to blend in with the crowd. But everybody's going to be looking at you," he said in a thick voice.

She blushed becomingly. "Don't be silly."

"Stop arguing. I'm starving."

He gave her the sandals he'd also purchased. While she sat down to put them on, he reached into his pocket and touched the letter he'd written her. His detailed instructions for getting out of Mythos were going to make her angry. But he couldn't help that. Anyway, he wasn't going to be around for the explosion.

They held hands as they strolled down to the plaza, stopping to look at windows full of tableware, cloths and classical statues. When they came to restaurants, they inspected the menus posted outside.

"Not much variety in the food," Elizabeth observed, after they'd looked at several similar offerings.

"So let's go for ambience." He pointed toward a tavern where outdoor tables with decorative tile tops were arranged under a wooden arbor flowering with bougainvillea vines. Traditional bouzouki music spilled through the restaurant doorway into the cool evening air. He could relax with his wife for one evening at this place, Zeke told himself. No one had figured out they were in this town—yet.

Still, he made a quick inventory of the other patrons. Some were obviously tourists. Others looked like local residents—a good sign, he decided as he began to speak to the maître d'. His fluent Greek earned them a table at the back of the arbor, where they could watch the action but still be private.

Zeke ordered lamb souvlaki and Elizabeth decided on moussaka. As Zeke ate his salad, he kept glancing at Elizabeth, wanting to fix this evening and her loveliness in his memory.

"So how are we getting to the town where Irena's staying?" she asked, reaching across the table to touch his hand.

He managed to coolly finish chewing and swallowing a piece of green pepper. "I've arranged to drive a shipment of olive oil and olives to a dealer up there."

She tipped her head a little to one side. "Why would they hire you instead of a local driver?"

He leaned forward and lowered his voice. "They're not paying me. I'm paying them. They think I need to transport some cargo of my own to Delvina."

Her eyes widened. "You mean you bribed them?"

"Yeah. With Icarus's money."

She grinned. "Glad to hear you're putting it to good use."

Their main course arrived, and he dug into the grilled meat and vegetables with enthusiasm.

Elizabeth watched him eat. "That looks good."

"We can share."

He enjoyed the intimacy of transferring some of his dinner to her plate and taking some of hers.

"I guess you know the roads," she said after a few bites of his grilled lamb.

He laughed. "There aren't many on the island, once you get out of town. You'll like the mountain scenery," he added, knowing that he had no intention of exposing her to the scenery or anything else on Mythos besides their room.

The silent observation made him realize that a slightly uneasy feeling had been tickling the edge of his awareness.

"Is something wrong?" Elizabeth asked, setting down her fork.

"I...don't know," he said, sorry that she had picked up on his mood. Casually, he looked around. The scene hadn't changed, except that another couple had taken a table several yards away. He gave them a quick inspection. They didn't look like a threat, so he went back to his food. But as he worked his way through the dinner, he kept feeling like a column of ants was climbing the back of his neck.

His hand tightened on his fork. Glancing up quickly, he caught sight of a narrow-eyed man standing at the edge of a nearby building. Zeke didn't recognize him. But as soon as the watcher realized he'd been spotted, he faded casually back into the shadows. He could simply be enjoying the plaza, Zeke supposed, although he wouldn't bet on it.

He got out a wad of drachmas—more than the bill, and put them on the table.

Elizabeth looked at him questioningly.

"We're leaving."

"Why?"

"We may have been spotted. Stand up when I do, and stick close to me."

He hadn't wanted to frighten her, but her expression changed to alarm as she glanced in the direction he'd been looking and spotted the watcher.

"Let's go." Zeke pushed back his chair and walked rapidly to her side of the table. Grasping her arm, he ushered her out the back of the restaurant and down one of the side streets leading from the plaza. Glad he'd taken the time to familiarize himself with the layout of the town, he chose a route that led away from the bed-and-breakfast where they were staying.

The ancient pavement was uneven, and one of Elizabeth's sandals hit a spot where two stones didn't quite meet. She started to pitch forward, but Zeke held firmly to her arm, keeping her from losing her footing entirely. A little gasp escaped her lips, and Zeke wanted to stop and make sure she was all right, but he could hear the sound of footsteps following relentlessly up the narrow street. It wasn't someone out for a casual stroll. It was someone in a hurry, more than likely the man he'd spotted watching them. So he kept them moving at a fast walk.

A couple of stray cats darted in front of their path. Moments later, they met another couple strolling in the opposite direction. Zeke steered Elizabeth to the right side of the cramped lane, barely slackening his pace as they rubbed shoulders with the man on one side and the wall of a house on the other. The man muttered a rude comment to Zeke about tourists parading through the streets like they owned the town. He ignored the gibe and plowed ahead.

He heard Elizabeth's breath coming hard, knowing it was as much from fear as from exertion. "You're doing great," he whispered. "There's a turn to the left about twenty feet ahead. After that, an archway leads to a narrow passageway on the right. We'll duck in there."

She didn't spare the breath to answer, taking two steps for every one of his as they rounded the corner. For a sickening moment, he thought he'd lost his bearings and made a mistake about the archway. Then he saw the opening yawning darkly between two narrow houses.

Quickening his pace, he darted through the entrance, tugging Elizabeth with him.

"Hurry," he hissed, literally pulling her along as he strode down the black tunnel. It opened onto a paved common area ringed by several houses. At the opposite end, was a similar covered passageway leading to another narrow street. If he'd been by himself, he might have dashed down the exit tunnel, come out on the other side and disappeared into the darkness. But he knew Elizabeth couldn't run fast enough to pull off the escape.

With narrowed eyes, he made an inventory of the area, praying for some kind of hiding place. Next to one of the houses was a wooden storage shed with the door standing half open. Zeke sprinted toward it and pulled Elizabeth inside. In the split second before he swung the door shut, he saw a jumble of old furniture and stacks of milled lumber. He pushed down a wooden peg that held the door closed, then wrapped his arms around Elizabeth. She clung to him in the darkness, trying to control her breathing, but her heart was pounding hard and fast against his chest. He dipped his head, pressing his lips against her cheek. They stood like that in the darkness, holding tight to each other.

Seconds after they'd ducked into the hiding place, he heard footsteps pelting down the passageway. Someone stopped in the open area, obviously trying to figure out which way they'd gone—or if they were still here. He heard a low oath as the man circled the area, went a little way down the exit passage and then came back. He was almost on top of their hiding place.

Zeke's arms tightened around Elizabeth, ready to shove her behind him if the door opened. He could feel her trembling, as she burrowed her face into his shoulder. Ears straining, he waited—sure that in the next second the flimsy door would fly open.

Instead, the footsteps retreated several paces, stopped, then moved down the far passage. In the darkness, Elizabeth raised her head. Zeke moved ever so slightly, pressing his finger to her lips. She nodded, silently holding her position as the seconds ticked by. Though it felt like an eternity, Zeke knew it was only a few minutes.

Elizabeth tipped her face toward his. "Can we open the door?" she whispered.

"Better wait."

"Who was behind us? Did you recognize someone in the restaurant?"

"No. But I saw a man watching us from the other side of the plaza."

She might have asked another question, but since Zeke's mouth was only an inch from hers, he took the opportunity to lightly brush her lips with his. She made a small, urgent sound in her throat that drove him wild, shifting the tension in his chest to the lower part of his body.

One hand cupped the back of her head. The other hauled her closer, so he could feel her slender body pressed more firmly along the length of his. The sudden sexual awareness drove everything from his mind except the feel of her.

Her fingers kneaded his shoulders, moved to his upper arms and back again, her touch feminine and erotic.

He forgot how they came to be in this dark enclosed place, the two of them. All he knew was that her hips moved restlessly against his and her lips were soft, warm and open, silently begging him for more. He obliged, deepening the kiss, using his tongue and his teeth and his lips in all the ways he'd come to know she liked.

She had been shy in bed with him. Now she brought his hands to her breasts, muffling a cry of pleasure as his fingers slid back and forth across her nipples. It wasn't enough. The clothing separating them was intolerable. His hands dipped into the V neck of her dress, stroking the tops of her breasts. She made a frustrated whimpering sound that turned the blood in his veins molten.

He was past the point where sanity ended and madness took over. Reaching for the hem of her dress, he pulled it up, bunching it around her waist and hastily stripping off her panties so that he could touch her the way he most wanted. She was hot and wet, and the stroking touch of his fingers seemed to make her body pulse and throb.

"Zeke, I need you," she gasped.

He remembered seeing an old chair lying on its side. Praying it had four good legs, he reached down, found it and set it upright.

"Help me. Unbuckle my belt," he growled.

She did, with quick shaky jerks of her fingers. And she didn't stop until she held him hot and throbbing in her hand. Sitting in the chair, he guided her forward, so that her legs were on either side of his.

She bent her knees, bringing him inside her with a sure, swift motion that robbed them both of breath. Then she was moving frantically above and around him, her gasps of pleasure muffled against his shoulder.

Nothing so intense could last for long. The explosive climax came quickly for both of them. Then she wilted against him, her face damp, her breath ragged.

Reality slammed back into him, as he realized where they were and what kind of insane chance they'd just taken. His long, low curse made Elizabeth's head jerk up.

He sat very still, listening. Apparently no one had discovered their trysting place. No thanks to himself. He'd made, wild passionate love to her only a few hours earlier. That should have satisfied him. Instead it had only fueled his need to do it all over again, as if loving her could change reality.

"What the hell am I thinking?" he asked himself.

She made a low, amused sound. "I guess you were thinking the same thing I was."

"We'd better go. This is hardly the place or the time for fooling around."

The words sent a shudder through her. "The man... chasing us. Who was he?"

"I'm not sure. Aristotle must be looking for us." He wasn't going to worry her further, by mentioning Cyril Agnapopolis. Still, he felt her body stiffen.

"I think it's safe to say we lost the guy," he added.

She stood, allowing him to get up. Glad she couldn't see his flushed face in the darkness, he adjusted his clothing.

Elizabeth reached down, feeling for something on the floor.

"What?"

"My panties," she said in a strangled voice. "I can't just leave them here."

He made a noncommittal sound as he moved the peg and opened the door, allowing a shaft of light to illuminate the scrap of feminine attire. Snatching up the evidence, she stuffed it into the purse that had also ended up on the ground.

When she started to step out of the shed, he held her back, searching the shadows. He might be going soft in the head, but he could still check out the area. They seemed to be alone. However, he led her farther away from the harbor before doubling back to their lodging. Then he unlocked the door and surveyed the area from the top of the steps before ushering her inside.

Bolting the door behind them gave him some sense of security. But he knew they weren't totally safe. If somebody was looking for them, a chance remark by their landlady about the young couple who had rented one of her rooms could lead to discovery. Still, staying inside was probably the best insurance for tonight.

A LOUD CLATTERING SOUND sent Elizabeth bolt upright in bed. As she looked wildly around in the gray light of early dawn, she saw Zeke standing by the door of their room, the expression on his face registering surprise. She was a bit surprised, too, since she hadn't been prepared for quite so much noise.

He dropped his duffel bag and stooped to pick up a drinking glass, fork and spoon that had clattered to the tile floor. "What the hell is this?"

She sat up in bed and stretched luxuriously, pretending

she wasn't fighting tension in every muscle. "Oh that? You just set off my alarm system."

"For what?"

"I think it's obvious. You were planning to skip out on me, weren't you?"

He strode across the few feet separating them and stood with his hands on his hips. "That's right. You can't go any farther with me."

"The hell I can't." She summoned her roughest language and matched his belligerent tone, although her stomach was tying itself in knots. "Were you going to let me wake up in a panic, when I realized you weren't here?" she asked in a low voice.

His gaze flicked to the table by the window. "I left you a note. And some money. It's only by sheer luck that you're still alive after the past few days you've spent with me."

"Not luck. Your excellent secret-agent skills," she said with sincerity.

"I missed your little trap," he ground out, gesturing toward the tableware on the floor.

"You weren't looking for any threats inside the room. You were focused on getting away."

"Right. I have to collect a shipment of olives and deliver them to Delvia."

As if the matter of who was going along had been settled, she climbed out of bed. Circling around him, she silently picked up the items in front of the door before turning back to him. "Give me a couple of minutes to get ready."

"You're not going."

"Nothing's changed," she said. "You said you needed me. You still do."

"It's getting more dangerous every minute. I thought bringing home my illegitimate daughter was a private matter. It looks like half the people on the island know I'm here. We can't even go out to dinner without being spotted."

"You warned me Aristotle's agents might be looking for us."

"It will confuse them if we split up," he tried. "You can charter a plane back to Athens and wait for us."

She knew darn well that the suggestion was only a ploy. "You said it was difficult to get a plane."

"It's easier from this end."

She raised her chin. "Zeke, we're wasting time. I'm not going to leave you in the middle of a crisis. You need me, and so does Ariadne. You're a stranger. She may be terrified to leave with you. But I'll know what to say to her. If she has me, she'll feel more secure."

Using his daughter's name got his attention, as she'd known it would. She saw him consider her logic, saw him waver.

"You know I'm right," she said in a firm voice.

"Maybe. But I still don't like it."

To hide the victorious look on her face, she turned away and reached for the envelope on the table. He grabbed it out of her hand before she could open it.

"I'd like to read it," she said.

"I'd rather you didn't." His expression was guarded.

What had he said in the note that he didn't want her to see, she wondered. Had he broken down and told her he loved her? Or had he said things he knew would devastate her? From the way he'd made love to her, she'd thought he'd admitted his feelings. Now she wanted to hear him say the words every woman wants to hear from the man she loves. Yet what if she were totally misreading him? What if she pushed him into a corner, and he said that there was still no future for the two of them? She didn't think she could cope with that. More important, she wasn't sure she could keep functioning in this dangerous arena, if she knew for sure that they were splitting up as soon as they got home.

"You'd better get dressed if you want to come along," he said gruffly.

"Right." She glanced toward the bathroom. "Give me your word you won't slip out when I close the door." At least she had to hear that much from him.

He sighed deeply. "I give you my word. I'll be here."

IRENA PRESSED A HAND over the little girl's mouth, lest she cry out and give them away.

"Wake up, little lamb."

Ariadne's eyes drifted open, and she stared at her aunt.

"We have to leave."

The little girl blinked. "So early?"

"We're going on a long trip."

When Irena pulled back the covers, the child shivered in the cool morning air. "Let's get dressed," Irena said, pulling the nightgown over the little girl's head and reaching for the sweater and slacks she'd selected.

"I'm hungry," Ariadne announced when she was dressed.

"I know. And I've packed some food for us. Some oranges and some cookies. We'll eat on the bus."

"I don't want to leave here. I don't like to ride on the bus," the child objected.

"We're going to a nice place."

"You said we could stay here."

"Stop arguing with me," Irena demanded, her own fear making her voice impatient. "We have to leave, and that's the end of it."

Ariadne's eyes filled with tears, and Irena drew her quickly into her embrace, hugging her tightly. "I'm sorry if I sound gruff," she said in a low voice. "I'm worried about getting to the bus on time. If we don't catch the early one, we won't get out of town for hours."

Ariadne nodded.

"We're going to go very quietly, so we don't wake anyone up."

Clutching the suitcase in one hand and Ariadne's little palm in the other, Irena led the way down the hall. They were almost to the courtyard when a door opened and a tall figure stepped out. It was too dark to see the gray hair and grizzled face. But she knew who it was.

Cyril Agnapopolis. She'd thought he was a perfect solution to her problem, and when he'd come into her room that first time and made love to her, it had been good, better than it had ever been with her deceased husband. She gave herself shamelessly to him after that, and she began to think she and Cyril might remain together. Then she saw the fax he'd left on his desk and realized he was only using her to trap Zeke Chambers. Her little world crumbled, yet she was forced to pretend everything was all right. She thought she'd fooled him. Now she was suddenly unsure.

"What are you doing?" he asked, his voice calm but sharp edged like a dagger.

"I—" She used up all the breath in her lungs before she could answer.

He lifted the shabby suitcase from her hand and set it on the floor. "You were so happy when I offered you a place to stay. Are you tired of my hospitality?" he asked.

Unable to speak, Irena shook her head.

He smiled at her, a smile as cold as his eyes. "We've had some good times together, you and I."

She cringed, as she heard the words. She'd thought their lovemaking had meant more to both of them.

He moved to Ariadne's side and tousled her dark hair. "You've had a good time staying with me, haven't you, little one?"

The child stood stiffly.

"Go back to your room," Cyril said to the little girl.

Ariadne glanced at her aunt.

"It's all right."

"But you said we were leaving."

"Go!" Irena croaked, and the child scurried away, her head bowed and her shoulders stiff.

She was left facing Cyril. Rigidly she stood in front of him.

"Why were you sneaking away?" he growled.

She shrugged. "I thought it would be safer for the child somewhere else."

He laughed, an ugly sound. "You're right, of course."

She turned her face beseechingly toward his. "Please, Cyril, I thought you felt something for me."

"I do," he said in a rough voice. "More than I expected I could feel."

She gathered her courage. "You and I could be happy together."

"I've given up on happiness."

"No—"

His eyes bore into hers. "When did you figure out I was using you?"

Why lie, she thought. "I saw a fax…"

"You should have stayed out of my office," he growled. "I thought you knew a woman's place."

"Please let us go. We haven't done anything to hurt you."

"I'm sorry, my dear." He sighed. "I can't do that. Chambers is already in Mythos. He should be here soon—to rescue his little girl, the child he never claimed before. He'll come here as soon as he figures out where I'm holding Ariadne."

Irena sucked in a strangled breath and forced herself to ask the question that had been nagging at her. "What did he do to you that you've taken so much time and effort to bring him to you?"

"Nothing. It was his father who made sure I went to jail for the crimes he committed. But the father's dead. So I must take my revenge on the son."

"Please don't destroy your life."

"Chambers's father already did that!"

"At least let me keep Ariadne safe."

He cupped his hand around her shoulder, the bony fingers pressing into her flesh. "When you and the little girl have played your part in luring Chambers here, I'll consider what to do with you.''

His rough touch made her tremble. They were alone in the darkened hall. Yet he bent down, and he brought his lips close to her ear, speaking so that only she could hear. "If you don't cooperate, I will be forced to do some very unfortunate things to the little girl. She's so sweet. It would be a shame to punish her for being born, don't you think? That would bring me down to Aristotle's level.''

Irena cringed away from him.

"Answer me!'' he demanded, the sticklike fingers anchoring her to reality.

She swallowed hard. "I'll help you,'' she promised, silently praying that she'd get another chance to take the child and run.

In the next moment, he dashed her hopes. "And I think we'd better make sure you don't try to sneak away. I picked this villa for a reason. There's a wine cellar in the basement—with a nice sturdy door and a stout lock.''

Chapter Fourteen

As Zeke led Elizabeth through the quiet streets, he was watchful and alert for signs that they were being followed. Although none of the people out and about at this early hour seemed interested in their presence, she didn't relax until they reached their destination. It was a warehouse on the edge of town, which looked like it could have been in use since Roman times. Several men were finishing loading plastic drums and buckets into a small truck. The vehicle was different from anything on the roads at home. The design was pretty much like an American van, but the rectangular storage area in back was both longer and wider. There were two seats in the front. Behind them, the cargo area was crammed with drums and covered buckets stacked in double rows, with barely room enough to squeeze between them.

"I thought you were coming alone," the foreman said to Zeke.

He shrugged. "My girlfriend won't be any trouble."

After a bit of persuasion and some more cash on Zeke's part, the man agreed to let her ride along.

After they'd pulled away, Zeke turned to her. "Can you handle one of these things?" he asked.

She watched him shift from first into second. "It's kind of like the truck on my uncle's farm, when we went there in the summers."

"Good."

"Aren't you going to drive?" she asked in a puzzled voice.

"I am planning on it." He looked down at his hands, which were wrapped around the wheel. "But every time I think I have things under control, something unexpected happens."

"What do you think could go wrong?" she asked, her voice coming out too high.

He shrugged. "I wish I could give you a good answer. About the only sure thing is that Sebastian isn't coming back from the dead."

Elizabeth felt her chest tighten, yet she responded with a weak smile. Zeke had planned on leaving her behind, and she'd insisted on coming. Now she didn't have the right to make things worse for him by acting frightened. Still, when he shifted into low gear and pulled onto the shoulder, she looked up nervously. "What are you doing?"

"Let's switch for a minute."

After he set the emergency brake and cut the engine, Elizabeth moved into the driver's seat and fumbled for the lever that adjusted the distance of the seat from the wheel. It took a moment to find it, but once she did, she was able to reach the clutch.

Zeke climbed into the passenger seat, watching closely as she put the transmission in first gear and started to move forward. When the truck bucked and stalled, she muttered an unladylike curse.

Concentrating on getting it right, she started all over again. This time the old skills came back to her more quickly.

Zeke didn't let her quit until she'd shifted through the four gears and taken the vehicle up to fifty miles an hour, which wasn't so bad on the four-lane road leading out of town.

"Okay," he finally said. "It looks like you can handle it. Pull over and we'll switch back."

The whole exercise had made her so nervous that whe
she started to climb out, she realized she'd forgotten to s
the emergency brake.

At least Zeke made no comment as he jerked the leve
up.

A minute later, they were on their way again. Only nov
she was too tense to sit back in her seat and relax.

The four-lane highway quickly narrowed into a two-lan
road as they started into the mountains. The surface wa
only in moderate repair, which made the vehicle bounce
and Elizabeth wondered how she'd do if she had to driv
up here. But there was no reason that was going to happer
she assured herself, as she ordered her muscles to loose
up. It was a beautiful, sunny day with mild temperatures
And she might as well enjoy the ride. As she stared at th
rugged mountains and blue water, she tried to return to th
fantasy that she and Zeke were on a pleasure trip.

But the ploy wasn't very successful. Zeke sat with hi
hands firmly on the wheel and his eyes on the road, as i
he were alone in the truck.

Elizabeth wanted to lay her hand on his arm and ask hir
to talk to her. It didn't have to be anything personal. Mayb
he'd even tell her about a movie he'd liked. Or a book. Ye
she was very conscious of having strong-armed her way o
this expedition. Small talk might distract her, but it wasn'
Zeke's style. So she kept her mouth shut and watched th
scenery. The vegetation was sparse, the ground rocky, an
she wondered if there were any cash crops on the islan
besides olives.

There were no other cars on the road, which woun
steadily upward. When she craned her head back, she ha
a spectacular view of the town and the harbor.

Soon they left the coast. As the narrow highway turne
inland, she spotted another one of the miniature building
she kept seeing along the shoulder. When they rounded
steep curve, she saw two more of the curiosities. They wer
a bit like dollhouses supported on three-foot legs, with glas

panels on the front and sides through which she could see various objects such as candles and pictures. The first one coming up was quite ornamental, with an elaborate peaked roofline. The second was old and weathered, with the glass on one side cracked.

"What are those?" she asked, pointing as they drew near.

"Shrines," Zeke answered. "When someone dies in an automobile accident, the family puts up a memorial at the spot where it happened."

Elizabeth swiveled backward to catch a better view of the ones they'd just passed—and the long downward slope where she could now see the remains of a rusted car. When she turned, she was facing another monument. "There must be a lot of accidents around here."

"Well, they're not big on guardrails," Zeke observed. "A lot of cars go over the edge."

He wasn't helping her nerves. Maybe he was unconsciously trying to make her sorry she'd come along. She found she was watching for the shrines, trying to judge the relative safety of each stretch of the twisting road.

She was looking over her shoulder at another death spot, when she heard Zeke make a sharp exclamation. Jerking forward, she saw that someone had dragged a wooden barrier across the pavement. A sign in Greek said, Road Closed.

Zeke began to slow down. "Now what?" he asked.

The apprehensive feeling that had been building all morning intensified as she looked from the roadblock to the hills. Although this seemed just like any other patch of what passed for an expressway between the coast and Dubina, something didn't feel right.

As the truck approached the roadblock, a man with a red flag stepped from around the bend. He was wearing a plaid shirt, jeans, sunglasses and a yellow hard hat that hid the top part of his face. Something about the cocky way he stood made her pay particular attention to him. As they

drew closer, she struggled to take in more details and saw
that he had a large ring on the hand holding the flag. A big
ugly ring, with a skull instead of a stone.

Elizabeth sucked in a sharp breath. That ring had burned
itself into her brain. It belonged to Cydon, the man who
had attacked her on the ship. The skull had scraped her
hand when she had tried to fend him off.

"No," she shouted. "Zeke, don't stop. It's Cydon. It's
a trap."

They were close enough now, so that she could even see
the scar on his cheek.

"Cydon!" Zeke spat out the name as he stepped on the
accelerator, aiming for the man with the flag. He jumped
back when Zeke swerved onto the shoulder, the truck's
fender taking off the left edge of the wooden barrier as the
vehicle sped past. Elizabeth looked back, watching Cydon
wave his clenched fist as the truck whipped sharply around
the curve.

Zeke's exclamation brought her facing front again. Three
more men were hidden around the bend. She couldn't hold
back a gasp as she recognized Captain Icarus, Tyrone and
the other crewman waiting expectantly by the side of an
old Chevy. Apparently they'd reached land safely and lost
no time making plans. Maybe the man who was following
her and Zeke last night had been working for *them*.

Zeke cursed, as he accelerated dangerously on the winding mountain road. As they whipped past, Icarus's face contorted, and he shouted something she was glad she couldn't
hear.

Twisting in her seat, Elizabeth saw Cydon sprinting
around the bend. When he reached the others, all four men
jumped into the Chevy. It was pointed in the wrong direction, probably because the captain had been confident that
the ruse would work.

Zeke skidded around another curve on two wheels,
blocking her view.

How long would it take the men from the *Amphitrite* to

turn the car around and come after them? She glanced frantically toward either side of the road, hoping for somewhere to hide—the way they'd done last night. But there were no side streets this high up in the mountains, and nowhere a truck could forge across the rocky terrain. The highway twisted through the mountains, with a sheer drop on one side and a cliff rising on the other. The shoulder was dotted with periodic shrines to remind Elizabeth that others had lost their lives along this route. Presumably nobody had been trying to outrun a bunch of murderous pirates.

With nowhere to go but forward, Zeke kept his foot to the floor. Still, she could hear the roar of an engine behind them. Icarus rounded a curve. He was gaining on them. Probably it was easier to drive the old Chevy on these roads than a truck full of cargo.

"What are we going to do?" she gasped.

Zeke kept driving, putting another curve between himself and the pursuers. "Got to stop them before they catch us," he growled. "Get ready for me to slam on the brakes. I'm climbing in the back. You scoot into the driver's seat and get going like sixty again."

Elizabeth opened her mouth to protest. She hadn't been all that good with the truck on a straight four-lane highway. Now Zeke was asking her to drive as fast as she could on this twisting mountain road. Yet she kept the protest locked in her throat. She'd rather go over the side of the cliff, than have Icarus and his gang catch them.

Zeke brought the truck to a bouncing halt and yanked up the brake. For an instant he turned toward Elizabeth, and the anguished expression on his face stole the breath from her lungs. At least he didn't say, "I told you so." Then he wormed his way between the bucket seats into the back of the vehicle. Elizabeth bounced behind the wheel, pulled the seat forward and stepped on the accelerator.

The truck made a grinding sound.

"Emergency brake," Zeke shouted.

She felt for the release as she glanced in the mirror. They

probably hadn't been stopped for more than a few seconds, but she could see the Chevy filling her whole field of vision.

Thank God, Zeke had made her practice. Her lip clamped between her teeth, she shoved the transmission into first and jolted forward.

More carefully, she shifted into second, her hands gripping the wheel as she negotiated the hairpin turns. Her heart leaped into her throat as she came around a corner and saw a sheer drop right in front of her. With a little moan, she yanked to the right and kept going, scraping the paint off the side as she veered against the rock. Probably Icarus and his men got a charge out of that. Probably they were waiting for her to mess up.

Behind her, Zeke was rattling cans of oil and buckets of olives. Sparing a glance in the mirror, she saw he'd opened the door. Wind whipped at his hair and clothing, threatening to tear him from the vehicle. Somehow, she kept herself from screaming as she plowed onward.

Zeke had already opened several of the containers. First, he dumped two tubs of olives onto the pavement. Then, he began pouring olive oil out the back door—making a mess of the road in back of them.

The truck gave a sudden jolt as it hit a pothole, almost sending him through the door again. Elizabeth gripped the wheel and tried to drive more steadily, but it was hard for her to manage such a large vehicle. With the poor condition of the road, the best she could do was keep the truck on the blacktop. In the rearview mirror, the Chevy loomed behind her, so close that she could see the murderous expression on Icarus's face. She and Zeke had stolen his ship. Now it seemed he would take any risk to get even.

As she watched, the Chevy skidded to the right, coming dangerously close to the drop off. She wanted to cheer. But the car didn't slow down.

In the next second, a series of loud reports made her gasp, and she realized with a sinking feeling that the noise had been gunshots. She wanted to shout at Zeke to close the door and come back into the front. If he was driving, maybe they could outrun Icarus now. But she told herself that he must know what he was doing. So she kept her mouth shut, and Zeke stayed where he was, tipping over buckets, spilling more and more olives and oil onto the twisting mountain road.

Elizabeth wanted to keep her eyes glued to him, but she was going to get them both killed if she didn't watch where she was going. So she kept her gaze forward, risking quick glances at Zeke. She had only taken her eyes from the road for a few seconds when the grade took a sudden downward turn, and she found herself heading straight toward a cluster of shrines.

Frantically, she hit the brake as she pulled the truck toward the right. Still, the left front tire left the pavement and began to bump along the shoulder, throwing the vehicle dangerously out of balance. All she could do was keep yanking on the wheel, sure that they were going to go over the side and plunge onto the rocks below. But at the last moment, she brought the truck back onto the pavement and continued her wild dash for freedom.

She had started to breathe out a sigh of relief when more shots sounded. Closer. Oh Lord, if Icarus and his crew couldn't drive her and Zeke off the road, they were going to riddle them with bullets.

She heard a loud exclamation from Zeke, and the air froze in her lungs.

He's been hit! He must have been hit. That was all she could think.

"Zeke!" she screamed.

"I'm okay," he called back, and she felt an enormous weight lift from her chest.

By force of will, she kept her foot on the accelerator and her eyes on the road. The last time she'd looked away they'd almost plunged over the edge of the cliff. She couldn't stop. She could only keep going and pray.

Zeke shouted in triumph.

In the mirror, she saw him raise one hand in victory. Daring to slow down, she watched the Chevy skid to the shoulder in what seemed like slow motion. Icarus spun the wheel frantically, but the car kept sliding inexorably toward the side of the road before leaving the pavement, skidding across the gravel and plunging over the edge. For several seconds, the world seemed frozen in silence. Then from far below, she heard the sound of an explosion. Seconds later, black smoke rose above the edge of the cliff.

With a sense of unreality, Elizabeth brought the truck to a bouncing stop. Her hand was shaking as she set the emergency brake with a jerk, thinking that she wouldn't want to roll over the edge, now that they'd dodged a hail of bullets and avoided being driven into the ravine.

As she sat behind the wheel sucking in drafts of air, Zeke enfolded her in his arms and she twisted around in her seat so she could hold on to him. Neither of them moved while they caught their breath.

"You did great," he said in a rough voice, leaning forward to press his cheek against the top of her head.

She held him tighter and moved her face against his. Now that the death ride was over, she felt giddy. "So did they teach you that trick with the olive oil in spy school?" she asked.

He gave a sharp laugh that made her raise her face toward him. His expression was bemused. "No. I remembered a scene in an old Walter Matthau movie. He was an ex-CIA agent getting revenge on his jerk of a boss. And he escaped from an FBI ambush the boss set up, by emptying a couple of barrels of crude oil from the back of his truck onto the road. The pursuers slid off into oblivion. Thank God, it worked with cooking oil."

Elizabeth made a sputtering sound. "You staked our lives on a scene from a movie?"

"Did you have a better idea?"

"No."

He kept his arms around her, and she heard him suck in a ragged breath. "It was a good trick, but I couldn't have done it without you," he finally said. "If you hadn't been here to drive the truck, they would have gotten me. Or I would have gone off the cliff trying to get away."

She was struck dumb—but only for a moment. "Are you admitting it would have been a mistake to leave me in town?" she asked.

"Yes," he said in a gravelly voice.

It was another perfect opportunity to say, I told you so. But she didn't. Instead, she squeezed his arm and leaned into his embrace.

He clasped her tightly, as if he had no intention of ever turning her loose. But finally he sighed and straightened. "We'd better put up a warning sign at both ends of this mess. I wouldn't want an innocent bystander going over the side on my account."

The thought sent a shiver though her as she relived the image of the Chevy skidding off the road and plunging down the cliff. "Icarus was—"

"A ruthless bastard who would have driven us over the edge if he could." Zeke finished her sentence.

While she thought about that, Zeke took out two of the barrels that were still full of olives and set them in the middle of the pavement, along with a red cloth he found in the glove compartment. Then he slowly drove back the way they'd come, repeating the process.

"Do you think Icarus and his men were out for revenge?" she asked. "Is that why they came after us?"

Zeke considered the questions. "The motive could have been revenge. Or they might have been sent to round us up, and when we didn't stop at the roadblock, they figured it was better to report that we drove over the side of the cliff than that we got away."

Elizabeth winced.

"I'm still wondering how everything fits together," Zeke

continued. "Every time we turn around, somebody knows just where to look for us."

She was working on that, when Zeke muttered a low curse.

"What?"

He shook his head in exasperation. "I guess we'll have to start dodging the guy who's expecting the shipment of olives. I don't have enough money with me to pay him for the cargo. I'll have to wire some."

"That's the least of our worries."

"It's trivial to us. For him, it's probably a good chunk of his year's income. He'll be cursing the day I walked into that warehouse and bribed his foreman to let me drive the cargo."

"You'll make it right when you can." Scooting to the left, she leaned her head against Zeke's shoulder. He had plenty of problems of his own, but he still had regrets about involving an innocent bystander.

They rounded a curve, and she could see a mountain village spread out below them. The houses were white, like the ones in town where they'd spent the night. But most of these had gabled red tile roofs instead of flat white ones. Zeke slowed, as they started down the grade. Before reaching town, they came to a place where a dirt track angled toward the left, following the course of a little stream. Zeke turned off the main road.

The stream hugged one side of the rutted lane. Boulders and clumps of bamboo pressed in along both sides, narrowing the passage so that it was barely wide enough for the truck. They bounced along for several hundred teeth-rattling feet, until they were hidden by a substantial outcropping of rock. Then Zeke cut the engine.

In the sudden quiet, it seemed to Elizabeth that she heard the sound of another vehicle being switched off.

"Did you hear something?"

"What?"

She shrugged. "Another car?"

He pulled at his ear. "No. But then I was pretty close to those gunshots. I'm not hearing perfectly at the moment."

She strained her ears, realizing her hearing wasn't up to par, either. "I guess it was an echo from the truck. Where are we?" she asked Zeke, as she looked around at the barren landscape.

"A prudent distance from town."

When he opened the door and climbed out, she followed. They were in a little clearing several hundred feet above the village—an excellent place to look down on the main square and some of the narrow streets. It must be market day. A row of stalls lined one side of the square, and women with baskets over their arms were haggling with vendors selling a variety of fruits and vegetables, as well as livestock still on the hoof.

Shading his eyes, Zeke stared at the scene below them. "I'm going to find out the address of the house where Irena was staying," he said. "It's on the outskirts of town, from what Jason could tell me. As soon as I establish the location, I'll come back and get you."

"Okay," she whispered, feeling a bit uncertain as they stood facing each other. Then Zeke closed the distance between them and folded her close. She felt a tremor go through him. "I'm glad you're here," he said in a thick voice. "And not only because you drove the truck. I'm glad you were willing to come on this expedition with me."

A strange, joyful feeling unfurled inside her. "It means a lot to hear you say that," she whispered.

"You and I have to talk. But we can't do it here or now."

She swallowed and raised her eyes to his, wishing he'd given her a hint of what he wanted to discuss.

His hold on her tightened. "I still don't think I'm doing you any favors at the moment."

"Let me be the judge of that."

He gave a short, hollow laugh. "You may change your

mind, when you hear the rest of it. Maybe it's not fair, but I want you to promise me something," he added, in a raspy whisper.

She braced herself. "Anything."

He was silent for several heartbeats. "Things keep happening. I could run into trouble. If something goes wrong...will you do your best to get Ariadne back home?"

She felt her throat clog. "We got away from Icarus. What else can happen?"

He shrugged. "I've given up trying to make predictions. But I'll feel better, if I hear your promise."

"I'll get Ariadne home," she agreed, silently telling herself that she was only saying it to relieve his mind.

Suddenly, another voice joined the conversation. "I'm afraid that's going to be impossible."

They both whirled. Elizabeth caught a flash of movement and saw a man step into the small clearing. He was slender and of medium height, with dark hair and dark eyes. She recognized him. It was the man who had found them in the restaurant and followed them through the streets last night. Now he was holding a gun—leveled at the center of her chest.

Chapter Fifteen

Beside her, Zeke went rigid. "Who the hell are you?" he challenged.

The newcomer gave a harsh little laugh. "It doesn't matter."

"It does to me," Zeke countered.

"If you insist on a name, you can call me John Smith."

"Sure." Zeke turned one palm up. "Okay, Mr. Smith, I'll pay you to leave my wife out of this. It's me you want."

"I'm already being paid. I doubt you can match the offer."

"Try me."

"No! We're wasting time."

Elizabeth saw fear in the man's eyes. Maybe he'd been afraid he'd end up like Sebastian.

"Who are you working for?" Zeke demanded.

The newcomer gave Zeke a parody of a smile. "You'll be meeting the gentleman soon enough," he said in an offhand way, yet he wasn't fooling Elizabeth.

"You were following us," she accused.

"When I lost you last night, I waited for you on the road. Glad you got away from those murderous sailors."

As she made a strangled sound, his eyes narrowed. "No more talking!"

He pulled a pair of handcuffs from his belt. "I'm going to toss these near your feet," he said to Elizabeth. "You

pick them up and put them on your husband. If you try
anything funny, I'll shoot you. You're expendable.''

A sick feeling churned inside her, as the handcuffs
bounced to the ground, clanking when they hit a small rock.
She shot a glance at Zeke, silently asking for guidance.
''Better do it,'' he growled.

Kneeling, she reached for the cuffs. In her imagination,
she had expected the metal to feel cold and clammy. Somehow it was worse to discover they were warm—from Mr.
Smith's body heat, she thought with a little shudder, as she
clenched her fingers around one of the rings. Shaking off
the dust, she turned toward Zeke. His face was set in a
rigid mask, which he probably thought was hiding his emotions. But she could see the anger below the controlled
surface, and she felt her heart squeeze. He had set out on
a rescue mission, and he had doggedly pursued that goal,
even when enemies had popped up at every turn to thwart
him. He was so close to success, yet it looked as if he had
run out of options.

He held out his hands, palms down, but the agony in his
eyes made Elizabeth's stomach knot. She stood rigid, trying
not to let her hands shake.

''Do it!'' Smith ordered. ''Or I'll shoot your arse and do
it myself.''

''Don't mess with him,'' Zeke whispered.

Teeth clamped to keep herself from screaming, Elizabeth
took a step forward, slid the cuffs around his wrists and
clicked them into place.

''Move away,'' the man with the gun ordered. ''Hurry.''

Elizabeth scrambled to obey, watching as Mr. Smith
strode forward, a look of relief and satisfaction on his face.
He must be feeling confident now, she judged, because his
total concentration was on Zeke. She had only seconds to
think about her next move. As the man turned his back on
her, she edged away, then made a sudden shift to the right,
putting a strategically situated boulder between herself and
the clearing.

Behind her, she heard feet scuffle, then the sound of a shot. The explosion was so close it made her ears ring, but the bullet only bounced off the rock.

Trying to be both fast and silent, Elizabeth turned and ran, taking a twisting path through the outcropping of rock and clumps of bamboo.

"You stupid cow! Come back," Smith shouted. "I've got the gun pointed at your husband's head. Come back or I'll put a bullet in his brain."

Elizabeth froze in midstride.

"You've got three seconds to get back here!"

Fighting sick fear, she pivoted and took a quick step in the direction from which she'd come. To her astonishment, she heard Zeke's voice, loud and strong. "Elizabeth, stay where you are. He's lying. He won't shoot me. He's gone to too much trouble to take me alive."

Smith dropped the English accent, snarling something guttural in Greek. "Come back!" he ordered again.

"No!" Zeke shouted. The order was followed by a thump and a groan.

Elizabeth's heart skipped a beat, then pounded against her ribs. Ears ringing, she scrunched down behind a clump of bamboo at the edge of the stream. It took every scrap of willpower she possessed to keep from shouting Zeke's name and giving away her hiding place—or from rushing back to the clearing to assure herself he was all right. Somehow she made herself stay hidden in the bamboo.

Agonizing seconds passed. The gunman cursed again. Nothing else happened for what seemed like an eternity. Then she heard several gruff orders issued in Greek, perhaps so she couldn't figure out what was being said. Her ears were still ringing from the gunshot, but by listening intently, she made out the sound of two sets of footsteps.

Not being able to see the action almost drove her crazy. She tried to follow Zeke and the other man's progress down the narrow road, but she lost track of them after a few moments. The next sound she heard was the opening and closing of a car door. An engine started but it was not the truck.

The other car! She remembered thinking she'd heard someone else stop on the road right after they did. But she convinced herself she was only imagining things.

As wheels spun and gravel crunched, she pictured the car backing up and turning around somewhere on the narrow track. Then silence descended, and she was alone. Elizabeth stayed where she was for half an hour. When it seemed no one was looking for her—or more properly when she couldn't stand hiding any longer—she made her way cautiously down the path toward the clearing. The truck was where they'd left it, with the keys still dangling from the ignition.

THE CAR STOPPED OUTSIDE a spacious white villa, isolated from the other houses in town and sited to command a panoramic view of the rugged mountains.

Zeke had little time to enjoy the vista, however, as he was quickly ushered inside and led into a sparsely furnished reception area. Moments later, a man with iron gray hair and a grizzled face strode in. He stood regarding Zeke with a look of deep satisfaction, before speaking.

"I am Cyril Agnapopolis. And you must be Zeke Chambers. It's good to finally meet you," he said, as if he were greeting an honored guest. He had been Zeke's father's partner in stealing and selling ancient artifacts from Mythos, but he and Zeke were meeting for the first time.

The pretense at hospitality ended when Agnapopolis pointed toward a heavy straight-back chair, and Mr. Smith pushed Zeke into the seat. He winced, fighting the throbbing inside his skull. The pain was the result of a swift blow to the back of his head—a punishment from Mr. Smith, for shouting to Elizabeth. His hands were still cuffed, and he landed with an ungraceful thud that emphasized his present situation. But at least Elizabeth had been smart enough to get away, he thought. Silently, he thanked God for small favors.

While he tried to look dignified, Agnapopolis settled himself smoothly into a well-padded desk chair. The gentle Mr. Smith stayed by the door with the gun at the ready. Agnapopolis paid him as much attention as a cheap copy of the *Winged Victory*.

Zeke studied his captor. He might look old, but he moved with the vigor of a man who had kept his lean, wiry body in shape.

"I went to a lot of trouble to get you to Mythos," he said with a satisfied smirk that deepened the lines around his mouth.

"I thought Sophia's husband, Aristotle, had that honor," Zeke answered, keeping his voice easy.

The old man smiled his cold smile. "They were a mismatched couple, don't you think? But he and Sophia might well have lived out a normal lifespan together, if I hadn't whispered a few words in his ear about her past—and yours."

Zeke tried to remain impassive, but he knew from Agnapopolis's pleased expression that his own face had betrayed his surprise. The realization made him reconsider the wisdom of remaining stoic. It might be more productive to exaggerate his reactions and let the old man feed off them.

"What do you know about me?" he asked, making his voice slightly querulous as he shifted his hands, pretending he was bothered by the handcuffs. Actually, it wasn't all that much of a pretense.

"Everything," Agnapopolis answered. "I've had private detectives dig up every scrap of available information about you."

Zeke doubted the revelations had been as extensive as the old man thought. His government work was classified. But he continued with his defensive demeanor. "Why?"

Agnapopolis's dark eyes bored into him. "I'll answer

that question when I'm ready. There are other things I war
you to know first.''

So the old man had been anticipating this interview, Zek
thought. He'd been playing it out in his mind, and he wasn
going to sacrifice a second of his enjoyment. Good.

Agnapopolis stood, and began to pace back and fort
across the marble floor. ''I know you started school a yea
late because your father dragged you along on a dig i
Honduras. That was the last time he took you to a workin
site. After that he began his criminal career. And he didn'
want any witnesses around. Not even his own son.

''I know you spent years in boarding schools. Your fam
ily was disgraced when he went to prison,'' he went or
apparently hitting what he considered the high point
''You've made yourself an expert in ancient and moder
Greek. You had an affair with Sophia nine months befor
her daughter was born. Aristotle was very interested in tha
piece of information. Apparently, she'd convinced him sh
was a virgin on her wedding night. He didn't like hearin
he'd been bamboozled.''

''That's what you told him?''

Agnapopolis answered with a smirk. ''His reaction wa
volcanic, wouldn't you say?''

''You endangered the life of an innocent child!'' Zek
retorted. The only thing that kept him from springing ou
of the chair and bashing the handcuffs against the old man'
face was his awareness of Mr. Smith and his gun. Smit
was listening with interest, and his weapon was trained o
Zeke.

''Your daughter got you here, didn't she? Actuall
Aristotle isn't all that interested in taking out his anger o
her. I simply made sure her Aunt Irena thought he was.''

Zeke didn't bother to hide his shock.

''But *I'll* kill her, if you don't do exactly what I say,'
Agnapopolis continued.

Zeke gritted his teeth. If he stayed focused on Ariadne
he would go insane. Instead, he tried to make sense of wha

ad happened over the past few days, in light of these new
evelations. "If you wanted me in Mythos, why did you
end Sebastian to attack me?"

Agnapopolis's features darkened. "He wasn't supposed
o attack you, only keep track of you and make sure you
lidn't change your mind. Apparently, he was using me to
get to you." He paused and gave Zeke a direct look. "He
aid for not following my instructions."

"Were Icarus and his crew working for you, too?" Zeke
sked. He might as well learn as much as he could, while
Agnapopolis was in a talkative mood.

The old man rolled his eyes. "Unfortunately, they were
o well known that both Pappas and I approached them. It
eems they were taking my money and his, too. I think they
vere going to auction you and your volunteer wife off to
he highest bidder."

Zeke sat up straighter. "Let's get to the point. What do
ou want from me? If it's information about where my
ather buried the treasure from the temple of Apollo, I don't
ave a clue. So you've wasted a lot of time and money."

Agnapopolis spread his hands. "I told Sebastian I was
fter treasure, but that was just a plausible story about why
was interested in you. I didn't need any more money from
he deal. My share of the profits was in a Swiss bank. It
gathered quite a lot of interest while I was rotting in
rison." As he said the last part, his voice turned gritty.

"I'm sorry your involvement with my father caused you
o much grief," Zeke said with sincerity. "I've spent my
ife trying to atone for his sins. I suppose you know about
hat?"

Agnapopolis ignored him, continuing his monologue as
f he'd never been interrupted. "In prison, I lived to take
ny revenge on your father. When I got out and found he
vas dead, I almost went insane. Then I realized you would
e his substitute."

Almost insane, Zeke thought. *A genuine nut case, was
nore like it.*

Agnapopolis kept ranting. Zeke found his mind drifting as he sat across from this man who hated him so much. The strange confrontation put things in perspective. He'd been afraid to tell Elizabeth he loved her, but he should have done it when he had the chance. Last night, maybe after he had made love to her so frantically. He knew she had wanted to hear it. He had wanted to say it, but he'd been afraid that if he told her, he wouldn't be able to leave her. Not saying the words hadn't made any difference. She had taught him the meaning of love, and now he might never get the chance to tell her.

"You came to see your daughter," Agnapopolis brought him back to the present with a jolt.

Zeke's eyes narrowed. "She'd better be unharmed."

"You're not in a position to give me orders."

"Is she all right?" Zeke insisted.

The old man smiled. "She's in good health. I'm afraid that her quarters aren't quite as luxurious as she's used to, however. Her aunt tried to run away with her early this morning. I had to lock them in a secure place."

Heedless of the man with the gun, Zeke stood. "Take me to her," he growled.

"That was my plan all along," Agnapopolis murmured. "I want you to meet her, get to know her. That will make the end of our little drama all the more poignant."

"What the hell are you planning?" Zeke growled.

"Partly, that will depend on you."

ELIZABETH LEANED INSIDE the driver's door of the truck, staring at the ignition keys dangling so temptingly a few feet in front of her. She started to slide behind the wheel, then changed her mind as she pictured herself turning the key and the vehicle exploding. The scenario was farfetched. Mr. Smith hadn't had time to rig a bomb, had he? Yet it didn't make sense that he'd left her the means to escape—unless he knew that driving the truck would be a fatal mistake. It would certainly make her conspicuous, she conceded. He could have men all over the roads looking for her. And he could send them back here, she realized with a sudden twinge. Whirling, she looked over her shoulder, scanning the landscape. No hostile faces popped up from behind any of the rocks. But that didn't mean she was safe.

Quickly, she scrambled inside the vehicle and climbed into the back where they'd stowed their luggage. Pulling open Zeke's bag, she brought out one of the rough-textured dark shirts he'd packed. It was too big for her, she thought, as she pulled her own knit top over her head and stuffed it into one of the empty olive buckets. But if searchers had been given a description of her clothing, they'd be thwarted.

As she pulled on the shirt, she closed her eyes and inhaled Zeke's scent. For a moment she went very still, imagining his arms wrapped around her. But she couldn't let herself be seduced by the compelling image. He was a captive, and she was on her own. She had promised to rescue Ariadne. Now she had to rescue him, too, she thought.

Buttoning the shirt, she cinched in the waist with her own belt. Then she rummaged in the bag and came up with the gun that had stood them in such good stead. Ready for action, she tucked the weapon into her waistband and covered it with the shirt. Now all she had to do was figure out where Mr. Smith had taken Zeke.

HOLDING AN OLD-FASHIONED lantern, Zeke walked down a flight of cement steps, his footsteps echoing hollowly. The stairs led to a dank basement where the temperature was ten degrees colder than the first floor of the villa. Mr. Smith walked directly behind him with the gun. Agnapopolis brought up the rear.

On the lower level, Agnapopolis unlocked a heavy wooden door.

"Inside," he ordered, pulling out a pistol that had been tucked into the waistband of his slacks. "And don't try

anything clever, or your daughter will be the first to g
it.''

Zeke considered his options. He had only one. Duckin
past Agnapopolis, he walked into the room. The mome
he was inside, the heavy door clanked shut. But he wa
hardly aware of being locked in.

As his eyes adjusted to the dim light, he searched th
small chamber and found a cot in the corner. Huddled o
it were a woman and a little girl who clung tightly to th
woman's skirt. As he stood facing them, he felt a tearin
sensation inside his chest. The little girl was Ariadne.

His child.

He had studied her solemn dark eyes, her narrow face
her dark hair in the photograph and tried to find his ow
features. But looking at a picture was only a dim approx
mation of seeing her in person.

Although he wasn't sure exactly what she'd inherite
from him, he felt the connection between them all the wa
to the depths of his soul.

He had thought about this moment so many times in th
past few days. Imagination had ill prepared him for th
dizzying rush of feeling that almost knocked him off hi
feet. He wanted to bolt across the room and scoop her up
keep her safe from all harm. But he didn't have that powe
And he knew he was likely to frighten her if he moved to
fast. So he clenched his hands at his sides and forced him
self to remain where he was.

The woman was staring at him, a dazed expression o
her face, as if she doubted her own senses. He had met he
before, a long time ago when he had lived in the Pappa
house. She had stayed out of his way, a woman of the ol
school, who wouldn't dream of acting forward with a ma
guest. Her sister, Sophia, had been quite different.

''Irena?''

She nodded uncertainly.

She looked a little like Sophia. She was a few year
older, he remembered. She wasn't as pretty, but there wa

a quiet appeal to her face. Or there would have been, he corrected himself, if her features hadn't been pinched with fright.

He took a step forward. "I'm Zeke. Zeke Chambers," he said in Greek. "Thank you for writing to me."

"I know who you are," she answered, holding out her hand and letting it drop back into her lap. "I'm sorry. I couldn't...keep her..." She let her voice trail off, as she looked down at the little girl.

"It's all right. You did your best," he said, wondering suddenly if Agnapopolis was listening to the conversation, feeding on the words and reactions. He decided it didn't matter.

The child began to whimper softly, and Zeke couldn't stop himself from crossing the eight feet of space that separated them. Slowly, he lowered himself to the floor in front of her.

"Didn't your Auntie Irena tell you about me?" he asked, surprised that he couldn't keep his voice from shaking.

"Yes," she whispered.

Slowly, slowly he moved his hand, watching it tremble as he brought it up to lightly touch her arm. The first contact sent a shiver through him. The child flinched, but didn't pull away.

"What did she tell you?" he asked.

The little girl focused her gaze somewhere in the vicinity of his right shoulder. "That you're going to take care of me."

"That's right," he managed.

"I don't like this place."

"I think we have to stay here for a little while."

She looked toward her aunt accusingly. "You said—"

"Hush," Irena instructed.

"It's okay," Zeke said quickly. "She's frightened."

So was he—for all of them. Perhaps he was the only one who knew how great was the danger. But he didn't want

Ariadne or her aunt to sense his anxiety. He gave the little
girl an encouraging smile.

She didn't smile back. She only stared at him.

But at least she was acknowledging his presence. He
swallowed hard. "Did your aunt tell you I live in a big
house with lots of dolls and toys a little girl would like?"
He didn't know where that idea had come from. It had
simply popped into his head. "And there's a nice woman
there," he added. "Elizabeth. She loves little girls. She's
told me how much she wants to meet you and help take
care of you."

Ariadne looked interested, yet she still clung tightly to
her aunt. Zeke wished Elizabeth was with him to smooth
the way. She'd know what to say to this frightened little
girl. Then he brought himself up short, remembering how
lucky he was that Elizabeth had gotten away from Mr.
Smith. He'd have to do this part himself.

He gave his daughter an encouraging smile. "Tell me
what kinds of toys you like to play with. Because if I don't
have them, I'll get them for you," he said in a choked
voice. "Anything. I'll do anything for you."

ELIZABETH TUCKED THE pistol into the waistband of her
slacks and covered it with the tails of the long shirt. Then
she tied her hair in a bandanna, which she'd decided was
more feminine and less conspicuous than Zeke's hat. Finally, she stuffed a wad of drachmas into her pocket.
Maybe she could use them for bribes, she thought, with a
wry twist of her mouth.

She also had a small carry bag of Zeke's. In it were the
pictures of Ariadne and her mother, Sophia. The best plan
she could think of was to ask some of the women at the
market if they'd seen the child with an older woman.

She decided it was prudent to stay off the road, so she
picked her way cautiously through the hills, moving downward on a series of footpaths toward the village. As she
rounded an outcropping of rock, a woman with a scarf very

much like her own stepped directly into her path. The scarf was pulled high around the newcomer's mouth and nose, hiding the lower part of her face. Above it, her eyes glittered with a dangerous intensity.

Pretending that she wasn't alarmed, Elizabeth kept her gaze lowered as she started to move out of the way.

"Wait. Stay here," the woman commanded. "You need my help." Raising her hand, she pulled her scarf off her head, revealing a strikingly beautiful face.

Elizabeth gasped and fell back a step, feeling dizzy and disoriented.

"You know me?"

"I—I—" she stammered, her mouth so dry she could say no more. The woman's face had been burned into her brain from the moment she'd first seen the pictures Irena had sent Zeke. It was Sophia, the woman Zeke had loved. Yet she couldn't be. Sophia was dead.

Chapter Sixteen

"You look like Sophia," Elizabeth breathed, her hand stilling as her gaze swept over the raven hair, the soft brown eyes, the even features. "But...but you can't be. Sophia was...was killed."

The woman shook her head and spoke slowly in a mixture of Greek and English. "You are correct. I am Sophia."

"But how?"

"Aristotle thought he killed me in a car accident. It was safer to let him go on thinking he'd gotten his revenge! Safer to let everybody think I was dead."

Elizabeth's head was spinning. Questions piled up inside her, but she wasn't even sure which one to ask first. Swallowing, she tried to pull herself together enough to think. What if Mr. Smith had sent this woman to find her—a woman who looked startlingly like Sophia. The scenario seemed implausible. Yet confronting this ghost was just as incredible. "How do I know who you really are?" she asked the question she should have posed in the first place.

The other woman gave her a wry little smile. "I believe you've answered your own question. You called me by name."

"I've seen Sophia's picture, but I've never met her. I—I could be wrong," she answered in halting Greek.

The newcomer's eyes narrowed. "And I could have let

you wander into the village and get caught by Cyril's men," she spat out.

"Why didn't you?" Elizabeth asked.

"You came here with Zeke. I think we can help each other."

Lucky for me, Elizabeth thought, looking into eyes that were coldly appraising. This woman knew how to get what she wanted.

"I saw that lout sneak up on the two of you. You were clever to get away."

Elizabeth nodded tightly, still trying to come to grips with the reality of Sophia. She was very beautiful; in fact, her picture didn't do her justice. Yet below the perfection of her features was a chilling quality. Zeke could never have fallen in love with someone like this, she told herself. Yet perhaps Sophia had been different when Zeke had known her. Perhaps her unhappy marriage had made her cold and calculating.

"Why don't you tell me what's going on?" Elizabeth managed. "How did you happen to see us captured?"

"I was waiting here—watching for Zeke. I knew he would come to the village to get Ariadne," the other woman continued. "I didn't expect anyone else to be with him. Who are you?"

Elizabeth hesitated, wondering just how much to reveal. "My name is Elizabeth…uh…Egan. Zeke and I have been friends for a long time," she finally said. "I agreed to help him bring his daughter home." She didn't want this woman to know that she was in love with Zeke, or that she'd actually married him as part of the agreement.

Sophia looked at her appraisingly. "Didn't you know that it would be dangerous to come to Mythos?"

"Yes." She could have said a good deal more, instead she tried to make her face a mask. Still, she had the unsettling feeling that Sophia's dark eyes could see into her head.

"Why are you helping Zeke?"

Elizabeth swallowed. "I was separated from my parents at an early age. I know what it's like to be a little girl alone and frightened."

"Ah."

Sophia's calm acceptance of the explanation gave Elizabeth pause. "But you're not dead," she pointed out. "You can take your daughter back."

"Not unless we can rescue her and Zeke," Sophia countered.

Elizabeth stared at her. Lord, what was really going on? Had she and Zeke come all this way and been attacked by murderers and pirates because of some crazy plot this woman had cooked up? What was she trying to do? Drawing herself up taller, she said, "I agree that we can help each other. But if we're going to work together, you'd better fill me in on what you know."

"I'm not sure where to start."

How about at the beginning? Did you seduce Zeke? Is that how you got yourself pregnant with his child? She'd been wanting to know that since she first heard about Sophia and her little girl. Yet the questions stayed locked behind her lips. Instead Elizabeth gestured toward the village below them. "How did you know Zeke would come here?"

"I had someone watching Irena, and I knew she had brought my daughter to this town. Unfortunately, my informant didn't figure out she was with an enemy of Zeke's. He's Cyril Agnapopolis." In response to Elizabeth's dark look, she asked, "You know about him?"

Elizabeth nodded. "I know he and Zeke's father worked together to smuggle antiquities out of the country."

Sophia snorted. "He took his chances selling his country's heritage, and he got caught. Then he blamed Zeke's father for his predicament and swore to get revenge. But the father is beyond his reach, so he goes after the son. He's responsible for all of this." Sophia waved her arm in a sweeping gesture, then went on in a rush of words. "He came to my husband and started babbling about my past with Zeke.'' She swallowed. ''The bastard told him I wasn't a virgin on my wedding night! Do you understand how a man like Aristotle would react to that news?''

Elizabeth nodded.

''He and I never loved each other. It was a marriage arranged by our families. When I couldn't give him a son, he beat me. After Cyril got his ear, things became much worse. I saw the cold hatred behind his eyes and knew I was in danger. I listened to his private conversations and learned that he was planning to get rid of me and marry someone else. That night before I was supposed to take a trip to Athens, I told him I knew about his conversation with Agnapopolis. I told him that Agnapopolis was right. Ariadne wasn't his. It was a calculated risk. I said I was leaving him. I knew I'd force him to make his move. But I was ready.''

Elizabeth tried to imagine a marriage like the one Sophia was describing.

Apparently unaware of the reaction she was producing, Sophia went on for several minutes, filling in Elizabeth, who listened with sick fascination. Sophia had carefully worked out all the details. She'd told the driver of her car that her husband was planning to get rid of her and didn't care who else got killed. He didn't believe her until she showed him the car's brakes were about to fail. When he realized Aristotle was going to murder him, too, he agreed to help Sophia. The two of them pushed the car over the cliff into deep water where it couldn't be recovered. She'd sold some of her jewelry and had enough money so she could pay him to disappear. She'd also paid a poor shepherd to say he'd seen them in the car when it plunged into the water.

Sophia finished and Elizabeth stared at her, thinking that it had taken guts—and considerable manipulative skills— to pull off such a risky plan.

''Does your sister think you're dead?'' she managed.

"Yes. Otherwise she wouldn't have sent for Zeke," Sophia answered, her voice sharp and practical. "I want to get out of the country. I want him to take me away where I'll be safe."

Elizabeth winced and knew Sophia had caught the response.

"You have other plans for Zeke?" Sophia asked.

"I told you. I want to help Ariadne."

Sophia regarded her steadily. "Now you'll help me, too."

"I think we both want to rescue Zeke. You know where that man took him?"

"To Cyril's."

"Show me where that is."

ZEKE CRADLED ARIADNE in his arms, the warm weight of her body remarkably comforting in this dark, cold place. It had been easier than he'd thought to win her over. She even trusted him enough to fall asleep. He'd had her laughing at some silly stories about elves playing tricks on people who invaded their hills. He hadn't even known where the fantasies came from. Maybe a children's book he'd read a long time ago.

His heart squeezed, as he stroked his fingers through the silky strands of his daughter's hair. It hadn't been so hard to get to know her. She was open. Trusting. So very sweet. And it seemed her mother had cared enough about her to shield her from the worst of Aristotle's anger. He had to give Sophia credit for that.

Sighing, he lowered his face to his daughter's neck and breathed in the clean scent of her skin, thinking about all the quiet and happy moments he'd already missed with her. He wanted to make up for lost time. And he would, he told himself sharply. Yet he knew he might only be spinning daydreams. He had no control of this situation. They were all at the mercy of Cyril Agnapopolis, the revenge-crazed man who had brought them here.

Ariadne stirred. "Shush, little one," he murmured, and she nestled more snugly against him.

She'd tried to stay awake for him, but she'd been exhausted. She'd fallen asleep after she'd made him tell her the ancient myth of Ariadne—how she'd helped Theseus and married Dionysus. He gathered from the way she prompted him that she already knew the story by heart. But he'd enjoyed sharing it with her.

He wanted to keep holding her, but he couldn't afford that luxury. Time was slipping through his fingers.

"Irena, can you take her?" he asked.

"Of course."

Shifting on the cot, he laid the child in her lap. Then he stood and stretched his cramped muscles before pacing across the ten-foot length of the cell.

The woman moved the sleeping girl so that Ariadne lay with her head in her lap and her legs on the rough wool blanket Agnapopolis had provided. She looked down at his daughter. "What is he going to do with us?" she asked.

"He's going to let you and Ariadne go," Zeke said. "He was only using you to get to me."

"If he's going to let us go, why hasn't he done it yet?"

Zeke shrugged and turned away, so that she couldn't see his face in the dim light from the lantern sitting on the floor in the corner. He wanted with every fiber of his being to believe Agnapopolis would set the woman and child free, now that they'd served his purpose. Yet his short interview with the man revealed he was dealing with someone ruthless. What if Agnapopolis planned to kill them first and make him watch? He shuddered, wishing he could dismiss that possibility. Once more, he silently thanked God that Elizabeth wasn't with him in this prison.

It took a few moments to compose himself. When he was sure he could speak without his voice cracking, he tried to sound coolly practical. "What do you know about Agnapopolis?" he asked.

He heard Irena swallow. "I thought he was a good

man," she whispered. "He said he wanted to help me, and I believed him. He can be kind," she added with regret in her voice. "I thought he cared for me. And I—I was hoping..." She didn't finish the sentence.

Yet Zeke heard the yearning in her voice. My God, it sounded like she'd fallen in love with the bastard. Too bad for her.

"He offered you a place to stay?" he asked.

"Yes. He said my parents had done him a service long ago, and now he wanted to repay them by helping me." She gestured helplessly. "I wanted so much to believe him. Now look what has happened."

"It's not your fault," Zeke whispered, wishing he could make things right for her. She was a good woman, who had been trying to do what she thought was best. She'd put herself in grave danger, the moment she'd run away with Ariadne. "Don't blame yourself. I'll always be grateful to you."

She wrapped her arms more tightly around the little girl. "You came all this way to get her. I knew you would come."

He nodded, struggling to breathe around the lump wedged in his chest. She had more faith in him then he'd had in himself. Unfortunately, he could see now that he'd never had a chance of success. Agnapopolis had planned things too carefully, marshaled too many resources. Even when the man had lost control of the situation, he'd had the determination and the capacity to recover.

Before Irena could see the anguish on his face, Zeke stooped and picked up the lantern, holding it high so he could examine the walls and ceiling of the cell. They were cement, probably very thick cement, since they formed part of the support structure of the house. When he wrapped his knuckles against them in several places, they seemed quite solid. He wasn't going to get through them in this century with anything less than plastic explosives. Even if he'd had explosives, he could hardly use them in such close confinement. Stepping toward the door, he examined the planks. They were also thick, but perhaps penetrable—if he had a couple of weeks to work on them. The metal hinges were large, with no rust, no corrosion. And the bolts that held them in place were—

He stopped short, afraid to let himself think there was a chance to get away. Yet he hadn't been mistaken. The top bolt on the uppermost hinge was a little loose. If he could work it free, he might be able to remove the door.

"I've found something," he whispered, turning back toward Irena.

"What?"

"I want to try and remove this hinge." He felt in his pockets. Agnapopolis had taken anything that might be useful...his coins, his pen knife, even his belt. "Do you have anything I can use on this?"

"What?"

"Something metal."

She looked blank for a moment, then reached under her scarf and produced a black hairpin. He took it in his hand, feeling the softness. It wasn't much to work with, but it was going to have to serve.

Quickly he began to twist at the bolt. From somewhere above him in the house came an ominous thumping sound. He froze and heard Irena draw in a sharp breath. The sound was followed by what appeared to be a shout.

Irena's eyes grew round. "What was that?" she asked.

"I don't know."

Turning back to the door, he began to work at the bolt with increased speed, fighting the ominous feeling that he was already out of time.

IT WAS A LONG WALK through the hills, as they worked their way cautiously upward toward the villa—particularly since Elizabeth and Sophia had to keep stopping, to avoid contact with other people.

The whole time, Sophia kept up a running monologue

about how unfair life had been to her. Elizabeth suppose
the woman was fighting a bad case of nerves, yet sh
couldn't imagine revealing so much to a total stranger. T
hear her tell it, Zeke was the only good thing that had eve
happened to her. He was the only one who had really love
her.

And she wanted him back.

Elizabeth kept telling herself that it was all a desperat
fantasy, since Zeke's version of events had been somewha
different. Yet the sick feeling still churned in her stomach
She'd convinced herself that over the past few days Zek
had come to care for her. Now the mother of his child ha
turned up alive and well and determined to win him back
And even if he'd started to feel something for his wife
everything had changed. He'd thought Sophia was dead
But he'd been wrong.

Elizabeth fixed her eyes on the resolute set of Sophia'
shoulders, terrified by the new equation that had been cre
ated. Zeke's lover was a woman of determination. Did sh
love him—or was she simply out to use him?

It sounded like the latter, Elizabeth told herself. But sh
suspected Sophia was very good at playing the part of a
woman thrilled to be reunited with the man she loved
Would Zeke see through that? Or would he be blinded by
his own feelings, she wondered with a gulp.

But she was getting ahead of the story, Elizabeth re
minded herself. First she had to get Zeke out of Cyri
Agnapopolis's clutches. And she had a better chance o
doing that with Sophia's help. Unless Sophia was playing
some terrible game of her own, Elizabeth realized with a
shiver. What if the woman was deliberately leading her int
a trap? If so, she was doing a pretty convincing job o
making the journey difficult.

"Almost there," Sophia whispered, pointing to a low
building spread out along the side of a hill. It gleame
whitely in the last rays of the setting sun.

Elizabeth stared at the light pouring through the win

dows, trying to spot some people inside. She could detect no movement and knew she'd have to get closer—which would be dangerous.

"What does Agnapopolis look like?" she whispered.

The other woman gave her a quick description of a gray-haired man with a lined face.

"Okay. I'll go first. Keep close to me."

Sophia didn't protest. Apparently, she was perfectly happy to leave the riskiest part to someone else.

After saying a quick little prayer, Elizabeth scurried forward through tall grass and low bushes, keeping as close to the ground as possible. Casting a quick glance over her shoulder, she could see Sophia a good ten yards behind her.

Thankful there were no spotlights on the exterior of the house, she moved forward. But the growing darkness proved to be a hazard, she discovered when she bashed her knee against a rock. She had to clench her teeth to keep from crying out.

She noticed with a little inward shrug that Sophia didn't rush to her aid. When the pain subsided, she maneuvered forward again, this time more cautiously.

The house was larger than most of the ones she'd seen in Mythos. It had a rectangular central structure with smaller wings jutting out on either side. She was at the back, she surmised, since the access road and the parking area were on the other side.

As silently as she could, Elizabeth climbed a low wall into a flower-filled courtyard and made her way to the closest windows, in the left-hand wing. Raising her head cautiously above the sill, she discovered that she was looking into a dining room, which was empty. The well-equipped kitchen was nearby, also vacant.

Moving along the perimeter, she came to a large room furnished with comfortable couches, chairs and oriental rugs. Her heart leaped and began to pound faster, when she saw Zeke sitting on one of the couches, holding a dark-haired girl on his lap. She must be Ariadne, his daughter—the reason they had both come here. Elizabeth lingered on the pair for several moments, rejoicing in the child's easy posture. She trusted Zeke already, and the rapport between them made Elizabeth feel a warm glow. Still, she clenched her hands when she saw a bruise across his cheek. Otherwise, he seemed to be all right—except for the tense set of his face. But the harsh lines softened as he looked down at his daughter. Beside him on the couch was a woman who resembled Sophia. That must be the aunt, Irena. To their left was the gray-haired man Sophia had described. Cyril. Standing behind him was the notorious Mr Smith—looking ashen, Elizabeth noted with a spurt of satisfaction.

And he wasn't the only part of the picture that seemed out of kilter to Elizabeth. Everyone else in the room was facing another man who had his back to the window. Apparently, he was speaking to the group, since she could hear the low hum of his voice. When he turned slightly to the left, Elizabeth saw that it wasn't his spellbinding oratory holding everybody's attention. It was the gun in his hand.

Sophia had entered the garden and was staring at the group inside the room. She gave a little gasp. "Aristotle, Holy Mother, it's Aristotle," she croaked.

"Your husband?" Elizabeth asked.

"Yes."

Elizabeth put her finger to her lips. Taking care not to alert the group facing in her direction, she moved stealthily along the wall to a spot where a sliding-glass door was open a crack. By straining her ears, she could hear some of what was going on inside.

"I have first claim on Chambers," Aristotle was saying. "He ruined my wife."

Cyril growled a negative response she couldn't catch.

Then Zeke broke into the conversation. "You can stop fighting over me," he said wearily, and inclined his head toward the aggrieved husband. "I'll go with you, but I want your word that Ariadne will be unharmed."

He was giving the impression of a man at the end of his rope. Yet Elizabeth knew him better than anyone else in that room, and she knew he wasn't simply going quietly with Aristotle. He had some plan. If she only knew what it was, she could help him.

"I don't have to guarantee anything to anyone, especially not you," Aristotle countered.

Zeke's face darkened. "She hasn't done anything to you!"

Irena stood. With a defiant look at both men, she picked up Ariadne and carried her out of the room.

"Come back," Aristotle bellowed.

Irena continued down the hall and out of sight. Long seconds ticked by. Finally, Irena returned, but she didn't have the girl with her. "She doesn't need to hear any more of this," she said in a grim voice. "One of the maids is tucking her into bed."

Cyril opened his mouth and closed it again. Aristotle gestured to Zeke. "Come on."

"What can we do?" Sophia whispered.

Elizabeth stared through the window. Was this what Zeke had planned? She didn't know. And she didn't know what would happen to Ariadne and Irena once Zeke left the room. Taking several steps back, she reached under her shirt and pulled out the gun that had been hidden all this time.

Sophia's eyes widened. "Where did you get that?" she hissed.

"Zeke." She kept her eye on Aristotle. What if she shot him in the back? The plan had a simple appeal, yet he might still be able to shoot Zeke. "Duck down," she warned Sophia.

Silently, Sophia dodged to the left, pressing herself against the garden wall. Elizabeth raised the pistol and aimed at the top of the window, firing two shots and shattering the glass. Her finger kept clicking the trigger until she realized that the gun must be out of bullets.

It was almost impossible to follow the sequence of events she set in motion. Aristotle whirled in a half crouch, his face contorted and his own weapon pointed high, as he squeezed off several shots where he apparently imagined the attack had originated. A split second after Aristotle fired, Zeke sprang toward the intruder's back. Almost at the same time, Cyril scrambled to open the drawer of the table next to the sofa. He came out with a gun in his hand, and pivoting, he aimed it at Zeke.

Chapter Seventeen

"God, no!" Elizabeth screamed, her finger still wrapped around the trigger of the now useless pistol as she pushed open the sliding-glass door. The only thing she knew, as she lunged into the scene of chaos, was that she had to save Zeke.

But Irena was closer to the action. As Elizabeth watched wide-eyed, the other woman threw herself between Cyril and Zeke.

"Get out of the way!" the old man screamed. "Get out of the way, you fool. I'm going to kill him, even if I have to kill you, too."

She raised her chin, staring at him defiantly "No. Zeke Chambers is a good man, and I won't let you do it."

"Move, woman!"

She shook her head. "I won't. Not just for him. For you. I won't let you go back to prison. I care about you too much."

For a terrible moment, Cyril stood with his face contorted and the gun leveled at her chest. Then he muttered an oath. Slowly, slowly, he lowered his hand and dropped the pistol with a thunk on the rug. Then his knees seemed to buckle, and he sank onto the couch.

The moment the weapon left his fingers, Elizabeth sprinted forward and picked it up. When she straightened

with the pistol in her hand, she aimed it toward Mr. Smith
who looked as if he was coming out of a trance.

Irena knelt in front of Cyril, and he cradled her head in
his lap, stroking her hair. "I thought…I thought prison had
turned me into a monster," he murmured. "But I couldn't
shoot you. I couldn't."

"I love you," she whispered back, her voice soft. Yet
her own amazement showed on her face.

Elizabeth wrenched her gaze away from the tender scene
as a lamp crashed to the floor and shattered.

Looking to her right, she saw Zeke struggling with Aristotle—who had knocked over the lamp table with his foot.
The two men rolled across the floor, battling with the fury
of old rivals finally granted a confrontation. But Zeke was
by far the younger and stronger. It took only a few more
seconds for him to deliver a knockout blow to the other
man's chin.

When Aristotle went slack, Zeke sprang up and stared at
Elizabeth, the look in his eyes slightly dazed.

Cyril twisted toward Mr. Smith. "No more attacks on
Chambers," he said.

"But—"

"No more!"

It was over. It was finally over. Elizabeth put down the
gun and took a step toward Zeke, but before she could cross
the house, Sophia sprinted through the sliding-glass door.

"Zeke. Thank the Holy Mother. Zeke," she cried, dash-
ing toward him.

If he'd looked dazed before, it was nothing compared to
his reaction now. His mouth dropped open, and he reached
to steady himself with a hand against the wall. "Sophia,"
he gasped out. "I thought. But you're—"

"I'm alive," she interrupted. "And I've been waiting all
this time for you. Now we can finally be together."

He shook his head, as if he didn't understand what she
was saying.

Elizabeth stood rooted to the spot, hardly daring to
breathe as she waited for him to speak.

When he remained silent, Sophia took another step forward. "Zeke, it's not too late," she continued. "Now we can finally be together."

He found his voice. "No." The syllable came out harsh and grating.

Sophia made a low sound. "You love me. We were meant for each other."

He shook his head. "I was never in love with you. But I was lonely and I wanted to be close to someone. You knew that, didn't you? You took advantage of me. I guess you thought I was going to marry you. Then your family interfered."

Elizabeth stood with her heart pounding, barely able to believe what she was hearing. All this time she'd thought Zeke loved Sophia. But he hardly sounded like a man reunited with his lost love.

"Zeke—what are you saying?" Sophia gasped out.

"I'm saying you had me so confused I wasn't sure whether I was coming or going. It's taken me a long time to find out what real love is. But I have—with Elizabeth."

"Oh, Zeke," Elizabeth whispered, overwhelmed.

"You can't be in love with her," Sophia screamed, color rising in her face.

"But I am. I was crazy not to admit it years ago." Turning away from Sophia, he started toward Elizabeth, who was so stunned she couldn't move. The warm look in his eyes released her, and she found that her legs would work, after all. Throwing herself toward Zeke, she landed squarely in his arms. With a glad exclamation, she buried her face against his shoulder. His hands came up to support her and they clung together, as she tried to shut out everything else but him.

"God, you were magnificent bursting into the house like that," he growled.

"I didn't know what else to do." She wanted to be alone with him. She wanted everybody else in the room to vanish.

"No," Sophia screamed. "No." Her anguished voice

penetrating the cocoon Elizabeth had tried to wrap around herself and Zeke.

Zeke tensed, yet he didn't raise his head toward Sophia.

"You don't want me?" she spat at him. "But you came all this way to get your daughter."

His gaze was stony as he stared at her. "Yes," he answered. "I knew I had an obligation to our child. And when I found her, I knew there was more between us than a simple obligation."

Sophia laughed mirthlessly. "Well, the joke is on you. She's not yours. She's Aristotle's. You have nothing to do with her. Nothing."

The blood drained from Zeke's face. "You're lying! Ariadne's my daughter."

She laughed. "That's what I wanted you to believe, because I thought you would take the two of us away. But it's not true. If you don't want me, you have no claim on Ariadne."

Zeke's face was ashen.

"She'll say anything," Elizabeth whispered. "That doesn't mean it's true." She was reaching for Zeke's hand, when Aristotle spoke.

"Sophia, you're finished toying with people's lives."

The focus of attention in the room shifted one more time. Aristotle sat on the floor, a gun in his hand, a gun pointed toward Sophia. While all eyes had been riveted elsewhere, he had quietly inched across the floor and picked up the weapon Zeke had knocked away during the fight.

The gray-haired husband sighed, as his gaze shifted away from Sophia for a second and then back again. "I thought I wanted to punish Zeke Chambers for poisoning our marriage. I see now that you fooled him the way you fooled me. I would have killed him—because of you."

"Holy Mother," Sophia whimpered, reaching out her hand toward her husband.

His expression was stony as he pulled the trigger—once, twice, three times. She screamed, staggered backward, and fell to the floor, the front of her dress red with blood.

Irena cried out in anguish, and rushed to the side of her injured sister. Dropping to her knees, she grabbed Sophia's hand, squeezing and chafing it.

"Sophia! Please, Sophia," she said over and over.

Zeke and Elizabeth were only a few steps behind. When they reached the side of the fallen woman, it was quickly obvious there was nothing they could do. Aristotle had dispatched his wife as efficiently as an executioner. His face was gray, and he blinked rapidly as if he'd suddenly realized what he'd done. Carefully, he set the gun on a table beside the sofa.

Cyril came down beside Irena on the floor, his arm around her shoulder, drawing her away from the body as she began to weep, her slender frame shaking. "I tried to do my best for you," she whispered to her sister. "Now look what's happened."

"It's not your fault," Cyril murmured.

"Yes, it is. I didn't do the right things when she was little."

"Don't blame yourself. Never that," he said. "She was never made to be happy. Now she is at peace."

Elizabeth drew closer to Zeke. "Thank God, Irena took Ariadne out of the room," she murmured.

"Yes," he agreed. "But I've got to go to her. She must be frightened, wondering what's happened. God, what if she comes running out here?"

She squeezed his hand. "We'll go together."

As they stood, Elizabeth realized she was hearing the wail of a siren in the darkness outside. She blinked as she saw a small black-and-white cruiser pull into the parking lot. It seemed impossible that the police could get there so fast after the shooting. Then she decided one of the servants must have become alarmed by the scene in the living room and called the police.

Uniformed officers ran toward the house, guns drawn, as they stared through the window at the grisly scene spread before them.

Cyril pushed himself up, squared his shoulders and

strode toward the front door. As the officers burst into the room, Aristotle stepped forward.

"I'm the one you want," he said in a firm voice. "I have killed my adulterous wife. She bore another man's baby five years ago. When she realized I knew about the child's father, she schemed to have me think she was killed in an automobile accident and made plans to run off with her old lover. Only she didn't know he'd already married someone else and was coming back to Mythos with his wife to claim his offspring."

Elizabeth felt Zeke's body stiffen. Her own head was spinning. Aristotle's explanation didn't match the facts she'd already heard from Sophia. Had Sophia lied about Aristotle's part in the accident? Had she arranged it herself as part of a plan to escape from her loveless marriage? And what about Ariadne—whose child was she?

"He and his wife are right there," Aristotle continued, pointing toward Zeke and Elizabeth.

After a low, apologetic discussion with the officers, Aristotle's hands were cuffed. To her amazement the authorities seemed sympathetic to his motives, and in a soft voice the senior policeman began asking questions. Sometimes Aristotle answered, sometimes Cyril.

Elizabeth tried to follow the conversation, but she was only partly successful. She gathered the explanations being given by both men were a continuation of the story Aristotle had begun. How ironic that they were working together, she thought.

Zeke kept shifting his stance and glancing down the hall. Finally, he broke into the interrogation to say he'd like to make sure his daughter was all right. He and Elizabeth were given permission to leave the room, but not the house.

He drew her into the bedroom wing, but stopped after a few steps and ushered her just inside an empty room. When he turned, they fell into each other's arms.

She'd been barely holding herself together. Now that they were alone, she let her body sag into his. His arms came up to support her, but he braced himself against the wall, his whole body trembling.

"Thank the Lord, you're safe," she murmured.

"Me?" He gave a harsh laugh. "I've given up counting the times I almost got you killed."

"Not you."

He pulled back so his eyes could meet hers. "Don't you understand? There was never any chance I could rescue Ariadne—not with all the forces allied against me," he said in a hard voice.

"You didn't know that!"

He ignored her and plowed on. "But I went ahead, taking terrible risks, unacceptable risks, because I felt guilty."

"No," she interrupted. "It wasn't just guilt. You realized you loved Ariadne. You couldn't admit it at first, but you'd figured out that bringing her to live with you would be the right thing for both of you."

His eyes were bright. "I guess I did, didn't I?" Then his expression sobered again and he raked a hand through his hair. "But I dragged you with me on *Mission Impossible.*"

"Zeke, you're the one who still doesn't get it. I wouldn't let you leave me behind."

His fingers dug into her shoulders. "You didn't realize how much danger there was."

"Stop!" she ordered. "Of course I did. As soon as Sebastian showed up. But now it's over. We're both safe and sound."

"But—"

She pressed her fingers to his lips. "Let's stick with the important stuff. You said you loved me. Was it true?"

"Yes."

"Oh, Zeke."

He let out a long sigh. "I'm trying to do the right thing."

"You always do. That's one of your inborn traits." She reached up to tenderly brush back a lock of his hair. "It makes you a very moral man. It also gets you in trouble. But I'm here to save you again. I'm not going to let you push me away because you think it's the right thing to do. You can't get rid of me that easily.''

"How could I be moral when my father was a thief?''

"Your father chose that life. You chose something different. You made yourself what you are—the man I love.''

"God, I love you. You taught me what love means.'' His hands tightened on her arms. "Every time you had to choose between what was best for me and what was best for you, you...you chose me.'' He sounded as if he still couldn't believe that was possible.

"And you did the same thing with Ariadne,'' she pointed out.

He looked utterly startled. "I—I guess I did.''

"So why not stop beating yourself up? Why not relax and enjoy what you deserve?'' She gave him the confident look she'd manufactured on their wedding night, then pulled his head down for a long, satisfying kiss.

When it was over, she grinned. "I guess that's settled. We're staying married. Now all we have to worry about is raising your daughter.''

His features twisted. "I don't know what to think anymore. What if Sebastian was right? What if...what if she's not mine?''

"When I crept up to the house, I saw you holding her on the sofa. I saw the look in your eyes and the way she was clinging to you.''

"I got to spend some time with her,'' he said in a soft voice. "She's a wonderful child.''

"And she's your daughter, as much as I was the Egans' daughter. Whether you made her or not, you've earned the right to be her father.''

He was silent for several seconds, his eyes misty. "I kept telling myself I hadn't learned a damned thing over the past few years. I was wrong. I learned how to pick my women.''

"Right. So let's go collect the little one. She's probably frightened, and hoping you'll be the one to come to tell her everything's all right.''

Epilogue

A smile played around Elizabeth's lips as she stood in the doorway of her cozy family room. Neither her husband nor her daughter knew she was watching them. They were too busy finger painting.

It had been easy for Elizabeth and Zeke to legally adopt Ariadne, since Aristotle had made no claim on her. He was still in prison, serving a short sentence for manslaughter, the only crime that an all-male jury was willing to find him guilty of. And he'd stuck to his story about Sophia. Maybe his version was true, but as Elizabeth looked over at Zeke and his daughter, she knew it didn't really matter if they'd ever learn the truth.

Ariadne and Zeke sat in the middle of a large area of the carpet that had been covered with sheets of newspaper, each of them hunched over a work of art in progress.

Ariadne's hands were smeared with red, yellow, green and blue paint. Zeke had confined himself to yellow and red. He was swirling red pigment to form the curled top of a series of Ionic columns. His daughter was making a garden full of many different flowers.

She glanced over at her father's effort, her face serious. "You don't have enough colors."

"I'm just making a temple," he replied. "Do you know what kind of columns it has?"

Ariadne peered at his work. "Ionic," she tossed out.

"Right. When I finish, you can decorate it with flowers."

"I like flowers."

"And you're much better than I am at painting them."

"I know. Mommy says you're too conventional."

"Oh, does she?"

Ariadne giggled.

Elizabeth cleared her throat. "You two look like you're having fun."

They both glanced up and spotted her in the doorway. "Make a picture with us," Ariadne said.

Elizabeth stared at their messy hands and the paint smeared around the edges of the pictures. "I can't. I'm fixing lunch. I only stopped by to say you need to be cleaned up in fifteen minutes."

"Oh, Mommy," Ariadne protested.

"If you paint, you have to clean up," Elizabeth reminded her.

"Right," Zeke agreed, sticking his fingers in the bowl of water he'd set out. When they were reasonably clean, he dried them on an old towel.

"Which picture do you like best?" Ariadne asked.

Elizabeth walked over to inspect several completed works of art. She pointed to one of Ariadne's. "This one has a wonderful sense of color, and I like the designs."

The little girl puffed out her chest.

"Wash your hands if you want chicken noodle soup."

"Yum." Ariadne began enthusiastically splashing in the bowl. Above her head, Zeke and Elizabeth smiled at each other.

"After I put on the flowers, can we send the picture of the temple to Aunt Irena and Uncle Cyril?"

"Yes," Elizabeth answered. She and Zeke had kept up the connection with Irena—and her new husband. Although Cyril had started off wanting revenge on Zeke, his love for Irena had changed him more than he'd realized. At the crisis point he'd had the wisdom to choose life with her, rather than staying on the self-destructive path he'd set for himself. He'd even written for permission to bring his wife or a visit. Zeke and Elizabeth had asked them to let Ariadne settle in a little more firmly first. She was adjusting well to life with her new parents. Zeke and Elizabeth had decided until she was older, it was better not to let her know how her mother had died. So they'd continued Irena's story that Sophia had gone away—and given Ariadne to a mommy and daddy who could take good care of her.

Zeke had never bothered to have any blood tests that would tell him for sure whether he and Ariadne were flesh and blood. He'd agreed with Elizabeth. It didn't matter. Either way, she was their child.

Since his uncle had left him with a good income, he'd been able to take some time off work. Besides settling into family life, his major occupation had been supervising the remodeling of Elizabeth's house. Until the job was finished two months ago, they'd rattled around in his stone-and-timber rancher.

"Go wash your hands with soap and water," Zeke said. "I'll clean up the newspaper."

Ariadne scrambled up and headed for the bathroom. Elizabeth bent to help Zeke with the papers.

When he stole a kiss, she leaned over and whispered in his ear. "Are you going to suggest nap time after lunch?"

"How did you guess?"

"Didn't you tell me it's easier to get little girls to cooperate, when Mom and Dad take a nap, too?"

"Absolutely." They exchanged a secret grin.

"Are you happy?" Zeke murmured.

"Do you have to ask? Of course I am."

"I like to hear you tell me."

"I'm happier than I've ever been in my life," she said.

"I—" His voice choked up, and he stopped for several seconds. "I am, too. I didn't know what having the two of you would mean to me." He rubbed his knuckles against his wife's cheek. "What do you think? Maybe we should start telling Ariadne how she's going to like being a big sister."

"I think we've got some time. I haven't even been t
the doctor yet."

"But you're pretty sure."

"Yes."

Zeke gave her a lingering kiss that ended when Ariadn
came bouncing out of the bathroom holding up her clea
hands. "I'm ready for chicken noodle soup."

Then she saw the way her mom and dad were lookin
at each other. "Come on, you guys! Don't get all mush
We have to eat lunch."

"Mushy is good," Zeke told her as they headed towar
the kitchen.

And there's more 43 LIGHT STREET!

Turn the page for a bonus look at what's in store
for you in the next "43 Light Street" book by
Rebecca York, coming to you in July 1998.

NOWHERE MAN

Only from Rebecca York and Harlequin Intrigue!

Prologue

Kathryn Kelley hesitated in the doorway to the darkened room, a small figure dwarfed by the silent, eerie space beyond. *Where were the lights?* she wondered, her gaze probing the watery darkness. Though she could see nothing she could feel a thick, chemical-tinged mist wafting toward her out of the blackness. It sent shivers over her skin as it collided with the cooler air of the hallway. Trying to dispel the sudden chill, she rubbed her hands along the thick sleeves of her robe.

It was Friday evening, and since the moment she'd opened her eyes on Monday, she'd sensed that something was wrong. She'd tried to ignore the oppressive sensation, but it was like a storm gathering around her. The feeling of apprehension made her turn quickly and glance over her shoulder to confirm that the corridor behind her was empty.

Of course it was empty! She made a wry face, annoyed at the tricks her mind was playing.

"What's wrong with you?" she asked, her voice echoing in the darkness beyond the door. With a quick decisive movement, she switched on the lights and marched inside. Shrugging out of her robe, she secured her mane of red hair with a band at the back of her neck, kicked off her shoes, and executed a perfect dive into the turquoise rectangle of the swimming pool.

The cold was a momentary shock to her system as she

shot downward into the pool, then came up to blink wate
out of her blue eyes. Straightening her limber body, sh
began a rapid crawl stroke. She'd been on the swim tea
in high school, and swimming had remained her exercis
of choice. In fact, she'd selected her Baltimore apartme
because the renovation of the Cecil Arms in the sixties ha
included a pool on the top floor.

By ten-thirty the pool was closed to tenants, but Kathry
had negotiated a lease that allowed her to use the facili
after hours. Willing the tension out of her muscles, she c
rapidly through the water. Still, she couldn't outdistance th
demons of the day. She'd been an expert witness in a chi
custody trial. Although she'd kept her cool on the stand
her testimony against Patrick Collins's father had made he
stomach churn.

Just thinking about the boy caused her to lose he
rhythm. With Patrick, she'd slipped over the line of pro
fessional detachment once again. It was getting harder an
harder to maintain the distance that shut her off from an
other person's pain. So she swam in the Cecil Arms priva
pool like the victim of a shipwreck flailing toward an un
reachable shore. And she let her mind wander to fantasie
of trading in her psychology practice for a flower shop lik
the guy in *Bed of Roses*. Maybe the management at 4
Light Street would rent her space in the lobby.

She didn't hear the door open. But a jolt went throug
her as she saw the overhead lights and the ones along th
side of the pool wink out. Stopping dead, she held he
breath, barely treading water, as her gaze scanned the floo
to-ceiling windows along the far wall. Below her, light
twinkled in other apartment buildings she could see, ye
this room at the top of the Cecil Arms was dark.

"Is somebody there?" She could hear her pulse pound
ing in her ears and the reverberations of her voice from th
walls and ceiling of the large room.

No one answered, and she felt goose bumps rise on he
arms. She wanted to believe someone was playing a crue
practical joke on the lady who went swimming in the eve

ing. The explanation didn't wash. In a blinding moment of panic, all the anxiety of the week coalesced into a terrible moment of certainty. She knew on a gut level who had turned off the lights, knew who had been stalking her. Now it made sense.

"James?" she quavered.

He made her beg for the answer.

"James?"

"Got ya!" a familiar, low voice echoed off the water.

She had been hoping against hope it wasn't true. Now she pictured a slender man with blond hair and blue eyes standing between her and the only door, the only escape route.

James Harrison. He had a charming smile and an easy manner, unless you looked below the surface to the rotten core carefully hidden inside.

She hadn't wanted to believe he was back. Yet deep in her subconscious she must have known. He'd been confined to the Indiana Institution for the Criminally Insane for the past three years, and he'd sworn to get even with Dr. Kelley for helping put him there.

She'd moved away, started over again in a new place with a new job and new friends. And time had dulled the memory of the curses he'd hurled at her. Until this week, she'd felt safe.

A small splash told her he had eased into the water, was stroking toward her. She dove deep, praying she had a chance to escape. Surfacing at the edge of the pool, she felt along the side, found the metal ladder and began to scramble up. But he must have been planning this carefully, must have studied the layout of the pool. Strong hands closed around her thighs, dragging her back down.

She had time for only a quick gasp of air before he pulled her under, pushing her below with the weight of his body. Trapped, she flailed in panic. But the thick, watery world muted the impact of her blows.

Frantically, she tried to struggle upward, but his hands held her under. Then for a moment he let her up, long

enough for her to get a blessed gasp of oxygen before he
pulled her down into the dark water again.

She knew then that he was toying with her, prolonging
her agony for his own sick satisfaction. With all her
strength, she tried to pull free. She tried to hit him. He only
shifted her in his grasp, his fingers like tentacles on her
water-slick flesh.

Her chest was bursting, and bright dots danced before
her eyes. Soon it would be impossible to hold her breath,
and the water would fill her lungs. James Harrison would
finally get his wish—her death. Yet she kept fighting him.

Her flailing hand brushed the edge of his swimsuit. She
followed the fabric downward until she encountered sensitive male flesh, then dug her nails into him, squeezing
with all her remaining strength. Through the muffling water, she heard him scream. His grasp loosened and she
wrenched away, putting distance between them. Breaking
the surface, she gasped for life-giving air.

"You bitch!" He made a grab for her, his fingers grazing
her shoulder. Hardly able to think, she maneuvered into
open water, heading for the opposite ladder. When his hand
touched her foot, she screamed and kicked harder.

Before he could catch up again, the lights flashed on.
Blinded, Kathryn kept flailing toward the far side of the
pool.

Seconds later a voice boomed over the water. "What the
hell's going on in here?"

Reaching the ladder, Kathryn gave a heartfelt cry of
thanks and quickly climbed up. But she didn't get any farther. As the air filled her lungs, she crumpled over and lay
panting on the cold cement. In the glow from the overhead
lights, all her eyes could make out was an indistinct figure
standing in the doorway.

"Listen up. You'd better have a good explanation, or
I'm going to call the police."

Even with the echo bouncing off the walls, she recognized the voice. It was Mr. Clemson, the building superintendent. "God, yes, call the police," she croaked.

A flash of movement on the other side of the pool made her cringe toward the wall. She saw James vault out of the water, hurtle toward Mr. Clemson, and pause to give him a mighty shove before charging through the door and disappearing.

The building superintendent went sprawling and landed hard on his back.

Finding her legs, Kathryn wobbled toward the wall phone near the door and dialed 911.

*   *   *   *   *

Don't miss this next 43 Light Street tale—
#474 NOWHERE MAN—
coming to you in July 1998. Only from Rebecca York
and Harlequin Intrigue!

Christmastime...

When rediscovering
lost loves brings a
special comfort, and helping
to deliver a precious bundle
is a remarkable joy.

Comfort and Joy

brings you gifts
of love and romance
from four talented
Harlequin authors.

A brand-new Christmas collection,
available at your favorite retail store
in November 1997.

HARLEQUIN®

HARLEQUIN WOMEN KNOW ROMANCE WHEN THEY SEE IT.

And they'll see it on **ROMANCE CLASSICS**, the new 24-hour TV channel devoted to romantic movies and original programs like the special **Romantically Speaking—Harlequin™ Goes Prime Time.**

Romantically Speaking—Harlequin™ Goes Prime Time introduces you to many of your favorite romance authors in a program developed exclusively for Harlequin® readers.

Watch for **Romantically Speaking—Harlequin™ Goes Prime Time** beginning in the summer of 1997.

If you're not receiving ROMANCE CLASSICS, call your local cable operator or satellite provider and ask for it today!

Escape to the network of your dreams.

See Ingrid Bergman and Gregory Peck in *Spellbound* on Romance Classics.

HARLEQUIN®

I N T R I G U E®

COMING NEXT MONTH

#441 HER HERO by Aimée Thurlo
Four Winds
Navajo healer Joshua Blackhorse was the one man who could help
Nydia Jim keep a promise to her son—and save a life. But when she
arrived in Four Winds she found Joshua accused of a terrible crime.

#442 HEART OF THE NIGHT by Gayle Wilson
Driven by a need she told herself was professional curiosity,
Kate August delved into the mystery of Thorne Barrington, the only
living victim of a serial bomber. But for what need did she follow him
into the darkness, determined to find the heart of the mystery…and
the man?

#443 A REAL ANGEL by Cassie Miles
Avenging Angels
It was Rafe Santini's job to stop an outbreak of a deadly virus.
Making love to his earthly assistant Jenna wasn't part of his duties. In
all his years as an Avenging Angel, Rafe had never been tempted by
the sins of the flesh. Why now, when so many lives were at stake?

#444 FAMILY TIES by Joanna Wayne
When Ashley's husband was nearly killed, she went into hiding,
taking with her the best part of Dillon Randolph—his baby. It took
three years for Dillon to find her and now he wanted her and his child
to come home to Texas. Surely now it'd be safe to be together
again…or was it?

Look us up on-line at: http://www.romance.net

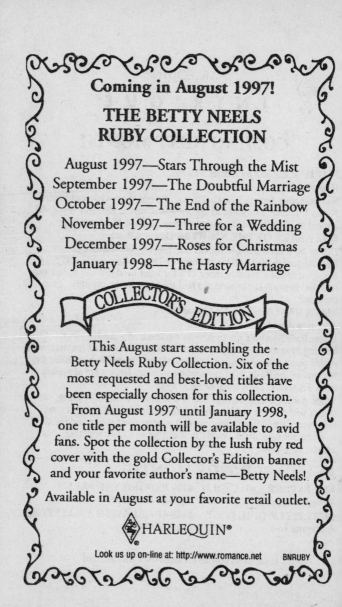

Coming in August 1997!

THE BETTY NEELS RUBY COLLECTION

August 1997—Stars Through the Mist

September 1997—The Doubtful Marriage

October 1997—The End of the Rainbow

November 1997—Three for a Wedding

December 1997—Roses for Christmas

January 1998—The Hasty Marriage

COLLECTOR'S EDITION

This August start assembling the
Betty Neels Ruby Collection. Six of the
most requested and best-loved titles have
been especially chosen for this collection.
From August 1997 until January 1998,
one title per month will be available to avid
fans. Spot the collection by the lush ruby red
cover with the gold Collector's Edition banner
and your favorite author's name—Betty Neels!

Available in August at your favorite retail outlet.

HARLEQUIN®

Look us up on-line at: http://www.romance.net

BNRUBY